EVERYMAN'S LIBRARY

EVERYMAN,
I WILL GO WITH THEE,
AND BE THY GUIDE,
IN THY MOST NEED
TO GO BY THY SIDE

JANE AUSTEN

Northanger Abbey

EVERYMAN'S LIBRARY

Alfred A. Knopf New York Toronto

109

THIS IS A BORZOI BOOK

PUBLISHED BY ALFRED A. KNOPF, INC.

First included in Everyman's Library, 1906
Introduction, Bibliography, and Chronology © 1992 by David
Campbell Publishers Ltd.

ISBN 0-679-41715-X
LC 92-52895

Library of Congress Cataloging-in-Publication Data
Austen, Jane, 1775–1815.
Northanger Abbey / Jane Austen.
p.   cm.—(Everyman's library)
ISBN 0-679-41715-X : $15.00 ($19.00 Can.)
I. Title.

PR4034.N7   1992   92-52895
823'.7—dc20   A933   CIP

Printed and bound in Germany

INTRODUCTION

Northanger Abbey is at once Jane Austen's first and last complete novel. Drafted in 1798-9, the novel (then called *Susan* and later *Catherine*) was revised, sold for ten pounds to Crosby & Co., and advertised for publication in 1803. Crosby & Co., however, never printed the manuscript, and although Austen bought it back in 1809, it was not to appear until 1817, five months after her death.[1] Clearly, the editor who decided not to publish Austen's first novel made a mistake for which literary history can hardly forgive him. But mistakes can be instructive, and his invites us to consider how this little novel – once considered no more than a fledgling effort of limited interest – not merely encompasses but in a sense also inspires Austen's canon. Abounding in youthful hilarity, *Northanger Abbey* is, among other things, a parody of gothic fiction, and as such it is obviously affiliated with the exuberant literary parodies among Austen's 'juvenile' productions, such as *Love and Freindship* [sic] (1790). But the accident of its publication alongside *Persuasion* alerts us to how much *Northanger Abbey* has in common with Austen's late work as well, especially with the unfinished *Sanditon*, which shares not only its determination to detach a heroine from her home, its depiction of resort life, and its bluntness of tone, but also its conspicuous preoccupation with reading.[2] It is this last feature which I consider particularly significant. *Northanger Abbey* narrates a young heroine's 'entrée into life', but it also constitutes a young author's 'entrée' into literature. In 1803, Austen could have made this entrance with a number of other works in manuscript: she could have revised *First Impressions* (the early version of *Pride and Prejudice*, which she had already tried and failed to get published six years earlier); she could have turned to *Lady Susan* or to *Elinor and Marianne* (later, *Sense and Sensibility*). It is tempting to argue – though this is, after all, only speculation – that faced with a choice among all these estimable, now-lost manuscripts, Austen opted to initiate her career with *Northanger Abbey* because in addition to being a good novel it alone was also a manifesto of her artistic program, one which was to retain its pertinence for years to come.

As recently as a generation ago, this claim would have struck many as rather strained. Austen seemed to be the most demure of novelists, a homely songbird indifferent to her art, as Henry James described her, with a mixture of querulousness and condescension.[3] Most appreciations dwelled with evident satisfaction on Austen's supposed modesty about her art, as if inviting us to reward her with our admiration in part because she herself had no pretensions to greatness: Austen was archly ironic, to be sure, but never would she exhibit anything so unladylike or so unseemly as ambition or a sense of artistic self-importance. In an oft-quoted section of *A Memoir of Jane Austen* (1870), J. E. Austen-Leigh recollects how Austen quickly put away or hid her drafts whenever the creaky door announced that visitors were coming. According to his representation, Austen is the good aunt, cheerfully surrendering herself to the casual interruptions that beset her as she worked in the common sitting-room. She naturally considered the entertainment of children such as himself of greater importance than artistic application.

Some of Austen's own statements would appear to support this view. Austen defended her niece's youthful attempts at composition by averring, reportedly, that 'writing stories was a great amusement, and *she* thought a harmless one, though many people, she was aware, thought otherwise', encouragement which sounds painfully uncomfortable to modern ears.[4] Finally, Austen's famous characterization of her fiction as a 'little bit (two inches wide) of Ivory' – even granting that it reads ironically in context – retreats from the grand and ambitious to the diminutive and the unassuming. This retreat implies an awareness that the imperative of female modesty did not cease to apply at the edge of a lady's writing table.[5] But *Northanger Abbey* gives us quite another picture. Far from being self-deprecatory about her compositions, Austen was plainly aggrieved by the novel's non-appearance. The 'Advertisement' to *Northanger Abbey*, written in 1816 in order to account for its belatedness, makes no attempt to conceal her lingering mortification. 'That any bookseller should think it worth while to purchase what he did not think it worth while to publish seems extraordinary,' Austen writes irritably, and that the book 'was even advertised' only later to be unaccountably withdrawn adds insult to injury.

If the neglect of thirteen years could not diminish the author's concern for *Northanger Abbey*, the reason has much to do with the fact that the novel itself is a spirited defense of novels. 'Yes, novels,' the narrator taunts towards its outset, daring the glib insults of reviewers who make a profession out of disparaging the novelist's art. In light of *Northanger Abbey*'s inaugurating position in Austen's career, we would do well to consider this bravura vindication of fiction that occupies its fifth chapter. Not for Austen the professions of diffidence contemporary novelists often employed in order to conciliate the critics: 'I will not adopt that ungenerous and impolitic custom so common with novel writers, of degrading by their contemptuous censure the very performances, to the number of which they are themselves adding'. Scorning such self-censure, she, on the contrary, goes on the offensive. It is reviewers, not novelists, who are the 'threadbare' ones, so warped by 'pride, ignorance, and fashion' that they 'eulogize' with 'a thousand pens' the 'nine-hundredth abridger of the History of England', to say nothing of the umpteenth anthologist of the same dozen lines from 'Milton, Pope, and Prior' along with a 'paper from the Spectator, and chapter from Sterne', while pooh-poohing with 'common cant' the labours of novelists which have 'only genius, wit, and taste to recommend them'. That unobtrusive little word 'only' packs the power of Austen's ironic punch.

With the benefit of some two hundred years of literary history behind us, the most recent of which have illuminated as well as challenged the very foundations on which cultural study itself is usually placed, we can now see that Austen is engaging in canon-reformation. When what we now call the novel emerged in England at the end of the seventeenth century, it was decried as a vulgar and potentially revolutionary form with no entitlement to the name literature, written and largely read by persons of both sexes without a classical education. The debate about the value of novels relative to other literary forms had not stopped by Austen's time, though its terms changed somewhat as novels themselves came increasingly to be considered a feminine medium. At stake in Austen's high-spirited defense – and its playful humor does not qualify its underlying seriousness – is not only the artistic dignity of novels, which had been assailed by cultural arbiters who refuse to recognize such 'labours' as literature at all, but also the legitimacy of the social vision of people who wrote them, people formerly excluded from the ranks of authorship and denied the distinction and the privilege of authority. The debate in which Austen is engaging is not essentially different from the controversy occurring on both sides of the Atlantic today in the press, in politics, and in the academy, as to whether the works of women, so-called 'minorities', and non-western peoples can be considered great literature in the same sense that the works of Homer and Shakespeare are.

Writing at the dawning of liberal feminism, and a generation after figures such as Mary Wollstonecraft and Catherine Macaulay, Austen does not make a theoretical issue of the way in which sexual bias *per se* motivates the exclusion of works by women from the dignified ranks of great literature. Nevertheless, all the examples she cites indicate her awareness that the writing, reading and assessing of literature are gendered activities, and that women's activities on all these fronts are unfairly devalued. When reviewers, novelists, and novelistic characters themselves throw their books aside and sigh ' "Oh! it is only a novel!" ' Austen (lingering ironically once again on 'only') paraphrases their disclaimer in a way that both explodes its legitimacy and shows her own hand:

'It is only Cecilia, or Camilla, or Belinda; or, in short, only some work in which the greatest powers of the mind are displayed, in which the most thorough knowledge of human nature, the happiest delineation of its varieties, the liveliest effusions of wit and humour are conveyed to the world in the best chosen language.'

It is not just the novel in general, but the emergent female tradition of the novel in particular that the narrator touts here with stunning superlatives. No reader will fail to catch the astonishingly self-assured implication that *Northanger Abbey* belongs to the tradition represented by sister-novelists Frances Burney and Maria Edgeworth. Novels of manners like Burney's *Evelina* (1778), *Cecilia* (1782), *Camilla* (1796), and Edgeworth's *Belinda* (1801) dramatize an intelligent, unaffected, and sheltered girl's first encounters with the perplexing and often brutal realities of the contemporary social world. Catherine Morland's 'entrée into life' at Bath, her attempts to learn about its rituals, to fathom its mysteries, to account for its contradictions, and finally to face its corruptions, are unquestionably modelled on the experiences of these earlier fictional counterparts.

But what about Ann Radcliffe, the most eminent author of the kind of fiction spoofed in *Northanger Abbey*? Do her novels – which typically narrate outlandishly extreme and vaguely supernatural goings-on in far-away places long ago – have a place in the tradition Austen champions? Or does *Northanger Abbey* engage in the same degrading attempt at advancement through negation that the narrator explicitly deplores, scapegoating gothic novelists like Radcliffe in order to spare novelists of manners like Edgeworth, Burney, and – by implication of course – Austen herself? The majority of scholars have maintained the latter, characterizing *Northanger Abbey* as an anti-gothic novel, which establishes its norms of sanity, moderation, and civility by ridiculing and reversing the excesses of books such as Radcliffe's *The Mysteries of Udolpho* (1794) and *The Italian* (1797). Superficially, there is much to support this view. By the late 1790's, the gothic novel had already become a conspicuously formulaic genre, and as such was often the butt of critical satire. The *Magasin encyclopédique* of 1797, for example, listed the following as a '*Recipe*' for a gothic novel:

An old castle, half of it crumbling down,
A long corridor, with numerous doors many of which must be hidden,
Three corpses weltering in their blood,
Three skeletons carefully wrapped up,
An old woman hanged, stabbed several times in her throat,
Robbers and ruffians galore,
A sufficient dose of whispers, stifled moan and frightful din.[6]

This list of 'ingredients', which is to be 'well mixed and

divided into three parts or volumes' by the cook/novelist, is manifestly similar in mood to much of the parody in *Northanger Abbey*. Catherine, for example, can't get her mind off the skeleton of Laurentini in *Mysteries of Udolpho*. When she learns that she is to journey to Northanger Abbey, she is overcome with the thrilling expectation of encountering its 'long, damp passages, its narrow cells and ruined chapel'. She even goes so far as to hope to discover there 'some awful memorials to an injured and ill-fated nun'. Henry Tilney, himself a parodist of sorts, jokingly encourages the gullible young Catherine to look for other 'horrors that a building such as "what one reads about" may produce' – such as 'peals of thunder' and 'frightful gusts of wind'; remote and dimly lit bedchambers walled with 'sliding pannels and tapestry'; hidden doors 'secured by massy bars and a padlock'; ponderous chests and cabinets 'which no efforts can open'; heart-stopping excursions through secret subterraneous corridors disclosing the obligatory 'dagger ... drops of blood ... [and] instrument of torture'.

Austen appears bent on satirizing the conventions of Radcliffean fiction by inciting her heroine to gothic expectations with the sole purpose of disappointing them. Northanger Abbey, for example, far from moldering into a sublime pile, is fully modernized, 'improved', and spruce, its pointed windows repaned with transparent glass admitting the reassuring brilliance of sunlight. The bedchamber into which Catherine is ushered is comfortable and cheery, with no lurid tapestries or mouldy velvet drapery in sight. The large chest she discovers there contains neatly folded hats and bonnets rather than the human remains of murder most foul, and the black cabinet is impossible to pry open only because Catherine herself had locked rather than unlocked it to begin with. Once open, it is discovered to contain a roll of manuscript pages comprising not the memoirs of a mysterious sufferer, but a laundry list and a farrier's bill.

But Austen's joke is not on Catherine's supposed obsession with gothic paraphenalia alone. *Our* gothic expectations about her are thoroughly mocked well before poor Catherine has the foggiest notion what gothic novels are, her library evidently containing nothing more modern than *Sir Charles Grandison*.

INTRODUCTION

The very first line of the novel – 'No one who had ever seen Catherine Morland in her infancy, would have supposed her born to be an heroine' – thus calls attention to our gothic preconceptions, not to hers. The haplessly ordinary Catherine is not, we discover, a poor orphan; she is plain, rather than lovely; dull rather than precocious; and far from exhibiting any incipient symptoms of heroic femininity – such as a fondness for nursing dolls, animals and flowers – she is a tomboy, hating 'confinement and cleanliness', and loving 'nothing so well in the world as rolling down the green slope at the back of the house'. Even after Catherine grows into young womanhood, she fails to exhibit that proclivity towards heroic inanition we (still) expect in heroines – in Radcliffe's novels, for example, only servants express solicitude for their bellies. Indeed, she returns home after a disappointing ball most unheroically to appease her 'extraordinary hunger' and consign herself not to a sleepless and tear-drenched pillow, but to a 'sound sleep' of nine refreshing hours. As the foregoing amply shows, it is not for nothing that so many readers have concluded that Austen's agenda in *Northanger Abbey* was to sweep aside the extravagant claptrap of gothic fiction and to replace them with her own circumscribed but also fresher and more realistic art.

But *Northanger Abbey* does not ultimately repudiate the gothic novel, and to mistake Austen on this point is to miss the richness, not to mention the joke, of *Northanger Abbey*. It is also to misapprehend Austen's celebrated irony in general. The opening chapter describes how Catherine 'fell miserably short of the true heroic height' only to assert that this 'young lady is to be a heroine' anyway. Austen makes no fast distinction between the gothic novel and the novel of manners. After all, Edgeworth and Burney were thoroughly imbued with Radcliffe's novels, and Austen launches into her encomium on the female novelistic tradition when Catherine retires to read Radcliffe's fiction – not theirs. Establishing a sense of artistic solidarity in a hostile critical climate – 'Let us not desert one another,' she declares, 'we are an injured body' – the narrator hoists the Augustan male literary establishment on its own petard by upbraiding works already regarded as veritable classics of Augustan prose: the *Spectator* essays. Austen was surely aware that the *Spectator* was celebrated for its polish, 'always equable,' as Samuel Johnson had put it in the *Life of Addison*, 'and always easy ... always luminous ... familiar but not coarse, and elegant but not ostentatious'. But her attack on the *Spectator*, which might seem to be purely gratuitous censure, is actually a strategically brilliant turn, for she proceeds to assail the very model of stylistic moderation on precisely the same grounds that gothic novels were – and still are – routinely attacked. Catherine herself later observes that respectable 'Mr. Allen had been used to call [gothic novels] unnatural and overdrawn'. But as the narrator would have it here, it is the *Spectator*, not *The Mysteries of Udolpho*, that is gross and exaggerated, saturated with 'improbable circumstances, unnatural characters' and language so 'coarse as to give no very favourable idea of the age that could produce it'. *Northanger Abbey* will go on to show that novels – and this includes gothic novels – actually give a clear, if unfavorable, picture of the age, accurately reflecting the way things are as she and novelists like her saw them.

This lengthy and sophisticated tribute to the feminine fictional tradition is no casual or momentary intrusion, to be indulged and then promptly forgotten. Rather, it states in a detached and self-conscious way the central contention of the novel: readers' different senses of propriety and plausibility, of the strange, the probable, the natural, the linguistically coarse or appropriate – and with all of these, of course, their different assessments of literary value – depend on their own authority, that is, on their relationship to established power. How one reads novels, Austen's novel will show, depends then on how one reads one's culture and one's place within it.

Northanger Abbey is a gothic novel about novels – about writing them, as we have seen above, but just as importantly about reading them. It dramatizes a heroine's encounters with the uncanny not by reversing but rather by rejuvenating and ultimately reaffirming gothic conventions. Despite what the narrator, adopting gothic discourse, describes as Catherine's 'strange' ordinariness, and despite the unaccountable 'perverseness' of her neighbourhood in failing to supply her with a hero-sweetheart, both she and we will learn to recognize the gothic outlines of her story as we learn how to read properly. Catherine, of course, seems a wholly naive reader, of both her world and her novels. She is comically endearing in part because she is as haunted and perplexed by the mysteries of Bath as she is by those of *Udolpho*. She starts out as a reader content with surfaces: Isabella professes a lofty disdain for the maneuvers of men, and Catherine, believing her older and wiser friend, simply overlooks her coquettish and transparently mercenary pursuit of them; her brother declares that rattles like John Thorpe are favored by women, and so Catherine suppresses her own irritation in his company; General Tilney professes an indifference to money, so Catherine does not believe he will object to Isabella's poverty.

More than inexperience is at issue in Catherine's readiness to take people at their word, for Catherine is rather trustful than merely credulous. In other words, 'with all the civility and deference of the youthful female mind', Catherine has faith in the truthfulness, the wisdom and the good-will of persons who stand in a relationship of authority to her. If such a person is a 'self-assured man', she is especially 'fearful of hazarding an opinion of her own' in opposition to him, no matter how ludicrous or offensive he may be; if he represents the 'high authority' of an eldest brother, his views will be hard to resist, no matter how blinkered and selfish; and if he is a father and a general to boot, his being 'perfectly agreeable and good-natured, and altogether a very charming man, did not admit of a doubt', no matter how oppressive his company. No proto-revolutionary, Catherine relies wholly on her elders and betters – 'he could not propose any thing improper for her', she remarks of General Tilney with a girlish trust that seems painfully pathetic in light of his eventual viciousness towards her.

Catherine may be trustful – from the start we are told that her mind is marked by 'youth and diffidence' – but she is not stupid. Before long her confidence ruptures. Once the disparity between profession and fact becomes too conspicuous for her to overlook, she begins to experience her world as a troubling and baffling place, and to become, in short, a gothic heroine beset by mysteries. She cannot 'avoid a little suspicion' of Isabella's duplicity; she feels 'astonishment' – which along with awe and terror are mandatory gothic sentiments – at Thorpe's exaggerations and contradictions; she is 'distressed, but not subdued' by the heartless and unprincipled attempts of her brother and friends to pressure her into breaking her engagement with the Tilneys; and she is 'puzzled' by the constraint Henry and Eleanor seem to suffer in their father's company. The gothic novel is before all else devoted to dramatizing the intuition of horrible truths concealed beneath imposing surfaces, to exposing how persons and institutions ostensibly devoted to the protection of the powerless instead coerce and betray them in the interests of greed and dominion. These examples – along with the novel's pervasive and entirely non-parodic use of gothic keywords relative to agony, captivity, torment, violence, submission – show how carefully Austen has used the language of gothic fiction to expose a horrible truth about daily life in Regency England.

Catherine experiences greed, betrayal, and dominion aplenty in Bath. But one of the novel's least appreciated jokes is the fact that even though she sometimes verges on connecting the world of gothic novels and the world of Bath – meditating 'by turns, on broken promises and broken arches, phaetons and false hangings, Tilneys and trap doors' – she does *not* see herself as the budding gothic heroine she is. Unlike characters in other novels written at least in part to mock the extravagancies of fiction and its female readers – one thinks of Lady Arabella in Charlotte Lennox's *The Female Quixote* (1752) and Cherubina in Eaton Stannard Barrett's exceptionally nasty *The Heroine* (1813) – Catherine is unable to imagine herself a gothic heroine until she is placed squarely and quite literally within a gothic abbey. *We* are able to perceive John Thorpe's boorish and brutal determination to force Catherine on a carriage ride with him despite her vociferous refusal – a refusal which prompts him merely to laugh and smack his whip – as a genuinely oppressive variant on the standard gothic abduction scene. *We* can discern in the neglect Catherine experiences at the Allens' hands a distant relative to the profound and haunting isolation endured by gothic heroines. And *we* can recognize the corporeal as well psychological violence to which James and the Thorpes resort to force her compliance with their schemes as a transposition of the gothic scene of torture which the heroine virtuously withstands.

The gothic frame established from the outset of the novel – to which Catherine, of course, has no access – invites us to conclude that gothic modulations may intensify the horror of daily life, but they do not distort it beyond all recognition. Until the conclusion of the novel, Catherine, by contrast, cannot realize this, and for the same reason that she is dumbfounded by Henry Tilney's comparison of dancing and marriage. A literalist through and through, she refuses Henry Tilney's simile because marriage and dancing 'are so very different', and no amount of elaboration on his part will make her budge. Similarly, mistaking gothic conventions for unmediated representation, she concludes that gothicism is something that happens only on stormy nights in medieval abbeys rather than ballrooms at Bath; that fierce ruffians cannot be the good friends of trusted brothers; that gothic villainy consists of nothing less than the imprisonment and murder of women.

For Henry Tilney the case stands quite differently. He regards gothic novels as nothing but an inventory of machinery. Henry is just as jaded about Bath chit-chat, considering the discourse of ordinary life and gothic fiction similarly stale and risible. Because Henry Tilney is often taken for Austen's surrogate, it is important to examine his attitudes on this score. When Catherine first meets Henry, he forms 'his features into a set smile, affectedly softening his voice ... with a simpering air' and delivers himself of a brief dramatic parody of banal Bath prattle. Yet when Catherine and Eleanor later meet, they exchange civilities identical to the chatter Henry ridicules: 'not an observation was made, nor an expression used by either which had not been made and used some thousands of times before, under that roof, in every Bath season'. Inasmuch as the narrator specifically praises Catherine and Eleanor's conversation for its 'simplicity, and truth', we must conclude that even clichéd, hyper-conventionalized discourse can be worthwhile, productive, and dignified – a conclusion which says as much about small-talk as it does about gothic novels.

Clearly, Henry Tilney is no authority on language, as pertains to life or literature, even though he presents himself as such. Despite his general benignity and good-humour, he is at times dangerously Thorpe-like in his presumption upon the authority attributable to his education, his age, his calling as a clergymen, and his sex. Men in *Northanger Abbey*, like Sir Thomas and Edmund in *Mansfield Park*, have a real mania for measurement, for determining the precise boundaries of time, of space, or – in Henry's case – of words. Having in his first conversation with Catherine not only caricatured Bath conversation but also chided women's letters for a 'general deficiency of subject, a total inattention to stops, and a very frequent ignorance of grammar', Henry immediately establishes himself as a stickler for words, bristling at every verbal transgression. Redundance (as in 'promised so faithfully', exaggeration (as in 'amazement'), semantic flattening (as in 'nice'), and definitional blurring (as in teachers 'tormenting' rather than 'instructing') turn Tilney into a linguistic despot of sorts, bent on 'overpower[ing]' offenders – the word is not without a gothic resonance – with the law of lexicographers and rhetoricians, in particular 'Johnson and Blair'.

Henry's patrol over proper usage culminates as Catherine and his sister, Eleanor, misunderstand each other when Catherine alludes to 'something very shocking' about to 'come out in London', something including 'murder and every thing of the kind'. Catherine of course is referring to the latest gothic novel, but Eleanor thinks only of the London riots which government troops – including her brother, Captain Frederick Tilney – may be called in to suppress. For Tilney, this *malentendu* demonstrates a typically feminine carelessness of thought and language, a carelessness at once regrettable and amusing. 'Perhaps,' he observes, 'the abilities of women are neither sound nor acute – neither vigorous nor keen.' Gallantly stepping in to assist woman in her weakness, and vaunting his manliness and his lucidity in such a way as to imply their intrinsic connection he asserts that: 'I will prove myself a man, no less by the generosity of my soul than the clearness of my head.' The playful solemnity of his tone notwithstanding, Henry is authorized to consider feminine discourse – in conversation, and in books – mistaken or absurd, and thus ever in need of his watchful arbitration.

But in linking political and literary unrest – the riotous crowds of London and the riotous pages of gothic novels – Catherine and Eleanor's unruly language has actually served them quite well, for both forms of excess are responses to unacceptable rule. The abusiveness of rule is, of course, the very premise of the gothic world. The linguistic regulations Tilney observes have no relevance in the gothic world, where words have been wrenched from their customary moorings, alas; where promises are not faithful, exaggerations are not excessive, and education is torment. The illegitimacy of rule, however, is exactly what Henry cannot imagine. His own position of authority – indeed his very clarity of and capacity for speech – depend on accepting the fitness of the prescribed order. This is why Henry is so appalled to learn that Catherine – her gothicizing imagination licensed by Northanger Abbey itself – suspects his father of murdering his mother:

'If I understand you rightly, you have formed a surmise of such horror as I have hardly word to – Dear Miss Morland, consider the dreadful nature of the suspicions you have entertained. What have you been judging from? Remember the country and the age in which we live. Remember that we are English, that we are Christians. Consult your own observation of what is passing around you – Does our education prepare us for such atrocities? Do our laws connive at them? Could they be perpetrated without being known, in a country like this, where social and literary discourse is on such a footing; where every man is surrounded by a neighbourhood of voluntary spies, and where roads and newspapers lay every thing open? Dearest Miss Morland, what ideas have you been admitting?'

For a moment, Henry, that master of words, is stupefied. Not all the words of Johnson and Blair can help him utter the 'horror' that gothic novels have invited Catherine to believe with such breezy nonchalance: that a modern Englishman, a law-abiding Christian living in full view of neighbours whose esteem he values, could nevertheless be plausibly suspected of killing his wife. The terms of Henry's indignation recapitulate the charges against gothic fiction – improbable circumstances, unnatural characters, and coarse language – that Austen deftly turned back on the Augustan masters in Chapter Five. They force us to recognize that people on the outside of ostensibly civilizing institutions he trusts may have different ideas about what is natural, probable, or overstated; that figureheads of domestic as well as political order can present a menacingly double image to girls like Catherine. Catherine herself, for the moment still caught up in the literalness of murder, will soon be brought to an appreciation of the figurative and moral truth of her suspicion. Cold-hearted, rapacious, mean-spirited, unprincipled and tyrannical, General Tilney *is* a gothic villain. He did in some legitimate sense of the term 'kill' his unhappy wife, not by locking her up and starving her to death, but rather by quashing her voice – note that General Tilney is a great interrupter, forcing opposition into silence – and stifling her vitality, much as he visibly crushes the spirits of his children. His subsequent behavior bears out Catherine's suspicion.

At the climax of *Northanger Abbey*, General Tilney banishes Catherine unprotected into the night solely because she is discovered not to be as rich as he had foolishly imagined. This act falls short of the grandeur of murder, to be sure. But to underrate its seriousness is to imply that important gentlemen are not to be judged by their treatment of poor girls, a devaluation which the female tradition of the novel gothically protests. Judged in historical terms, General Tilney's expulsion of Catherine is grossly uncivil in the deepest sense, exhibiting insolence towards inferiors, indifference to the good opinion of neighbours, and a contempt for the rules of hospitality, gentlemanliness, and decency, particularly towards women. When Catherine sees General Tilney working in his study at night, furrowing his brow and pondering the interests of national security in a dangerously unstable time, her mind leaps to Radcliffe's arch-villain, Montoni. Catherine does not ponder the conjunction gothic literature prompts her to sense. But we must, for it is perceptive. In addition to being the heroine's guardian and persecutor,

Montoni is the chief of a savage band of *condottieri* carving up the countryside of Italy during the civil wars. In associating General Tilney with Montoni, Catherine is sensing his doubleness, for he is a figure of order as well as the agent of lawlessness. By the novel's end, Catherine concludes that gothic novels taught her what no one and nothing else would. They have brought her to the essential, though not the literal, truth about a figure who represents national as well as domestic order: 'in suspecting General Tilney of either murdering or shutting up his wife, she had scarcely sinned against his character, or magnified his cruelty'.

To Henry, as we have seen, the haunting doubleness of gothic fiction is semantically and politically impossible. Hence his dismissal of gothic novels as shallow if entertaining artifice, devoid of any claim to verisimilitude. Catherine's vision of General Tilney as a respectable father *and* as a gothic villain is to him as inadmissable as her linkage of the verbs 'to torment' and 'to instruct' is absurd. But Catherine's final appraisal of General Tilney is allowed to stand as correct, unqualified by the narrator, unchallenged by Henry himself. This ultimately pro-gothic conclusion shows that, ironically enough, it is not Catherine, but Henry Tilney who turns out to have been the naive reader, blinded by his own privilege to the unsettling truths gothic novels made visible to Catherine. The major purpose of Austen's prefatory 'Advertisement' is to apologize for 'those parts of the work which thirteen years have made comparatively obsolete', thus obscuring her design: 'The public are entreated to bear in mind that thirteen years have passed since it was finished, many more since it was begun, and that during that period, places, manner, books, and opinions have undergone considerable changes.' As several scholars have demonstrated, Austen carefully accumulates details about contemporary England – there are more in this novel than in any other – which darken the portrait of General Tilney and his household: General Tilney's hothouses devoted to the cultivation of pineapples for the rich; his practice of enclosure, with its infamously disastrous effects on the rural poor; his arrogantly high-handed treatment of servants; the family's references to riots caused by food shortages and political unrest, together with vague suggestions about the General's involvement in 'the affairs of the nation'; and Henry's satisfied allusion to the Treasonable Practices Act of 1794 which permitted a 'neighbourhood of voluntary spies' to report anyone for seditious speech.[7] Informed readers of Austen's day would recognize in these details symptoms of social ills endemic to the ruling class. The docile Catherine, chastened by Henry's scolding, had made us smile when she opined that Radcliffe's characters are not to be found in 'the central part of England' – though, 'if hard pressed, she would have yielded the northern and western extremities' along with Italy and the south of France. But surely Henry's call-down, itself a version of it-can't-happen-here, is less sophisticated and more wrong, and it is not merely the outcome of the plot, but the evidence of his own household – evidence which he cannot 'read' – that proves this.

Yet Henry Tilney was destined from the first chapter to be the 'hero' of this novel, and he does not disappoint us. Defying his father's wrath, he keeps faith with Catherine, journeying to Fullerton to ask her hand in a marriage his father will not allow. In her final *homage* to the gothic, Austen brings her novel out of this unhappy impasse by flaunting gothic conventions. Reminding us that the 'tell-tale compression of pages' means 'that we are all hastening together to perfect felicity', she appeases the General's worldly vanity by marrying Eleanor off to a fabulously wealthy Viscount, non-existent till the eleventh hour. ('My own joy on the occasion is very sincere,' the narrator remarks, garrulously.) She affirms the 'rules of composition' by assigning to his ownership the washing bills Catherine had mistaken for a woeful memoir. She enlarges the income of the Morlands' estate enough to satisfy the General's 'greedy speculation'. And, most importantly of all, she establishes a happy ending by deliberately fudging the novel's central problem, ironically averring that the General's 'unjust interference' actually helped rather than hindered Catherine and Tilney. The stylized excess of these quintessentially gothic gestures of closure – where all the strings are tied up, where all the problems are solved, where villains turn out to be nice guys, where all the characters retire to conjugal bliss – reminds us that we are in the never-never-land of comedy rather than the 'midland counties of England'. The obviously hasty, extravagant, and overdetermined felicity of the conclusion suggests that comic resolutions may be more fictive than gothic terrors, that fantasies about happiness may be less credible than fantasies about suffering and persecution.

Northanger Abbey is, then, a delightful novel, but also a serious one, and the first completely to master the stylistic method that would become the hallmark of its author's art: irony. Austenian irony is no mere matter of sarcastically saying x while meaning y. On the contrary, it is two-sided, functioning somewhat like a Mobius strip, where two apparently discrete and opposite planes are manipulated into a mind-bending coextensiveness. Consider, for example, the following exchanges in *Northanger Abbey*:

Mrs Allen was one of that numerous class of females, whose society can raise no other emotion than surprise at there being any men in the world who could like them well enough to marry them. She had neither beauty, genius, accomplishment, nor manner. The air of gentlewoman, a great deal of quiet, inactive good temper, and a trifling turn of mind, were all that could account for her being the choice of a sensible, intelligent man, like Mr. Allen.

The advantages of natural folly in a beautiful girl have been already set forth by the capital pen of a sister author [Burney]; – and to her treatment of the subject I will only add in justice to men, that though to the larger and more trifling part of the sex, imbecility in females is a great enhancement of their personal charms, there is a portion of them too reasonable and too well informed themselves to desire any thing more in woman than ignorance.

Brain-twisters of sorts, these examples both turn on and turn against the very persons we expected them to champion, prompting us to do a double-take just when we thought we had caught the drift and slackened our concentration. In a passage which seems devoted to satirizing Mrs Allen's stupidity, it is the sensible and intelligent Mr Allen who ends up looking decidedly more like his wife in having chosen her for her very weaknesses; and 'reasonable and well-informed men' men, far from being morally and intellectually segregated from their trifling brethren, are brought into disturbing juxtaposition with them for preferring merely ignorant rather than downright stupid women.

Northanger Abbey accomplishes as a whole what these passages do in a smaller compass. Opposing the 'alarms of romance' to the 'anxieties of common life', and to all appearances siding artistically with the latter, the novel finally brings them into an illuminating and troubling conjunction. The gothic novel itself was devoted to defamiliarizing the common so as to bring its alarming strangeness into view. But by the time Austen took up her pen, its strangeness itself had become so familiar as to be dismissed as convention alone. Gothic strangeness itself had to be defamiliarized, and the only way to do so was to make it ordinary. In adapting the fictional norms of gothic to Regency England, Austen was thus rehabilitating them. Even Henry Tilney, of course, enjoyed gothic novels: 'The Mysteries of Udolpho, when once I had begun it, I could not lay down again.' But Austen's claims for Radcliffe's fiction, as for Edgeworth's, Burney's and her own, go well beyond the pleasure of a good 'read'. She reclaims a fictional tradition the better to examine 'strange' truths about familiar life, sharpening our discernment and enlarging our understanding by obliging us to be attentive readers of books and worlds that we, like Henry Tilney, erroneously think we already understand. In so doing, *Northanger Abbey* makes good its assertion that novels are works 'in which the greatest powers of the mind are displayed ... in the best chosen language'. It was an awesome beginning.

Claudia L. Johnson

NOTES

1. The chronology of Austen's early work has been a matter of controversy. For an explanation, see A. Walton Litz, *Jane Austen: A Study of her Artistic Development*, Oxford University Press, New York, 1965, pp. 171–80; and B. C. Southam, 'Mrs. Leavis and Miss Austen: The "Critical Theory" Reconsidered', *Nineteenth-Century Fiction*, 17, 1961, 21–32. Six years before selling *Northanger Abbey* to Crosby & Co. Austen had taken steps to attract the publisher Cadell in *First Impressions*, but Cadell was not interested.

2. Although Austen's 'Advertisement' of 1816 suggests an intention to publish, in 1817 Austen wrote that 'Miss Catherine is put upon the Shelve for the present, and I do not know that she will ever come out' in a letter to Fanny Knight, 13 March 1817. Scholars opine that Austen suspended publication plans because she feared the literary and political allusions of *Northanger Abbey* would not wear well. This decision may have made Austen freer to let the mood of *Northanger Abbey* rub off on *Sanditon*.

3. See B. C. Southam, ed., *Jane Austen: The Critical Heritage*, Routledge & Kegan Paul, London, 1968, Vol. 2, pp. 229–30.

4. *Persuasion, with a Memoir of Jane Austen*, ed. D. W. Harding, Penguin Books, Baltimore, 1965, p. 187.

5. Letter to J. Edward Austen, 16 December 1816. For a discussion of female modesty as it both enabled and limited women writers, see Mary Poovey, *The Proper Lady and the Woman Writer*, University of Chicago Press, Chicago, 1984.

6. I am indebted to Litz, p. 60, for this brilliant gothic parody, which as he notes, employs a translation from D. P. Varma, *The Gothic Flame*, London, 1957, pp. 179–80.

7. For these insights into the political allusions in *Northanger Abbey*, I am indebted to B. C. Southam's seminal, 'General Tilney's Hot-Houses', *Ariel*, 2, 1971, 52–62, and to Robert Hopkin's still indispensable 'General Tilney and Affairs of State: The Political Gothic of *Northanger Abbey*', *Philological Quarterly* 57, 1978, 213–24. For a fuller discussion of the political character of *Northanger Abbey*, see my *Jane Austen: Women, Politics, and the Novel*, Chicago and London, 1988.

SELECT BIBLIOGRAPHY

Jane Austen has attracted massive and sometimes uncritical attention since the pioneer work of R. W. Chapman in the 1920s. The brief selection below covers texts, interest in her life and time, letters, and general critical appraisals which include *Northanger Abbey*; some of these have specific sections or chapters devoted to the novel.

Texts There are three good annotated editions. The first is the Chapman edition (begun in 1923), in five volumes to which a sixth was subsequently added. These were revised by Mary Lascelles (1965-7) and became the Oxford Illustrated edition. Derived from this is the World's Classics edition, edited and with new notes and introductions (1990). There is also the Penguin English Library edition, which began with *Persuasion* in 1965. Of the Jane Austen companions, easily the best and most up to date is *The Jane Austen Handbook*, Athlone Press, 1986, edited by J. David Grey. The range is impressive: it is a detailed filling in of Jane Austen's background and foreground. The standard edition of *Jane Austen's Letters* is that by R. W. Chapman, Oxford University Press, 1952.

Biographies which merit attention begin with *A Memoir of Jane Austen* by her nephew J. E. Austen-Leigh, Richard Bentley, 1870, expanded 1871 (ed. R. W. Chapman, Oxford University Press,, 1926); it is elegant, charming, pious, and just avoids being cloying. His son William and R. A. Austen-Leigh published *Jane Austen, Her Life and Letters: A Family Record*, 1913 (reprinted Russell, New York, 1965), a responsible, scholarly work. Elizabeth Jenkins' *Jane Austen: A Biography*, Gollancz, 1938, is an intelligent, perceptive commentary on the period and tells a convincing, graphic story. Lord David Cecil's *Portrait of Jane Austen*, Penguin, 1978, is a balanced account, comfortable and comforting. Park Honan's *Jane Austen: Her Life*, Weidenfeld, 1987, is excellent, the result of dedicated and sympathetic research. It is particularly strong on family background.

Criticism Jane Austen criticism has changed immensely over the past two hundred years. B. C. Southam's *Jane Austen: The Critical Heritage*, 2 vols., Routledge, 1968-87, anthologizes every important commentary that appeared from Austen's own time through the first part of our century, and also provides an extensive analysis of how appraisals have changed. Most full-length studies of Jane Austen devote a separate chapter to *Northanger Abbey*. For some excellent discussions of Austen's stylistic devlopment and formal mastery, see Mary Lascelles, *Jane Austen and Her Art*, Oxford University Press, 1939; A. Walton Litz, *Jane Austen: A Study of Her Artistic Development*, Oxford University Press, 1965, and Joseph Wiesenfarth, *The Errand of Form: An Assay of Jane Austen's Art*, Fordham University Press, 1967. Book-length studies considering Austen's novels in relation to the political controversies of her time include Marilyn Butler, *Jane Austen and the War of Ideas*, Oxford University Press, 1975, rev. 1987, which argues for Austen's sternly Tory sympathies; and Claudia L. Johnson, *Jane Austen: Women, Politics, and the Novel*, University of Chicago Press, 1988, which emphasizes Austen's progressive stances, particularly as regards women. Other studies focusing on Austen's representation of women's experience include Mary Poovey's important *The Proper Lady and the Woman Writer*, University of Chicago Press, 1984, which analyses the ideology of female propriety; Alison Sulloway, *Jane Austen and the Province of Womanhood*, University of Pennsylvania Press, 1989, which places Austen's novels in the context of contemporary debates about women, concluding that she was a moderate feminist. Marvin Mudrick's *Jane Austen: Irony as Defense and Discovery*, Princeton University Press, 1952, still sets the terms for many discussions of Jane Austen and her ostensibly cold irony, and Michael Sadleir's *The Northanger Novels*, English Association Pamphlet No. 68, 1927, is still useful in acquainting the general reader to the reading-list of gothic thrillers alluded to in *Northanger Abbey*.

CHRONOLOGY

Readers wishing to know more of Jane Austen's family background and the achievements of her brothers should consult Park Honan's *Jane Austen: Her Life* (1987).

DATE	AUTHOR'S LIFE	LITERARY CONTEXT
1770		Wordsworth born.
1771		Sir Walter Scott born.
		Smollett: *Sir Humphrey Clinker*.
		Death of Gray.
1772		Coleridge born.
1773		Earl of Chesterfield dies.
1774		Death of Goldsmith.
		Dr Johnson: *A Journey to the Western Isles*.
1775	Born at Steventon, Hampshire, on 16 December (five brothers, one sister, Cassandra).	Charles Lamb, J. M. W. Turner born.
1776		Gibbon: *Decline and Fall of the Roman Empire*.
1777		
1778		Hazlitt born.
		Burney: *Evelina*.
1779		Johnson: *Lives of the Poets* (completed 1781).
1780		
1781		
1782		Burney: *Cecilia*.
1783		Crabbe: *The Village*.
1784–5	At Abbey School, Reading, with Cassandra.	Dr Johnson dies.
1785		Cowper: *The Task*.
1786	Leaves Abbey School (December).	Burns' first poems.
1788	Visits Sevenoaks (July).	Byron born.
1789		Blake: *Songs of Innocence*.
1790		
1791		John Wesley dies.
		Boswell: *Life of Johnson*.
1792		Shelley born.
1793		
1794	Comte de Feuillide, husband of her father's niece Eliza, executed (February) in the Terror in Paris.	Radcliffe: *The Mysteries of Udolpho*.

Boston Tea Party.

American War of Independence – Battle of Bunker Hill. Washington in command of American army.

Adam Smith's *Wealth of Nations*. American Declaration of Independence (4 July).
Burgoyne surrenders to American forces at Saratoga.

The Gordon Riots.
Franco–American victory at Yorktown.
Peace with the United States.
Treaty of Versailles.
Pitt the Younger becomes Prime Minister.

Cartwright invents power weaving.

George III declared insane. Impeachment of Warren Hastings (acquitted 1795).
French Revolution – storming of the Bastille.
Burke's *Reflections on the French Revolution*.

Paine's *Rights of Man*.
Britain goes to war with France.
Suspension of the Habeas Corpus Act. French relieve Toulon (artillery commanded by young Napoleon Bonaparte).

DATE	AUTHOR'S LIFE	LITERARY CONTEXT
1795	Writes *Elinor and Marianne* in the form of letters.	Keats born. Matthew Gregory Lewis: *The Monk*.
1796	*First Impressions* (later *Pride and Prejudice*) begun (October).	Burney: *Camilla*. Burns dies.
1797	Visits Bath (November). Begins *Sense and Sensibility* (November). *First Impressions* offered to Cadell. *Susan*, later *Northanger Abbey*, written.	Burke, Horace Walpole and Mary Wollstonecraft die. Radcliffe: *The Italian*.
1798	Visits Godmersham with Cassandra.	Wordsworth and Coleridge: *Lyrical Ballads*.
1799	Stays in Bath (May–June) with her mother.	Lewis: *Tales of Terror*.
1800		Cowper dies. Maria Edgeworth: *Castle Rackrent*.
1801	Again visits Bath (May) with her family. Family settles (autumn) in Bath.	Lewis: *Tales of Wonder*. Maria Edgeworth: *Belinda*.
1802	Visits (summer) to Dawlish and Sidmouth.	Scott: *Minstrelsy of the Scottish Border*.
1803	*Susan* (*Northanger Abbey*) sold to Crosby (spring).	
1804	Visits Lyme (September). Death of Mrs Lefroy (16 December).	
1805	Father dies (21 June). *Lady Susan/The Watsons* probably written.	Scott: *The Lay of the Last Minstrel*.
1806	Family move to Southampton (autumn).	
1807	Family settled in Castle Square, Southampton. With mother and Cassandra at Chawton (September).	Wordsworth: *Poems*. Crabbe: *The Parish Register*.
1808	Idea of moving to Chawton (October).	Scott: *Marmion*.
1809	Settled happily at Chawton (July).	Byron: *English Bards and Scotch Reviewers*.
1810		Scott: *The Lady of the Lake*.
1811	*Mansfield Park* begun (February, finished summer 1813). *Sense and Sensibility* published (November) by Egerton.	
1812	*Pride and Prejudice* sold to Egerton (November).	Byron: *Childe Harold* (completed 1818). Crabbe: *Tales in Verse*. Dickens born.

CHRONOLOGY

Naval mutinies at the Nore and Spithead.

Pitt introduces income tax. Malthus' *An Essay on the Principle of Population*. Nelson defeats French at Aboukir Bay.
Repressive acts against radicalism passed. Napoleon appointed First Consul.
Napoleon defeats the Austrians at Marengo.

First census taken. Defeat of Pitt.

Peace of Amiens with France.

War resumed with France.

Return of Pitt as Prime Minister. French invasion of England planned (Napoleon Emperor of France). Anglo–Russian Alliance (joined by Austria 1805).
French fleet defeated by Nelson at Trafalgar (Austro–Russians defeated at Austerlitz).
Blockade of Britain. Death of Pitt.

Franco–Russian alliance against England.

Napoleon captures Madrid.

Wellesley defeats the French at Talavera. French victory over English at Walcheren. Moore's defence of Corunna.

French cleared out of Portugal.

Madrid recaptured. War with the United States. End of Napoleon's Russian campaign – retreat from Moscow.

DATE	AUTHOR'S LIFE	LITERARY CONTEXT
1813	*Pride and Prejudice* published (January). Visits London (September). Second edition of *Pride and Prejudice* (November). Second edition of *Sense and Sensibility* (November).	Byron: *The Giaour*.
1814	*Emma* begun (21 January; finished 29 March 1815). *Mansfield Park* published (May) by Egerton.	Scott: *Waverley*.
1815	*Persuasion* begun (summer; finished August 1816). *Emma* published (December) by John Murray.	Trollope born. Scott: *Guy Mannering*. Byron: *Hebrew Melodies*. Wordsworth: *The White Doe of Rylstone*, poems.
1816	*Quarterly Review* – Scott's laudatory notice of *Emma* (March). Second edition of *Mansfield Park*.	Scott: *The Antiquary* and *Old Mortality*. Peacock: *Headlong Hall*. Coleridge: *Christabel* and *Kubla Khan*. Shelley: *Alastor*.
1817	Writes *Sanditon* (January–March). Dies at Winchester (18 July). *Northanger Abbey* and *Persuasion*, with a Biographical Notice of the Author published (December?) by John Murray (dated 1818).	Byron: *Tasso* and *Manfred*. Coleridge: *Biographia Literaria* and *Sibylline Leaves*. Keats: *Poems*.
1818		Scott: *Heart of Midlothian*. Mary Shelley: *Frankenstein*. Peacock: *Nightmare Abbey*.
1819		Byron: *Don Juan* (completed 1824). Wordsworth: *Peter Bell*.
1820		Shelley: *Prometheus Unbound* and *The Cenci*. Keats: *Lamia, Isabella, The Eve of St Agnes* and the *Odes*. Clare: *Poems Descriptive of Rural Life and Scenery*. Scott: *Ivanhoe*. Southey: *Life of Wesley*.
1821		Keats dies. Shelley: *Adonais*.

CHRONOLOGY

HISTORICAL EVENTS

Robert Owen: *A New View of Society*.

Peace with America. The Allies take Paris.

Napoleon returns from Elba. Allies defeat Napoleon at Waterloo. Peace of Vienna.

Spa Fields riot. Economic depression.

Princess Charlotte dies.

Peterloo Massacre. Birth of Queen Victoria.

ADVERTISEMENT,

BY THE AUTHORESS,

TO

NORTHANGER ABBEY.

———

THIS little work was finished in the year 1803, and intended for immediate publication. It was disposed of to a bookseller, it was even advertised, and why the business proceeded no farther, the author has never been able to learn. That any bookseller should think it worth while to purchase what he did not think it worth while to publish seems extraordinary. But with this, neither the author nor the public have any other concern than as some observation is necessary upon those parts of the work which thirteen years have made comparatively obsolete. The public are entreated to bear in mind that thirteen years have passed since it was finished, many more since it was begun, and that during that period, places, manners, books, and opinions have undergone considerable changes.

VOLUME ONE

NORTHANGER ABBEY.

CHAPTER I.

No one who had ever seen Catherine Morland in her infancy, would have supposed her born to be an heroine. Her situation in life, the character of her father and mother, her own person and disposition, were all equally against her. Her father was a clergyman, without being neglected, or poor, and a very respectable man, though his name was Richard—and he had never been handsome. He had a considerable independence, besides two good livings—and he was not in the least addicted to locking up his daughters. Her mother was a woman of useful plain sense, with a good temper, and, what is more remarkable, with a good constitution. She had three sons before Catherine was born ; and instead of dying in bringing the latter into the world, as any body might expect, she still lived on—lived to have six children more —to see them growing up around her, and to enjoy excellent health herself. A family of ten children will be always called a fine family, where there are heads and arms and legs enough for the number ; but the Morlands had little other right to the word, for they were in general very plain, and Catherine, for many years of her life, as plain as any. She had a thin awkward figure, a sallow skin without colour, dark lank hair, and strong features ;— so much for her person ;—and not less unpropitious for heroism seemed her mind. She was fond of all boys' plays, and greatly preferred cricket not merely to dolls, but to the more heroic enjoyments of infancy, nursing a dormouse, feeding a canary-bird, or watering a rose-bush. Indeed she had no taste for a garden ; and if she
gathered

gathered flowers at all, it was chiefly for the pleasure of
mischief—at least so it was conjectured from her always
preferring those which she was forbidden to take.—Such
were her propensities—her abilities were quite as extraordinary. She never could learn or understand any thing
before she was taught; and sometimes not even then,
for she was often inattentive, and occasionally stupid.
Her mother was three months in teaching her only to
repeat the " Beggar's Petition ; " and after all, her next
sister, Sally, could say it better than she did. Not that
Catherine was always stupid,—by no means ; she learnt
the fable of " The Hare and many Friends," as quickly
as any girl in England. Her mother wished her to learn
music ; and Catherine was sure she should like it, for
she was very fond of tinkling the keys of the old forlorn
spinnet ; so, at eight years old she began. She learnt
a year, and could not bear it ;—and Mrs. Morland, who
did not insist on her daughters being accomplished in
spite of incapacity or distaste, allowed her to leave off.
The day which dismissed the music-master was one of
the happiest of Catherine's life. Her taste for drawing
was not superior ; though whenever she could obtain the
outside of a letter from her mother, or seize upon any
other odd piece of paper, she did what she could in that
way, by drawing houses and trees, hens and chickens, all
very much like one another.—Writing and accounts she
was taught by her father; French by her mother : her
proficiency in either was not remarkable, and she shirked
her lessons in both whenever she could. What a strange,
unaccountable character !—for with all these symptoms of
profligacy at ten years old, she had neither a bad heart
nor a bad temper ; was seldom stubborn, scarcely ever
quarrelsome, and very kind to the little ones, with few
interruptions of tyranny ; she was moreover noisy and
wild, hated confinement and cleanliness, and loved
nothing so well in the world as rolling down the green
slope at the back of the house.

Such was Catherine Morland at ten. At fifteen, appearances

ances were mending ; she began to curl her hair and long
for balls ; her complexion improved, her features were
softened by plumpness and colour, her eyes gained more
animation, and her figure more consequence. Her love of
dirt gave way to an inclination for finery, and she grew
clean as she grew smart ; she had now the pleasure of
sometimes hearing her father and mother remark on her
personal improvement. " Catherine grows quite a good-
looking girl,—she is almost pretty to day," were words
which caught her ears now and then ; and how welcome
were the sounds ! To look *almost* pretty, is an acquisition
of higher delight to a girl who has been looking plain the
first fifteen years of her life, than a beauty from her cradle
can ever receive.

Mrs. Morland was a very good woman, and wished to
see her children every thing they ought to be ; but her
time was so much occupied in lying-in and teaching the
little ones, that her elder daughters were inevitably left
to shift for themselves ; and it was not very wonderful
that Catherine, who had by nature nothing heroic about
her, should prefer cricket, base ball, riding on horseback,
and running about the country at the age of fourteen, to
books—or at least books of information— for, provided
that nothing like useful knowledge could be gained from
them, provided they were all story and no reflection, she
had never any objection to books at all. But from fifteen
to seventeen she was in training for a heroine ; she read
all such works as heroines must read to supply their
memories with those quotations which are so serviceable
and so soothing in the vicissitudes of their eventful lives.

From Pope, she learnt to censure those who

" bear about the mockery of woe."

From Gray, that

" Many a flower is born to blush unseen,
" And waste its fragrance on the desert air."

From Thompson, that

———— " It is a delightful task
" To teach the young idea how to shoot."

And

And from Shakspeare she gained a great store of information—amongst the rest, that

> ———— " Trifles light as air,
> " Are, to the jealous, confirmation strong,
> " As proofs of Holy Writ."

That

> " The poor beetle, which we tread upon,
> " In corporal sufferance feels a pang as great
> " As when a giant dies."

And that a young woman in love always looks

> ———— " like Patience on a monument
> " Smiling at Grief."

So far her improvement was sufficient—and in many other points she came on exceedingly well; for though she could not write sonnets, she brought herself to read them; and though there seemed no chance of her throwing a whole party into raptures by a prelude on the pianoforte, of her own composition, she could listen to other people's performance with very little fatigue. Her greatest deficiency was in the pencil—she had no notion of drawing—not enough even to attempt a sketch of her lover's profile, that she might be detected in the design. There she fell miserably short of the true heroic height. At present she did not know her own poverty, for she had no lover to pourtray. She had reached the age of seventeen, without having seen one amiable youth who could call forth her sensibility; without having inspired one real passion, and without having excited even any admiration but what was very moderate and very transient. This was strange indeed! But strange things may be generally accounted for if their cause be fairly searched out. There was not one lord in the neighbourhood; no—not even a baronet. There was not one family among their acquaintance who had reared and supported a boy accidentally found at their door—not one young man whose origin was unknown. Her father had no ward, and the squire of the parish no children.

But when a young lady is to be a heroine, the perverseness of forty surrounding families cannot prevent her. Something

Something must and will happen to throw a hero in her way.

Mr. Allen, who owned the chief of the property about Fullerton, the village in Wiltshire where the Morlands lived, was ordered to Bath for the benefit of a gouty constitution;—and his lady, a good-humoured woman, fond of Miss Morland, and probably aware that if adventures will not befal a young lady in her own village, she must seek them abroad, invited her to go with them. Mr. and Mrs. Morland were all compliance, and Catherine all happiness.

CHAPTER II.

In addition to what has been already said of Catherine Morland's personal and mental endowments, when about to be launched into all the difficulties and dangers of a six weeks' residence in Bath, it may be stated, for the reader's more certain information, lest the following pages should otherwise fail of giving any idea of what her character is meant to be ; that her heart was affectionate, her disposition cheerful and open, without conceit or affectation of any kind—her manners just removed from the awkwardness and shyness of a girl ; her person pleasing, and, when in good looks, pretty—and her mind about as ignorant and uninformed as the female mind at seventeen usually is.

When the hour of departure drew near, the maternal anxiety of Mrs. Morland will be naturally supposed to be most severe. A thousand alarming presentiments of evil to her beloved Catherine from this terrific separation must oppress her heart with sadness, and drown her in tears for the last day or two of their being together ; and advice of the most important and applicable nature must of course flow from her wise lips in their parting conference in her closet. Cautions against the violence of such noblemen and baronets as delight in forcing young ladies away to some remote farm-house, must, at such a moment, relieve the fulness of her heart. Who would not think so ? But Mrs. Morland knew so little of lords and baronets, that she entertained no notion of their general mischievous-ness, and was wholly unsuspicious of danger to her daughter from their machinations. Her cautions were confined to the following points. " I beg, Catherine, you will always wrap yourself up very warm about the throat, when you come from the Rooms at night ; and I wish you would try

try to keep some account of the money you spend ;—
I will give you this little book on purpose."

Sally, or rather Sarah, (for what young lady of common
gentility will reach the age of sixteen without altering
her name as far as she can ?) must from situation be at
this time the intimate friend and confidante of her sister.
It is remarkable, however, that she neither insisted on
Catherine's writing by every post, nor exacted her promise
of transmitting the character of every new acquaintance,
nor a detail of every interesting conversation that Bath
might produce. Every thing indeed relative to this
important journey was done, on the part of the Morlands,
with a degree of moderation and composure, which
seemed rather consistent with the common feelings of
common life, than with the refined susceptibilities, the
tender emotions which the first separation of a heroine
from her family ought always to excite. Her father,
instead of giving her an unlimited order on his banker, or
even putting an hundred pounds bank-bill into her hands,
gave her only ten guineas, and promised her more when
she wanted it.

Under these unpromising auspices, the parting took
place, and the journey began. It was performed with
suitable quietness and uneventful safety. Neither robbers
nor tempests befriended them, nor one lucky overturn to
introduce them to the hero. Nothing more alarming
occurred than a fear on Mrs. Allen's side, of having once
left her clogs behind her at an inn, and that fortunately
proved to be groundless.

They arrived at Bath. Catherine was all eager delight ;—
her eyes were here, there, every where, as they approached
its fine and striking environs, and afterwards drove
through those streets which conducted them to the hotel.
She was come to be happy, and she felt happy already.

They were soon settled in comfortable lodgings in
Pulteney-street.

It is now expedient to give some description of Mrs.
Allen, that the reader may be able to judge, in what

manner

manner her actions will hereafter tend to promote the
general distress of the work, and how she will, probably,
contribute to reduce poor Catherine to all the desperate
wretchedness of which a last volume is capable—whether
by her imprudence, vulgarity, or jealousy—whether by
intercepting her letters, ruining her character, or turning
her out of doors.

Mrs. Allen was one of that numerous class of females,
whose society can raise no other emotion than surprise at
there being any men in the world who could like them
well enough to marry them. She had neither beauty,
genius, accomplishment, nor manner. The air of a gentlewoman, a great deal of quiet, inactive good temper, and
a trifling turn of mind, were all that could account for
her being the choice of a sensible, intelligent man, like
Mr. Allen. In one respect she was admirably fitted to
introduce a young lady into public, being as fond of going
every where and seeing every thing herself as any young
lady could be. Dress was her passion. She had a most
harmless delight in being fine ; and our heroine's entrée
into life could not take place till after three or four days
had been spent in learning what was mostly worn, and
her chaperon was provided with a dress of the newest
fashion. Catherine too made some purchases herself, and
when all these matters were arranged, the important
evening came which was to usher her into the Upper
Rooms. Her hair was cut and dressed by the best hand,
her clothes put on with care, and both Mrs. Allen and her
maid declared she looked quite as she should do. With
such encouragement, Catherine hoped at least to pass
uncensured through the crowd. As for admiration, it was
always very welcome when it came, but she did not
depend on it.

Mrs. Allen was so long in dressing, that they did not
enter the ball-room till late. The season was full, the
room crowded, and the two ladies squeezed in as well as
they could. As for Mr. Allen, he repaired directly to the
card-room, and left them to enjoy a mob by themselves.
                                                            With

With more care for the safety of her new gown than for the comfort of her protegée, Mrs. Allen made her way through the throng of men by the door, as swiftly as the necessary caution would allow ; Catherine, however, kept close at her side, and linked her arm too firmly within her friend's to be torn asunder by any common effort of a struggling assembly. But to her utter amazement she found that to proceed along the room was by no means the way to disengage themselves from the crowd ; it seemed rather to increase as they went on, whereas she had imagined that when once fairly within the door, they should easily find seats and be able to watch the dances with perfect convenience. But this was far from being the case, and though by unwearied diligence they gained even the top of the room, their situation was just the same ; they saw nothing of the dancers but the high feathers of some of the ladies. Still they moved on— something better was yet in view ; and by a continued exertion of strength and ingenuity they found themselves at last in the passage behind the highest bench. Here there was something less of crowd than below ; and hence Miss Morland had a comprehensive view of all the company beneath her, and of all the dangers of her late passage through them. It was a splendid sight, and she began, for the first time that evening, to feel herself at a ball : she longed to dance, but she had not an acquaintance in the room. Mrs. Allen did all that she could do in such a case by saying very placidly, every now and then, " I wish you could dance, my dear,—I wish you could get a partner." For some time her young friend felt obliged to her for these wishes ; but they were repeated so often, and proved so totally ineffectual, that Catherine grew tired at last, and would thank her no more.

They were not long able, however, to enjoy the repose of the eminence they had so laboriously gained.—Every body was shortly in motion for tea, and they must squeeze out like the rest. Catherine began to feel something of disappointment—she was tired of being continually pressed against

against by people, the generality of whose faces possessed
nothing to interest, and with all of whom she was so
wholly unacquainted, that she could not relieve the
irksomeness of imprisonment by the exchange of a
syllable with any of her fellow captives ; and when at
last arrived in the tea-room, she felt yet more the awkwardness of having no party to join, no acquaintance to claim,
no gentleman to assist them.—They saw nothing of Mr.
Allen ; and after looking about them in vain for a more
eligible situation, were obliged to sit down at the end of
a table, at which a large party were already placed,
without having any thing to do there, or any body to
speak to, except each other.

Mrs. Allen congratulated herself, as soon as they were
seated, on having preserved her gown from injury. " It
would have been very shocking to have it torn," said she,
" would not it ?—It is such a delicate muslin.—For my
part I have not seen any thing I like so well in the whole
room, I assure you."

" How uncomfortable it is," whispered Catherine, " not
to have a single acquaintance here ! "

" Yes, my dear," replied Mrs. Allen, with perfect
serenity, " it is very uncomfortable indeed."

" What shall we do ?—The gentlemen and ladies at
this table look as if they wondered why we came here—
we seem forcing ourselves into their party."

" Aye, so we do.—That is very disagreeable. I wish
we had a large acquaintance here."

" I wish we had *any* ;—it would be somebody to go to."

" Very true, my dear ; and if we knew anybody we
would join them directly. The Skinners were here last
year—I wish they were here now."

" Had not we better go away as it is ?—Here are no
tea things for us, you see."

" No more there are, indeed.—How very provoking !
But I think we had better sit still, for one gets so tumbled
in such a crowd ! How is my head, my dear ?—Somebody
gave me a push that has hurt it I am afraid."

" No,

" No, indeed, it looks very nice.—But, dear Mrs. Allen, are you sure there is nobody you know in all this multitude of people ? I think you *must* know somebody."

" I don't upon my word—I wish I did. I wish I had a large acquaintance here with all my heart, and then I should get you a partner.—I should be so glad to have you dance. There goes a strange-looking woman ! What an odd gown she has got on !—How old fashioned it is ! Look at the back."

After some time they received an offer of tea from one of their neighbours ; it was thankfully accepted, and this introduced a light conversation with the gentleman who offered it, which was the only time that any body spoke to them during the evening, till they were discovered and joined by Mr. Allen when the dance was over.

" Well, Miss Morland," said he, directly, " I hope you have had an agreeable ball."

" Very agreeable indeed," she replied, vainly endeavouring to hide a great yawn.

" I wish she had been able to dance," said his wife, " I wish we could have got a partner for her.—I have been saying how glad I should be if the Skinners were here this winter instead of last ; or if the Parrys had come, as they talked of once, she might have danced with George Parry. I am so sorry she has not had a partner ! "

" We shall do better another evening I hope," was Mr. Allen's consolation.

The company began to disperse when the dancing was over—enough to leave space for the remainder to walk about in some comfort ; and now was the time for a heroine, who had not yet played a very distinguished part in the events of the evening, to be noticed and admired. Every five minutes, by removing some of the crowd, gave greater openings for her charms. She was now seen by many young men who had not been near her before. Not one, however, started with rapturous wonder on beholding her, no whisper of eager inquiry ran round the room, nor was she once called a divinity by any body.
Yet

Yet Catherine was in very good looks, and had the company only seen her three years before, they would *now* have thought her exceedingly handsome.

She *was* looked at however, and with some admiration ; for, in her own hearing, two gentlemen pronounced her to be a pretty girl. Such words had their due effect ; she immediately thought the evening pleasanter than she had found it before—her humble vanity was contented— she felt more obliged to the two young men for this simple praise than a true quality heroine would have been for fifteen sonnets in celebration of her charms, and went to her chair in good humour with every body, and per- fectly satisfied with her share of public attention.

CHAP-

CHAPTER III.

EVERY morning now brought its regular duties ;—
shops were to be visited ; some new part of the town to
be looked at ; and the Pump-room to be attended, where
they paraded up and down for an hour, looking at every
body and speaking to no one. The wish of a numerous
acquaintance in Bath was still uppermost with Mrs.
Allen, and she repeated it after every fresh proof, which
every morning brought, of her knowing nobody at all.

They made their appearance in the Lower Rooms ;
and here fortune was more favourable to our heroine.
The master of the ceremonies introduced to her a very
gentlemanlike young man as a partner ;—his name was
Tilney. He seemed to be about four or five and twenty,
was rather tall, had a pleasing countenance, a very
intelligent and lively eye, and, if not quite handsome,
was very near it. His address was good, and Catherine
felt herself in high luck. There was little leisure for
speaking while they danced ; but when they were seated
at tea, she found him as agreeable as she had already
given him credit for being. He talked with fluency and
spirit—and there was an archness and pleasantry in his
manner which interested, though it was hardly understood by her. After chatting some time on such matters
as naturally arose from the objects around them, he
suddenly addressed her with—" I have hitherto been very
remiss, madam, in the proper attentions of a partner
here ; I have not yet asked you how long you have been
in Bath ; whether you were ever here before ; whether
you have been at the Upper Rooms, the theatre, and the
concert ; and how you like the place altogether. I have
been very negligent—but are you now at leisure to satisfy
me in these particulars ? If you are I will begin directly."

" You need not give yourself that trouble, sir."

" No

"No trouble I assure you, madam." Then forming his features into a set smile, and affectedly softening his voice, he added, with a simpering air, "Have you been long in Bath, madam?"

"About a week, sir," replied Catherine, trying not to laugh.

"Really!" with affected astonishment.

"Why should you be surprized, sir?"

"Why, indeed!" said he, in his natural tone—"but some emotion must appear to be raised by your reply, and surprize is more easily assumed, and not less reasonable than any other.—Now let us go on. Were you never here before, madam?"

"Never, sir."

"Indeed! Have you yet honoured the Upper Rooms?"

"Yes, sir, I was there last Monday."

"Have you been to the theatre?"

"Yes, sir, I was at the play on Tuesday."

"To the concert?"

"Yes, sir, on Wednesday."

"And are you altogether pleased with Bath?"

"Yes—I like it very well."

"Now I must give one smirk, and then we may be rational again."

Catherine turned away her head, not knowing whether she might venture to laugh.

"I see what you think of me," said he gravely—"I shall make but a poor figure in your journal to-morrow."

"My journal!"

"Yes, I know exactly what you will say: Friday, went to the Lower Rooms; wore my sprigged muslin robe with blue trimmings—plain black shoes—appeared to much advantage; but was strangely harassed by a queer, half-witted man, who would make me dance with him, and distressed me by his nonsense."

"Indeed I shall say no such thing."

"Shall I tell you what you ought to say?"

"If you please."

"I danced

" I danced with a very agreeable young man, introduced by Mr. King; had a great deal of conversation
with him—seems a most extraordinary genius—hope
I may know more of him. *That*, madam, is what I *wish*
you to say."

" But, perhaps, I keep no journal."

" Perhaps you are not sitting in this room, and I am
not sitting by you. These are points in which a doubt is
equally possible. Not keep a journal! How are your
absent cousins to understand the tenour of your life in
Bath without one? How are the civilities and compliments of every day to be related as they ought to be,
unless noted down every evening in a journal? How are
your various dresses to be remembered, and the particular
state of your complexion, and curl of your hair to be
described in all their diversities, without having constant
recourse to a journal?—My dear madam, I am not so
ignorant of young ladies' ways as you wish to believe me ;
it is this delightful habit of journalizing which largely
contributes to form the easy style of writing for which
ladies are so generally celebrated. Every body allows
that the talent of writing agreeable letters is peculiarly
female. Nature may have done something, but I am sure
it must be essentially assisted by the practice of keeping
a journal."

" I have sometimes thought," said Catherine, doubt-
ingly, " whether ladies do write so much better letters
than gentlemen! That is—I should not think the
superiority was always on our side."

" As far as I have had opportunity of judging, it appears
to me that the usual style of letter-writing among women
is faultless, except in three particulars."

" And what are they ? "

" A general deficiency of subject, a total inattention to
stops, and a very frequent ignorance of grammar."

" Upon my word ! I need not have been afraid of dis-
claiming the compliment. You do not think too highly
of us in that way."

" I should

" I should no more lay it down as a general rule that
women write better letters than men, than that they sing
better duets, or draw better landscapes. In every power,
of which taste is the foundation, excellence is pretty fairly
divided between the sexes."

They were interrupted by Mrs. Allen :—" My dear
Catherine," said she, " do take this pin out of my sleeve ;
I am afraid it has torn a hole already ; I shall be quite
sorry if it has, for this is a favourite gown, though it cost
but nine shillings a yard."

" That is exactly what I should have guessed it,
madam," said Mr. Tilney, looking at the muslin.

" Do you understand muslins, sir ? "

" Particularly well ; I always buy my own cravats,
and am allowed to be an excellent judge ; and my sister
has often trusted me in the choice of a gown. I bought
one for her the other day, and it was pronounced to be
a prodigious bargain by every lady who saw it. I gave
but five shillings a yard for it, and a true Indian muslin."

Mrs. Allen was quite struck by his genius. " Men
commonly take so little notice of those things," said she :
" I can never get Mr. Allen to know one of my gowns
from another. You must be a great comfort to your
sister, sir."

" I hope I am, madam."

" And pray, sir, what do you think of Miss Morland's
gown ? "

" It is very pretty, madam," said he, gravely examining
it ; " but I do not think it will wash well ; I am afraid
it will fray."

" How can you," said Catherine, laughing, " be so ——"
she had almost said, strange.

" I am quite of your opinion, sir," replied Mrs. Allen :
" and so I told Miss Morland when she bought it."

" But then you know, madam, muslin always turns to
some account or other ; Miss Morland will get enough
out of it for a handkerchief, or a cap, or a cloak.—Muslin
can never be said to be wasted. I have heard my sister
say

say so forty times, when she has been extravagant in buying more than she wanted, or careless in cutting it to pieces."

" Bath is a charming place, sir ; there are so many good shops here.—We are sadly off in the country ; not but what we have very good shops in Salisbury, but it is so far to go ;—eight miles is a long way ; Mr. Allen says it is nine, measured nine ; but I am sure it cannot be more than eight ; and it is such a fag—I come back tired to death. Now here one can step out of doors and get a thing in five minutes."

Mr. Tilney was polite enough to seem interested in what she said ; and she kept him on the subject of muslins till the dancing recommenced. Catherine feared, as she listened to their discourse, that he indulged himself a little too much with the foibles of others.—" What are you thinking of so earnestly ? " said he, as they walked back to the ball-room ;—" not of your partner, I hope, for, by that shake of the head, your meditations are not satisfactory."

Catherine coloured, and said, " I was not thinking of any thing."

" That is artful and deep, to be sure ; but I had rather be told at once that you will not tell me."

" Well then, I will not."

" Thank you ; for now we shall soon be acquainted, as I am authorized to tease you on this subject whenever we meet, and nothing in the world advances intimacy so much."

They danced again ; and, when the assembly closed, parted, on the lady's side at least, with a strong inclination for continuing the acquaintance. Whether she thought of him so much, while she drank her warm wine and water, and prepared herself for bed, as to dream of him when there, cannot be ascertained ; but I hope it was no more than in a slight slumber, or a morning doze at most ; for if it be true, as a celebrated writer has maintained, that no young lady can be justified in falling

in

in love before the gentleman's love is declared,* it must be very improper that a young lady should dream of a gentleman before the gentleman is first known to have dreamt of her. How proper Mr. Tilney might be as a dreamer or a lover, had not yet perhaps entered Mr. Allen's head, but that he was not objectionable as a common acquaintance for his young charge he was on inquiry satisfied ; for he had early in the evening taken pains to know who her partner was, and had been assured of Mr. Tilney's being a clergyman, and of a very respectable family in Gloucestershire.

* Vide a letter from Mr. Richardson, No. 97, vol. ii. Rambler.

CHAP-

CHAPTER IV.

WITH more than usual eagerness did Catherine hasten
to the Pump-room the next day, secure within herself of
seeing Mr. Tilney there before the morning were over,
and ready to meet him with a smile :—but no smile was
demanded—Mr. Tilney did not appear. Every creature
in Bath, except himself, was to be seen in the room at
different periods of the fashionable hours ; crowds of
people were every moment passing in and out, up the
steps and down ; people whom nobody cared about, and
nobody wanted to see ; and he only was absent. " What
a delightful place Bath is," said Mrs. Allen, as they sat
down near the great clock, after parading the room till
they were tired ; " and how pleasant it would be if we
had any acquaintance here."

This sentiment had been uttered so often in vain, that
Mrs. Allen had no particular reason to hope it would be
followed with more advantage now ; but we are told to
" despair of nothing we would attain," as " unwearied
diligence our point would gain ; " and the unwearied
diligence with which she had every day wished for the
same thing was at length to have its just reward, for
hardly had she been seated ten minutes before a lady of
about her own age, who was sitting by her, and had been
looking at her attentively for several minutes, addressed
her with great complaisance in these words :—" I think,
madam, I cannot be mistaken ; it is a long time since
I had the pleasure of seeing you, but is not your name
Allen ? " This question answered, as it readily was, the
stranger pronounced her's to be Thorpe ; and Mrs. Allen
immediately recognized the features of a former school-
fellow and intimate, whom she had seen only once since
their respective marriages, and that many years ago.
Their joy on this meeting was very great, as well it might,
since

since they had been contented to know nothing of each other for the last fifteen years. Compliments on good looks now passed ; and, after observing how time had slipped away since they were last together, how little they had thought of meeting in Bath, and what a pleasure it was to see an old friend, they proceeded to make inquiries and give intelligence as to their families, sisters, and cousins, talking both together, far more ready to give than to receive information, and each hearing very little of what the other said. Mrs. Thorpe, however, had one great advantage as a talker, over Mrs. Allen, in a family of children ; and when she expatiated on the talents of her sons, and the beauty of her daughters,—when she related their different situations and views,—that John was at Oxford, Edward at Merchant-Taylors', and William at sea,—and all of them more beloved and respected in their different stations than any other three beings ever were, Mrs. Allen had no similar information to give, no similar triumphs to press on the unwilling and unbelieving ear of her friend, and was forced to sit and appear to listen to all these maternal effusions, consoling herself, however, with the discovery, which her keen eye soon made, that the lace on Mrs. Thorpe's pelisse was not half so handsome as that on her own.

" Here come my dear girls," cried Mrs. Thorpe, pointing at three smart looking females, who, arm in arm, were then moving towards her. " My dear Mrs. Allen, I long to introduce them ; they will be so delighted to see you : the tallest is Isabella, my eldest ; is not she a fine young woman ? The others are very much admired too, but I believe Isabella is the handsomest."

The Miss Thorpes were introduced ; and Miss Morland, who had been for a short time forgotten, was introduced likewise. The name seemed to strike them all ; and, after speaking to her with great civility, the eldest young lady observed aloud to the rest, " How excessively like her brother Miss Morland is ! "

" The very picture of him indeed ! " cried the mother—
and

and " I should have known her any where for his
sister ! " was repeated by them all, two or three times
over. For a moment Catherine was surprized ; but Mrs.
Thorpe and her daughters had scarcely begun the history
of their acquaintance with Mr. James Morland, before
she remembered that her eldest brother had lately formed
an intimacy with a young man of his own college, of the
name of Thorpe ; and that he had spent the last week of
the Christmas vacation with his family, near London.

The whole being explained, many obliging things were
said by the Miss Thorpes of their wish of being better
acquainted with her ; of being considered as already
friends, through the friendship of their brothers, &c.
which Catherine heard with pleasure, and answered with
all the pretty expressions she could command ; and, as
the first proof of amity, she was soon invited to accept
an arm of the eldest Miss Thorpe, and take a turn with
her about the room. Catherine was delighted with this
extension of her Bath acquaintance, and almost forgot
Mr. Tilney while she talked to Miss Thorpe. Friendship
is certainly the finest balm for the pangs of disappointed
love.

Their conversation turned upon those subjects, of
which the free discussion has generally much to do in
perfecting a sudden intimacy between two young ladies ;
such as dress, balls, flirtations, and quizzes. Miss Thorpe,
however, being four years older than Miss Morland, and
at least four years better informed, had a very decided
advantage in discussing such points ; she could compare
the balls of Bath with those of Tunbridge ; its fashions
with the fashions of London ; could rectify the opinions
of her new friend in many articles of tasteful attire ;
could discover a flirtation between any gentleman and
lady who only smiled on each other ; and point out
a quiz through the thickness of a crowd. These powers
received due admiration from Catherine, to whom they
were entirely new ; and the respect which they naturally
inspired might have been too great for familiarity, had

not the easy gaiety of Miss Thorpe's manners, and her frequent expressions of delight on this acquaintance with her, softened down every feeling of awe, and left nothing but tender affection. Their increasing attachment was not to be satisfied with half a dozen turns in the Pump-room, but required, when they all quitted it together, that Miss Thorpe should accompany Miss Morland to the very door of Mr. Allen's house; and that they should there part with a most affectionate and lengthened shake of hands, after learning, to their mutual relief, that they should see each other across the theatre at night, and say their prayers in the same chapel the next morning. Catherine then ran directly up stairs, and watched Miss Thorpe's progress down the street from the drawing-room window; admired the graceful spirit of her walk, the fashionable air of her figure and dress, and felt grateful, as well she might, for the chance which had procured her such a friend.

Mrs. Thorpe was a widow, and not a very rich one; she was a good-humoured, well-meaning woman, and a very indulgent mother. Her eldest daughter had great personal beauty, and the younger ones, by pretending to be as handsome as their sister, imitating her air, and dressing in the same style, did very well.

This brief account of the family is intended to supersede the necessity of a long and minute detail from Mrs. Thorpe herself, of her past adventures and sufferings, which might otherwise be expected to occupy the three or four following chapters; in which the worthlessness of lords and attornies might be set forth, and conversations, which had passed twenty years before, be minutely repeated.

CHAP-

CHAPTER V.

CATHERINE was not so much engaged at the theatre that evening, in returning the nods and smiles of Miss Thorpe, though they certainly claimed much of her leisure, as to forget to look with an inquiring eye for Mr. Tilney in every box which her eye could reach ; but she looked in vain. Mr. Tilney was no fonder of the play than the Pump-room. She hoped to be more fortunate the next day ; and when her wishes for fine weather were answered by seeing a beautiful morning, she hardly felt a doubt of it ; for a fine Sunday in Bath empties every house of its inhabitants, and all the world appears on such an occasion to walk about and tell their acquaintance what a charming day it is.

As soon as divine service was over, the Thorpes and Allens eagerly joined each other ; and after staying long enough in the Pump-room to discover that the crowd was insupportable, and that there was not a genteel face to be seen, which every body discovers every Sunday throughout the season, they hastened away to the Crescent, to breathe the fresh air of better company. Here Catherine and Isabella, arm in arm, again tasted the sweets of friendship in an unreserved conversation ;—they talked much, and with much enjoyment; but again was Catherine disappointed in her hope of re-seeing her partner. He was no where to be met with ; every search for him was equally unsuccessful, in morning lounges or evening assemblies ; neither at the upper nor lower rooms, at dressed or undressed balls, was he perceivable ; nor among the walkers, the horsemen, or the curricle-drivers of the morning. His name was not in the Pump-room book, and curiosity could do no more. He must be gone from Bath. Yet he had not mentioned that his stay would be so short ! This sort of mysteriousness, which is always

so

so becoming in a hero, threw a fresh grace in Catherine's imagination around his person and manners, and increased her anxiety to know more of him. From the Thorpes she could learn nothing, for they had been only two days in Bath before they met with Mrs. Allen. It was a subject, however, in which she often indulged with her fair friend, from whom she received every possible encouragement to continue to think of him ; and his impression on her fancy was not suffered therefore to weaken. Isabella was very sure that he must be a charming young man ; and was equally sure that he must have been delighted with her dear Catherine, and would therefore shortly return. She liked him the better for being a clergyman, " for she must confess herself very partial to the profession ; " and something like a sigh escaped her as she said it. Perhaps Catherine was wrong in not demanding the cause of that gentle emotion—but she was not experienced enough in the finesse of love, or the duties of friendship, to know when delicate raillery was properly called for, or when a confidence should be forced.

Mrs. Allen was now quite happy—quite satisfied with Bath. She had found some acquaintance, had been so lucky too as to find in them the family of a most worthy old friend ; and, as the completion of good fortune, had found these friends by no means so expensively dressed as herself. Her daily expressions were no longer, " I wish we had some acquaintance in Bath ! " They were changed into—" How glad I am we have met with Mrs. Thorpe ! " —and she was as eager in promoting the intercourse of the two families, as her young charge and Isabella themselves could be ; never satisfied with the day unless she spent the chief of it by the side of Mrs. Thorpe, in what they called conversation, but in which there was scarcely ever any exchange of opinion, and not often any resemblance of subject, for Mrs. Thorpe talked chiefly of her children, and Mrs. Allen of her gowns.

The progress of the friendship between Catherine and Isabella was quick as its beginning had been warm, and they

they passed so rapidly through every gradation of increasing tenderness, that there was shortly no fresh proof of it to be given to their friends or themselves. They called each other by their Christian name, were always arm in arm when they walked, pinned up each other's train for the dance, and were not to be divided in the set ; and if a rainy morning deprived them of other enjoyments, they were still resolute in meeting in defiance of wet and dirt, and shut themselves up, to read novels together. Yes, novels ;—for I will not adopt that ungenerous and impolitic custom so common with novel writers, of degrading by their contemptuous censure the very performances, to the number of which they are themselves adding—joining with their greatest enemies in bestowing the harshest epithets on such works, and scarcely ever permitting them to be read by their own heroine, who, if she accidentally take up a novel, is sure to turn over its insipid pages with disgust. Alas ! if the heroine of one novel be not patronized by the heroine of another, from whom can she expect protection and regard ? I cannot approve of it. Let us leave it to the Reviewers to abuse such effusions of fancy at their leisure, and over every new novel to talk in threadbare strains of the trash with which the press now groans. Let us not desert one another ; we are an injured body. Although our productions have afforded more extensive and unaffected pleasure than those of any other literary corporation in the world, no species of composition has been so much decried. From pride, ignorance, or fashion, our foes are almost as many as our readers. And while the abilities of the nine-hundredth abridger of the History of England, or of the man who collects and publishes in a volume some dozen lines of Milton, Pope, and Prior, with a paper from the Spectator, and a chapter from Sterne, are eulogized by a thousand pens,—there seems almost a general wish of decrying the capacity and undervaluing the labour of the novelist, and of slighting the performances which have only genius, wit, and taste to recommend them. " I am

no

no novel reader—I seldom look into novels—Do not imagine that *I* often read novels—It is really very well for a novel." —Such is the common cant.—" And what are you reading, Miss —— ? " " Oh ! it is only a novel ! " replies the young lady ; while she lays down her book with affected indifference, or momentary shame.—" It is only Cecilia, or Camilla, or Belinda ; " or, in short, only some work in which the greatest powers of the mind are displayed, in which the most thorough knowledge of human nature, the happiest delineation of its varieties, the liveliest effusions of wit and humour are conveyed to the world in the best chosen language. Now, had the same young lady been engaged with a volume of the Spectator, instead of such a work, how proudly would she have produced the book, and told its name ; though the chances must be against her being occupied by any part of that voluminous publication, of which either the matter or manner would not disgust a young person of taste : the substance of its papers so often consisting in the statement of improbable circumstances, unnatural characters, and topics of conversation, which no longer concern any one living ; and their language, too, frequently so coarse as to give no very favourable idea of the age that could endure it.

CHAP-

CHAPTER VI.

The following conversation, which took place between the two friends in the Pump-room one morning, after an acquaintance of eight or nine days, is given as a specimen of their very warm attachment, and of the delicacy, discretion, originality of thought, and literary taste which marked the reasonableness of that attachment.

They met by appointment ; and as Isabella had arrived nearly five minutes before her friend, her first address naturally was—" My dearest creature, what can have made you so late ? I have been waiting for you at least this age ! "

" Have you, indeed !—I am very sorry for it ; but really I thought I was in very good time. It is but just one. I hope you have not been here long ? "

" Oh ! these ten ages at least. I am sure I have been here this half hour. But now, let us go and sit down at the other end of the room, and enjoy ourselves. I have an hundred things to say to you. In the first place, I was so afraid it would rain this morning, just as I wanted to set off ; it looked very showery, and that would have thrown me into agonies ! Do you know, I saw the prettiest hat you can imagine, in a shop window in Milsom-street just now—very like yours, only with coquelicot ribbons instead of green ; I quite longed for it. But, my dearest Catherine, what have you been doing with yourself all this morning ?—Have you gone on with Udolpho ? "

" Yes, I have been reading it ever since I woke ; and I am got to the black veil."

" Are you, indeed ? How delightful ! Oh ! I would not tell you what is behind the black veil for the world ! Are not you wild to know ? "

" Oh ! yes, quite ; what can it be ?—But do not tell me—I would not be told upon any account. I know it must

must be a skeleton, I am sure it is Laurentina's skeleton.
Oh! I am delighted with the book! I should like to
spend my whole life in reading it. I assure you, if it had
not been to meet you, I would not have come away from
it for all the world."

" Dear creature! how much I am obliged to you;
and when you have finished Udolpho, we will read the
Italian together; and I have made out a list of ten or
twelve more of the same kind for you."

" Have you, indeed! How glad I am!—What are
they all ? "

" I will read you their names directly; here they are,
in my pocket-book. Castle of Wolfenbach, Clermont,
Mysterious Warnings, Necromancer of the Black Forest,
Midnight Bell, Orphan of the Rhine, and Horrid Mysteries.
Those will last us some time."

" Yes, pretty well; but are they all horrid, are you
sure they are all horrid ? "

" Yes, quite sure; for a particular friend of mine,
a Miss Andrews, a sweet girl, one of the sweetest creatures
in the world, has read every one of them. I wish you
knew Miss Andrews, you would be delighted with her.
She is netting herself the sweetest cloak you can conceive.
I think her as beautiful as an angel, and I am so vexed
with the men for not admiring her!—I scold them all
amazingly about it."

" Scold them! Do you scold them for not admiring
her ? "

" Yes, that I do. There is nothing I would not do for
those who are really my friends. I have no notion of
loving people by halves, it is not my nature. My attach-
ments are always excessively strong. I told Capt. Hunt
at one of our assemblies this winter, that if he was to
tease me all night, I would not dance with him, unless
he would allow Miss Andrews to be as beautiful as an
angel. The men think us incapable of real friendship you
know, and I am determined to shew them the difference.
Now, if I were to hear any body speak slightingly of you,
I should

I should fire up in a moment :—but that is not at all likely, for *you* are just the kind of girl to be a great favourite with the men."

" Oh ! dear," cried Catherine, colouring, " how can you say so ? "

" I know you very well ; you have so much animation, which is exactly what Miss Andrews wants, for I must confess there is something amazingly insipid about her. Oh ! I must tell you, that just after we parted yesterday, I saw a young man looking at you so earnestly—I am sure he is in love with you." Catherine coloured, and disclaimed again. Isabella laughed. " It is very true, upon my honour, but I see how it is ; you are indifferent to every body's admiration, except that of one gentleman, who shall be nameless. Nay, I cannot blame you— (speaking more seriously)—your feelings are easily understood. Where the heart is really attached, I know very well how little one can be pleased with the attention of any body else. Every thing is so insipid, so uninteresting, that does not relate to the beloved object ! I can perfectly comprehend your feelings."

" But you should not persuade me that I think so very much about Mr. Tilney, for perhaps I may never see him again."

" Not see him again ! My dearest creature, do not talk of it. I am sure you would be miserable if you thought so."

" No, indeed, I should not. I do not pretend to say that I was not very much pleased with him ; but while I have Udolpho to read, I feel as if nobody could make me miserable. Oh ! the dreadful black veil ! My dear Isabella, I am sure there must be Laurentina's skeleton behind it."

" It is so odd to me, that you should never have read Udolpho before ; but I suppose Mrs. Morland objects to novels."

" No, she does not. She very often reads Sir Charles Grandison herself ; but new books do not fall in our way."

" Sir Charles Grandison ! That is an amazing horrid book

book, is it not ?—I remember Miss Andrews could not get through the first volume."

" It is not like Udolpho at all ; but yet I think it is very entertaining."

" Do you indeed !—you surprize me ; I thought it had not been readable. But, my dearest Catherine, have you settled what to wear on your head to-night ? I am deter- mined at all events to be dressed exactly like you. The men take notice of *that* sometimes you know."

" But it does not signify if they do ; " said Catherine, very innocently.

" Signify ! Oh, heavens ! I make it a rule never to mind what they say. They are very often amazingly impertinent if you do not treat them with spirit, and make them keep their distance."

" Are they ?—Well, I never observed *that*. They always behave very well to me."

" Oh ! they give themselves such airs. They are the most conceited creatures in the world, and think them- selves of so much importance !—By the bye, though I have thought of it a hundred times, I have always forgot to ask you what is your favourite complexion in a man. Do you like them best dark or fair ? "

" I hardly know. I never much thought about it. Something between both, I think. Brown—not fair, and not very dark."

" Very well, Catherine. That is exactly he. I have not forgot your description of Mr. Tilney ;—' a brown skin, with dark eyes, and rather dark hair.'—Well, my taste is different. I prefer light eyes, and as to complexion—do you know—I like a sallow better than any other. You must not betray me, if you should ever meet with one of your acquaintance answering that description."

" Betray you !—What do you mean ? "

" Nay, do not distress me. I believe I have said too much. Let us drop the subject."

Catherine, in some amazement, complied ; and after remaining a few moments silent, was on the point of reverting

reverting to what interested her at that time rather more
than any thing else in the world, Laurentina's skeleton ;
when her friend prevented her, by saying,—"For Heaven's
sake ! let us move away from this end of the room. Do
you know, there are two odious young men who have
been staring at me this half hour. They really put me
quite out of countenance. Let us go and look at the
arrivals. They will hardly follow us there."

Away they walked to the book ; and while Isabella
examined the names, it was Catherine's employment to
watch the proceedings of these alarming young men.

" They are not coming this way, are they ? I hope they
are not so impertinent as to follow us. Pray let me know
if they are coming. I am determined I will not look up."

In a few moments Catherine, with unaffected pleasure,
assured her that she need not be longer uneasy, as the
gentlemen had just left the Pump-room.

"And which way are they gone ? " said Isabella, turning
hastily round. " One was a very good-looking young man."

" They went towards the churchyard."

" Well, I am amazingly glad I have got rid of them !
And now, what say you to going to Edgar's Buildings
with me, and looking at my new hat ? You said you
should like to see it."

Catherine readily agreed. " Only," she added, " perhaps we may overtake the two young men."

" Oh ! never mind that. If we make haste, we shall pass
by them presently, and I am dying to shew you my hat."

" But if we only wait a few minutes, there will be no
danger of our seeing them at all."

" I shall not pay them any such compliment, I assure
you. I have no notion of treating men with such respect.
That is the way to spoil them."

Catherine had nothing to oppose against such reason-
ing ; and therefore, to shew the independence of Miss
Thorpe, and her resolution of humbling the sex, they set
off immediately as fast as they could walk, in pursuit of
the two young men.

CHAP·

CHAPTER VII.

HALF a minute conducted them through the Pump-yard to the archway, opposite Union-passage ; but here they were stopped. Every body acquainted with Bath may remember the difficulties of crossing Cheap-street at this point ; it is indeed a street of so impertinent a nature, so unfortunately connected with the great London and Oxford roads, and the principal inn of the city, that a day never passes in which parties of ladies, however important their business, whether in quest of pastry, millinery, or even (as in the present case) of young men, are not detained on one side or other by carriages, horsemen, or carts. This evil had been felt and lamented, at least three times a day, by Isabella since her residence in Bath ; and she was now fated to feel and lament it once more, for at the very moment of coming opposite to Union-passage, and within view of the two gentlemen who were proceeding through the crowds, and threading the gutters of that interesting alley, they were prevented crossing by the approach of a gig, driven along on bad pavement by a most knowing-looking coachman with all the vehemence that could most fitly endanger the lives of himself, his companion, and his horse.

" Oh, these odious gigs ! " said Isabella, looking up, " how I detest them." But this detestation, though so just, was of short duration, for she looked again and exclaimed, " Delightful ! Mr. Morland and my brother ! "

" Good heaven ! 'tis James ! " was uttered at the same moment by Catherine ; and, on catching the young men's eyes, the horse was immediately checked with a violence which almost threw him on his haunches, and the servant having now scampered up, the gentlemen jumped out, and the equipage was delivered to his care.

Catherine, by whom this meeting was wholly unexpected, received

received her brother with the liveliest pleasure ; and he, being of a very amiable disposition, and sincerely attached to her, gave every proof on his side of equal satisfaction, which he could have leisure to do, while the bright eyes of Miss Thorpe were incessantly challenging his notice ; and to her his devoirs were speedily paid, with a mixture of joy and embarrassment which might have informed Catherine, had she been more expert in the developement of other people's feelings, and less simply engrossed by her own, that her brother thought her friend quite as pretty as she could do herself.

John Thorpe, who in the mean time had been giving orders about the horses, soon joined them, and from him she directly received the amends which were her due ; for while he slightly and carelessly touched the hand of Isabella, on her he bestowed a whole scrape and half a short bow. He was a stout young man of middling height, who, with a plain face and ungraceful form, seemed fearful of being too handsome unless he wore the dress of a groom, and too much like a gentleman unless he were easy where he ought to be civil, and impudent where he might be allowed to be easy. He took out his watch : " How long do you think we have been running it from Tetbury, Miss Morland ? "

" I do not know the distance." Her brother told her that it was twenty-three miles.

" *Three*-and-twenty ! " cried Thorpe ; " five-and-twenty if it is an inch." Morland remonstrated, pleaded the authority of road-books, innkeepers, and milestones ; but his friend disregarded them all ; he had a surer test of distance. " I know it must be five-and-twenty," said he, " by the time we have been doing it. It is now half after one ; we drove out of the inn-yard at Tetbury as the town-clock struck eleven ; and I defy any man in England to make my horse go less than ten miles an hour in harness ; that makes it exactly twenty-five."

" You have lost an hour," said Morland ; " it was only ten o'clock when we came from Tetbury."

" Ten

"Ten o'clock! it was eleven, upon my soul! I counted every stroke. This brother of yours would persuade me out of my senses, Miss Morland; do but look at my horse; did you ever see an animal so made for speed in your life?" (The servant had just mounted the carriage and was driving off.) "Such true blood! Three hours and a half indeed coming only three-and-twenty miles! look at that creature, and suppose it possible if you can."

"He *does* look very hot to be sure."

"Hot! he had not turned a hair till we came to Walcot Church: but look at his forehand; look at his loins; only see how he moves; that horse *cannot* go less than ten miles an hour: tie his legs and he will get on. What do you think of my gig, Miss Morland? a neat one, is not it? Well hung; town built; I have not had it a month. It was built for a Christchurch man, a friend of mine, a very good sort of fellow; he ran it a few weeks, till, I believe, it was convenient to have done with it. I happened just then to be looking out for some light thing of the kind, though I had pretty well determined on a curricle too; but I chanced to meet him on Magdalen Bridge, as he was driving into Oxford, last term: 'Ah! Thorpe,' said he, 'do you happen to want such a little thing as this? it is a capital one of the kind, but I am cursed tired of it.' 'Oh! d——,' said I, 'I am your man; what do you ask?' And how much do you think he did, Miss Morland?"

"I am sure I cannot guess at all."

"Curricle-hung you see; seat, trunk, sword-case, splashing-board, lamps, silver moulding, all you see complete; the iron-work as good as new, or better. He asked fifty guineas; I closed with him directly, threw down the money, and the carriage was mine."

"And I am sure," said Catherine, "I know so little of such things that I cannot judge whether it was cheap or dear."

"Neither one nor t'other; I might have got it for less I dare say; but I hate haggling, and poor Freeman wanted cash."

"That

" That was very good-natured of you," said Catherine, quite pleased.

" Oh! d—— it, when one has the means of doing a kind thing by a friend, I hate to be pitiful."

An inquiry now took place into the intended movements of the young ladies ; and, on finding whither they were going, it was decided that the gentlemen should accompany them to Edgar's Buildings, and pay their respects to Mrs. Thorpe. James and Isabella led the way ; and so well satisfied was the latter with her lot, so contentedly was she endeavouring to ensure a pleasant walk to him who brought the double recommendation of being her brother's friend, and her friend's brother, so pure and uncoquettish were her feelings, that, though they overtook and passed the two offending young men in Milsom-street, she was so far from seeking to attract their notice, that she looked back at them only three times.

John Thorpe kept of course with Catherine, and, after a few minutes' silence, renewed the conversation about his gig—" You will find, however, Miss Morland, it would be reckoned a cheap thing by some people, for I might have sold it for ten guineas more the next day ; Jackson, of Oriel, bid me sixty at once ; Morland was with me at the time."

" Yes," said Morland, who overheard this ; " but you forget that your horse was included."

" My horse ! oh, d—— it ! I would not sell my horse for a hundred. Are you fond of an open carriage, Miss Morland ? "

" Yes, very ; I have hardly ever an opportunity of being in one ; but I am particularly fond of it."

" I am glad of it ; I will drive you out in mine every day."

" Thank you," said Catherine, in some distress, from a doubt of the propriety of accepting such an offer.

" I will drive you up Lansdown Hill to-morrow."

" Thank you ; but will not your horse want rest ? "

" Rest ! he has only come three-and-twenty miles to-day ;

day ; all nonsense ; nothing ruins horses so much as
rest ; nothing knocks them up so soon. No, no ; I shall
exercise mine at the average of four hours every day
while I am here."

" Shall you indeed ! " said Catherine very seriously,
" that will be forty miles a day."

" Forty ! aye fifty, for what I care. Well, I will drive
you up Lansdown to-morrow ; mind, I am engaged."

" How delightful that will be ! " cried Isabella, turning
round ; " my dearest Catherine, I quite envy you ; but
I am afraid, brother, you will not have room for a third."

" A third indeed ! no, no ; I did not come to Bath to
drive my sisters about ; that would be a good joke,
faith ! Morland must take care of you."

This brought on a dialogue of civilities between the
other two ; but Catherine heard neither the particulars
nor the result. Her companion's discourse now sunk
from its hitherto animated pitch, to nothing more than
a short decisive sentence of praise or condemnation on
the face of every woman they met ; and Catherine, after
listening and agreeing as long as she could, with all the
civility and deference of the youthful female mind, fearful
of hazarding an opinion of its own in opposition to that
of a self-assured man, especially where the beauty of her
own sex is concerned, ventured at length to vary the
subject by a question which had been long uppermost in
her thoughts ; it was, " Have you ever read Udolpho,
Mr. Thorpe ? "

" Udolpho ! Oh, Lord ! not I ; I never read novels ;
I have something else to do."

Catherine, humbled and ashamed, was going to apologize
for her question, but he prevented her by saying, " Novels
are all so full of nonsense and stuff ; there has not been
a tolerably decent one come out since Tom Jones, except
the Monk ; I read that t'other day ; but as for all the
others, they are the stupidest things in creation."

" I think you must like Udolpho, if you were to read
it ; it is so very interesting."

" Not

"Not I, faith! No, if I read any, it shall be Mrs. Radcliff's; her novels are amusing enough; they are worth reading; some fun and nature in *them*."

"Udolpho was written by Mrs. Radcliff," said Catherine, with some hesitation, from the fear of mortifying him.

"No sure; was it? Aye, I remember, so it was; I was thinking of that other stupid book, written by that woman they make such a fuss about, she who married the French emigrant."

"I suppose you mean Camilla?"

"Yes, that's the book; such unnatural stuff!—An old man playing at see-saw! I took up the first volume once, and looked it over, but I soon found it would not do; indeed I guessed what sort of stuff it must be before I saw it: as soon as I heard she had married an emigrant, I was sure I should never be able to get through it."

"I have never read it."

"You had no loss I assure you; it is the horridest nonsense you can imagine; there is nothing in the world in it but an old man's playing at see-saw and learning Latin; upon my soul there is not."

This critique, the justness of which was unfortunately lost on poor Catherine, brought them to the door of Mrs. Thorpe's lodgings, and the feelings of the discerning and unprejudiced reader of Camilla gave way to the feelings of the dutiful and affectionate son, as they met Mrs. Thorpe, who had descried them from above, in the passage. "Ah, mother! how do you do?" said he, giving her a hearty shake of the hand: "where did you get that quiz of a hat, it makes you look like an old witch? Here is Morland and I come to stay a few days with you, so you must look out for a couple of good beds some where near." And this address seemed to satisfy all the fondest wishes of the mother's heart, for she received him with the most delighted and exulting affection. On his two younger sisters he then bestowed an equal portion of his fraternal tenderness, for he asked each of them how they did, and observed that they both looked very ugly.

These manners did not please Catherine ; but he was James's friend and Isabella's brother ; and her judgment was further bought off by Isabella's assuring her, when they withdrew to see the new hat, that John thought her the most charming girl in the world, and by John's engaging her before they parted to dance with him that evening. Had she been older or vainer, such attacks might have done little ; but, where youth and diffidence are united, it requires uncommon steadiness of reason to resist the attraction of being called the most charming girl in the world, and of being so very early engaged as a partner ; and the consequence was, that, when the two Morlands, after sitting an hour with the Thorpes, set off to walk together to Mr. Allen's, and James, as the door was closed on them, said, " Well, Catherine, how do you like my friend Thorpe ? " instead of answering, as she probably would have done, had there been no friendship and no flattery in the case, "I do not like him at all;" she directly replied, " I like him very much ; he seems very agreeable."

" He is as good-natured a fellow as ever lived ; a little of a rattle ; but that will recommend him to your sex I believe : and how do you like the rest of the family ? "

" Very, very much indeed : Isabella particularly."

" I am very glad to hear you say so ; she is just the kind of young woman I could wish to see you attached to ; she has so much good sense, and is so thoroughly unaffected and amiable ; I always wanted you to know her ; and she seems very fond of you. She said the highest things in your praise that could possibly be ; and the praise of such a girl as Miss Thorpe even you, Catherine," taking her hand with affection, " may be proud of."

" Indeed I am," she replied ; " I love her exceedingly, and am delighted to find that you like her too. You hardly mentioned any thing of her, when you wrote to me after your visit there."

" Because I thought I should soon see you myself. I hope you will be a great deal together while you are in Bath. She is a most amiable girl ; such a superior understanding !

standing ! How fond all the family are of her ; she is evidently the general favourite ; and how much she must be admired in such a place as this—is not she ? "

" Yes, very much indeed, I fancy ; Mr. Allen thinks her the prettiest girl in Bath."

" I dare say he does ; and I do not know any man who is a better judge of beauty than Mr. Allen. I need not ask you whether you are happy here, my dear Catherine ; with such a companion and friend as Isabella Thorpe, it would be impossible for you to be otherwise ; and the Allens I am sure are very kind to you ? "

" Yes, very kind ; I never was so happy before ; and now you are come it will be more delightful than ever ; how good it is of you to come so far on purpose to see *me*."

James accepted this tribute of gratitude, and qualified his conscience for accepting it too, by saying with perfect sincerity, " Indeed, Catherine, I love you dearly."

Inquiries and communications concerning brothers and sisters, the situation of some, the growth of the rest, and other family matters, now passed between them, and continued, with only one small digression on James's part, in praise of Miss Thorpe, till they reached Pulteney-street, where he was welcomed with great kindness by Mr. and Mrs. Allen, invited by the former to dine with them, and summoned by the latter to guess the price and weigh the merits of a new muff and tippet. A pre-engagement in Edgar's Buildings prevented his accepting the invitation of one friend, and obliged him to hurry away as soon as he had satisfied the demands of the other. The time of the two parties uniting in the Octagon Room being correctly adjusted, Catherine was then left to the luxury of a raised, restless, and frightened imagination over the pages of Udolpho, lost from all worldly concerns of dressing and dinner, incapable of soothing Mrs. Allen's fears on the delay of an expected dressmaker, and having only one minute in sixty to bestow even on the reflection of her own felicity, in being already engaged for the evening.

CHAP-

CHAPTER VIII.

In spite of Udolpho and the dress-maker, however, the
party from Pulteney-street reached the Upper-rooms in
very good time. The Thorpes and James Morland were
there only two minutes before them ; and Isabella having
gone through the usual ceremonial of meeting her friend
with the most smiling and affectionate haste, of admiring
the set of her gown, and envying the curl of her hair,
they followed their chaperons, arm in arm, into the ball-
room, whispering to each other whenever a thought
occurred, and supplying the place of many ideas by
a squeeze of the hand or a smile of affection.

The dancing began within a few minutes after they
were seated ; and James, who had been engaged quite as
long as his sister, was very importunate with Isabella to
stand up ; but John was gone into the card-room to
speak to a friend, and nothing, she declared, should
induce her to join the set before her dear Catherine could
join it too : " I assure you," said she, " I would not
stand up without your dear sister for all the world ; for
if I did we should certainly be separated the whole evening." Catherine accepted this kindness with gratitude,
and they continued as they were for three minutes longer,
when Isabella, who had been talking to James on the
other side of her, turned again to his sister and whispered,
" My dear creature, I am afraid I must leave you, your
brother is so amazingly impatient to begin ; I know you
will not mind my going away, and I dare say John will
be back in a moment, and then you may easily find me
out." Catherine, though a little disappointed, had too
much good-nature to make any opposition, and the others
rising up, Isabella had only time to press her friend's
hand and say, " Good bye, my dear love," before they
hurried off. The younger Miss Thorpes being also dancing,

ing, Catherine was left to the mercy of Mrs. Thorpe and Mrs. Allen, between whom she now remained. She could not help being vexed at the non-appearance of Mr. Thorpe, for she not only longed to be dancing, but was likewise aware that, as the real dignity of her situation could not be known, she was sharing with the scores of other young ladies still sitting down all the discredit of wanting a partner. To be disgraced in the eye of the world, to wear the appearance of infamy while her heart is all purity, her actions all innocence, and the misconduct of another the true source of her debasement, is one of those circumstances which peculiarly belong to the heroine's life, and her fortitude under it what particularly dignifies her character. Catherine had fortitude too ; she suffered, but no murmur passed her lips.

From this state of humiliation, she was roused, at the end of ten minutes, to a pleasanter feeling, by seeing, not Mr. Thorpe, but Mr. Tilney, within three yards of the place where they sat ; he seemed to be moving that way, but he did not see her, and therefore the smile and the blush, which his sudden reappearance raised in Catherine, passed away without sullying her heroic importance. He looked as handsome and as lively as ever, and was talking with interest to a fashionable and pleasing-looking young woman, who leant on his arm, and whom Catherine immediately guessed to be his sister ; thus unthinkingly throwing away a fair opportunity of considering him lost to her for ever, by being married already. But guided only by what was simple and probable, it had never entered her head that Mr. Tilney could be married ; he had not behaved, he had not talked, like the married men to whom she had been used ; he had never mentioned a wife, and he had acknowledged a sister. From these circumstances sprang the instant conclusion of his sister's now being by his side ; and therefore, instead of turning of a deathlike paleness, and falling in a fit on Mrs. Allen's bosom, Catherine sat erect, in the perfect use of her senses, and with cheeks only a little redder than usual.

Mr.

Mr. Tilney and his companion, who continued, though slowly, to approach, were immediately preceded by a lady, an acquaintance of Mrs. Thorpe ; and this lady stopping to speak to her, they, as belonging to her, stopped likewise, and Catherine, catching Mr. Tilney's eye, instantly received from him the smiling tribute of recognition. She returned it with pleasure, and then advancing still nearer, he spoke both to her and Mrs. Allen, by whom he was very civilly acknowledged. " I am very happy to see you again, sir, indeed ; I was afraid you had left Bath." He thanked her for her fears, and said that he had quitted it for a week, on the very morning after his having had the pleasure of seeing her.

" Well, sir, and I dare say you are not sorry to be back again, for it is just the place for young people—and indeed for every body else too. I tell Mr. Allen, when he talks of being sick of it, that I am sure he should not complain, for it is so very agreeable a place, that it is much better to be here than at home at this dull time of year. I tell him he is quite in luck to be sent here for his health."

" And I hope, madam, that Mr. Allen will be obliged to like the place, from finding it of service to him."

" Thank you, sir. I have no doubt that he will.— A neighbour of ours, Dr. Skinner, was here for his health last winter, and came away quite stout."

" That circumstance must give great encouragement."

" Yes, sir—and Dr. Skinner and his family were here three months ; so I tell Mr. Allen he must not be in a hurry to get away."

Here they were interrupted by a request from Mrs. Thorpe to Mrs. Allen, that she would move a little to accommodate Mrs. Hughes and Miss Tilney with seats, as they had agreed to join their party. This was accordingly done, Mr. Tilney still continuing standing before them ; and after a few minutes consideration, he asked Catherine to dance with him. This compliment, delightful as it was, produced severe mortification to the lady ; and in
giving

giving her denial, she expressed her sorrow on the occasion
so very much as if she really felt it, that had Thorpe, who
joined her just afterwards, been half a minute earlier, he
might have thought her sufferings rather too acute. The
very easy manner in which he then told her that he had
kept her waiting, did not by any means reconcile her
more to her lot ; nor did the particulars which he entered
into while they were standing up, of the horses and dogs
of the friend whom he had just left, and of a proposed
exchange of terriers between them, interest her so much
as to prevent her looking very often towards that part of
the room where she had left Mr. Tilney. Of her dear
Isabella, to whom she particularly longed to point out
that gentleman, she could see nothing. They were in
different sets. She was separated from all her party,
and away from all her acquaintance ;—one mortification
succeeded another, and from the whole she deduced this
useful lesson, that to go previously engaged to a ball, does
not necessarily increase either the dignity or enjoyment
of a young lady. From such a moralizing strain as this,
she was suddenly roused by a touch on the shoulder, and
turning round, perceived Mrs. Hughes directly behind
her, attended by Miss Tilney and a gentleman. " I beg
your pardon, Miss Morland," said she, " for this liberty,—
but I cannot any how get to Miss Thorpe, and Mrs.
Thorpe said she was sure you would not have the least
objection to letting in this young lady by you." Mrs.
Hughes could not have applied to any creature in the
room more happy to oblige her than Catherine. The
young ladies were introduced to each other, Miss Tilney
expressing a proper sense of such goodness, Miss Morland
with the real delicacy of a generous mind making light
of the obligation ; and Mrs. Hughes, satisfied with having
so respectably settled her young charge, returned to her
party.

Miss Tilney had a good figure, a pretty face, and a very
agreeable countenance ; and her air, though it had not
all the decided pretension, the resolute stilishness of
                                                    Miss

Miss Thorpe's, had more real elegance. Her manners
shewed good sense and good breeding ; they were neither
shy, nor affectedly open ; and she seemed capable of
being young, attractive, and at a ball, without wanting
to fix the attention of every man near her, and without
exaggerated feelings of extatic delight or inconceivable
vexation on every little trifling occurrence. Catherine,
interested at once by her appearance and her relationship
to Mr. Tilney, was desirous of being acquainted with her,
and readily talked therefore whenever she could think
of any thing to say, and had courage and leisure for
saying it. But the hindrance thrown in the way of a very
speedy intimacy, by the frequent want of one or more of
these requisites, prevented their doing more than going
through the first rudiments of an acquaintance, by in-
forming themselves how well the other liked Bath, how
much she admired its buildings and surrounding country,
whether she drew, or played or sang, and whether she
was fond of riding on horseback.

The two dances were scarcely concluded before Catherine
found her arm gently seized by her faithful Isabella, who
in great spirits exclaimed—" At last I have got you. My
dearest creature, I have been looking for you this hour.
What could induce you to come into this set, when you
knew I was in the other ? I have been quite wretched
without you."

" My dear Isabella, how was it possible for me to get
at you ? I could not even see where you were."

" So I told your brother all the time—but he would
not believe me. Do go and see for her, Mr. Morland, said
I—but all in vain—he would not stir an inch. Was not
it so, Mr. Morland ? But you men are all so immoderately
lazy ! I have been scolding him to such a degree, my dear
Catherine, you would be quite amazed.—You know
I never stand upon ceremony with such people."

" Look at that young lady with the white beads round
her head," whispered Catherine, detaching her friend
from James—" It is Mr. Tilney's sister."

" Oh !

"Oh! heavens! You don't say so! Let me look at her this moment. What a delightful girl! I never saw any thing half so beautiful! But where is her all-conquering brother? Is he in the room? Point him out to me this instant, if he is. I die to see him. Mr. Morland, you are not to listen. We are not talking about you."

"But what is all this whispering about? What is going on?"

"There now, I knew how it would be. You men have such restless curiosity! Talk of the curiosity of women, indeed!—'tis nothing. But be satisfied, for you are not to know any thing at all of the matter."

"And is that likely to satisfy me, do you think?"

"Well, I declare I never knew any thing like you. What can it signify to you, what we are talking of? Perhaps we are talking about you, therefore I would advise you not to listen, or you may happen to hear something not very agreeable."

In this common-place chatter, which lasted some time, the original subject seemed entirely forgotten; and though Catherine was very well pleased to have it dropped for a while, she could not avoid a little suspicion at the total suspension of all Isabella's impatient desire to see Mr. Tilney. When the orchestra struck up a fresh dance, James would have led his fair partner away, but she resisted. "I tell you, Mr. Morland," she cried, "I would not do such a thing for all the world. How can you be so teasing; only conceive, my dear Catherine, what your brother wants me to do. He wants me to dance with him again, though I tell him that it is a most improper thing, and entirely against the rules. It would make us the talk of the place, if we were not to change partners."

"Upon my honour," said James, "in these public assemblies, it is as often done as not."

"Nonsense, how can you say so? But when you men have a point to carry, you never stick at any thing. My sweet Catherine, do support me, persuade your brother how

how impossible it is. Tell him, that it would quite shock you to see me do such a thing ; now would not it ? "

" No, not at all ; but if you think it wrong, you had much better change."

" There," cried Isabella, " you hear what your sister says, and yet you will not mind her. Well, remember that it is not my fault, if we set all the old ladies in Bath in a bustle. Come along, my dearest Catherine, for heaven's sake, and stand by me." And off they went, to regain their former place. John Thorpe, in the meanwhile, had walked away ; and Catherine, ever willing to give Mr. Tilney an opportunity of repeating the agreeable request which had already flattered her once, made her way to Mrs. Allen and Mrs. Thorpe as fast as she could, in the hope of finding him still with them—a hope which, when it proved to be fruitless, she felt to have been highly unreasonable. " Well, my dear," said Mrs. Thorpe, impatient for praise of her son, " I hope you have had an agreeable partner."

" Very agreeable, madam."

" I am glad of it. John has charming spirits, has not he ? "

" Did you meet Mr. Tilney, my dear ? " said Mrs. Allen.

" No, where is he ? "

" He was with us just now, and said he was so tired of lounging about, that he was resolved to go and dance ; so I thought perhaps he would ask you, if he met with you."

" Where can he be ? " said Catherine, looking round ; but she had not looked round long before she saw him leading a young lady to the dance.

" Ah ! he has got a partner, I wish he had asked *you*," said Mrs. Allen ; and after a short silence, she added, " he is a very agreeable young man."

" Indeed he is, Mrs. Allen," said Mrs. Thorpe, smiling complacently ; " I must say it, though I *am* his mother, that there is not a more agreeable young man in the world."

This

This inapplicable answer might have been too much for the comprehension of many ; but it did not puzzle Mrs. Allen, for after only a moment's consideration, she said, in a whisper to Catherine, " I dare say she thought I was speaking of her son."

Catherine was disappointed and vexed. She seemed to have missed by so little the very object she had had in view ; and this persuasion did not incline her to a very gracious reply, when John Thorpe came up to her soon afterwards, and said, " Well, Miss Morland, I suppose you and I are to stand up and jig it together again."

" Oh, no ; I am much obliged to you, our two dances are over ; and, besides, I am tired, and do not mean to dance any more."

" Do not you ?—then let us walk about and quiz people. Come along with me, and I will shew you the four greatest quizzers in the room ; my two younger sisters and their partners. I have been laughing at them this half hour."

Again Catherine excused herself ; and at last he walked off to quiz his sisters by himself. The rest of the evening she found very dull ; Mr. Tilney was drawn away from their party at tea, to attend that of his partner ; Miss Tilney, though belonging to it, did not sit near her, and James and Isabella were so much engaged in conversing together, that the latter had no leisure to bestow more on her friend than one smile, one squeeze, and one " dearest Catherine."

CHAP-

CHAPTER IX.

THE progress of Catherine's unhappiness from the events of the evening, was as follows. It appeared first in a general dissatisfaction with every body about her, while she remained in the rooms, which speedily brought on considerable weariness and a violent desire to go home. This, on arriving in Pulteney-street, took the direction of extraordinary hunger, and when that was appeased, changed into an earnest longing to be in bed ; such was the extreme point of her distress ; for when there she immediately fell into a sound sleep which lasted nine hours, and from which she awoke perfectly revived, in excellent spirits, with fresh hopes and fresh schemes. The first wish of her heart was to improve her acquaintance with Miss Tilney, and almost her first resolution, to seek her for that purpose, in the Pump-room at noon. In the Pump-room, one so newly arrived in Bath must be met with, and that building she had already found so favourable for the discovery of female excellence, and the completion of female intimacy, so admirably adapted for secret discourses and unlimited confidence, that she was most reasonably encouraged to expect another friend from within its walls. Her plan for the morning thus settled, she sat quietly down to her book after breakfast, resolving to remain in the same place and the same employment till the clock struck one ; and from habitude very little incommoded by the remarks and ejaculations of Mrs. Allen, whose vacancy of mind and incapacity for thinking were such, that as she never talked a great deal, so she could never be entirely silent ; and, therefore, while she sat at her work, if she lost her needle or broke her thread, if she heard a carriage in the street, or saw a speck upon her gown, she must observe it aloud, whether there were any one at leisure to answer her or not.

not. At about half past twelve, a remarkably loud rap drew her in haste to the window, and scarcely had she time to inform Catherine of there being two open carriages at the door, in the first only a servant, her brother driving Miss Thorpe in the second, before John Thorpe came running up stairs, calling out, " Well, Miss Morland, here I am. Have you been waiting long ? We could not come before ; the old devil of a coachmaker was such an eternity finding out a thing fit to be got into, and now it is ten thousand to one, but they break down before we are out of the street. How do you do, Mrs. Allen ? a famous ball last night, was not it ? Come, Miss Morland, be quick, for the others are in a confounded hurry to be off. They want to get their tumble over."

" What do you mean ? " said Catherine, " where are you all going to ? "

" Going to ? why, you have not forgot our engagement ! Did not we agree together to take a drive this morning ? What a head you have ! We are going up Claverton Down."

" Something was said about it, I remember," said Catherine, looking at Mrs. Allen for her opinion ; " but really I did not expect you."

" Not expect me ! that's a good one ! And what a dust you would have made, if I had not come."

Catherine's silent appeal to her friend, meanwhile, was entirely thrown away, for Mrs. Allen, not being at all in the habit of conveying any expression herself by a look, was not aware of its being ever intended by any body else ; and Catherine, whose desire of seeing Miss Tilney again could at that moment bear a short delay in favour of a drive, and who thought there could be no impropriety in her going with Mr. Thorpe, as Isabella was going at the same time with James, was therefore obliged to speak plainer. " Well, ma'am, what do you say to it ? Can you spare me for an hour or two ? shall I go ? "

" Do just as you please, my dear," replied Mrs. Allen, with the most placid indifference. Catherine took the
advice,

advice, and ran off to get ready. In a very few minutes
she re-appeared, having scarcely allowed the two others
time enough to get through a few short sentences in her
praise, after Thorpe had procured Mrs. Allen's admiration of his gig; and then receiving her friend's parting
good wishes, they both hurried down stairs. " My dearest
creature," cried Isabella, to whom the duty of friendship
immediately called her before she could get into the
carriage, " you have been at least three hours getting
ready. I was afraid you were ill. What a delightful ball
we had last night. I have a thousand things to say to
you ; but make haste and get in, for I long to be off."

Catherine followed her orders and turned away, but
not too soon to hear her friend exclaim aloud to James,
" What a sweet girl she is ! I quite doat on her."

" You will not be frightened, Miss Morland," said
Thorpe, as he handed her in, " if my horse should dance
about a little at first setting off. He will, most likely,
give a plunge or two, and perhaps take the rest for a
minute ; but he will soon know his master. He is full
of spirits, playful as can be, but there is no vice in him."

Catherine did not think the portrait a very inviting
one, but it was too late to retreat, and she was too young
to own herself frightened ; so, resigning herself to her
fate, and trusting to the animal's boasted knowledge of
its owner, she sat peaceably down, and saw Thorpe sit
down by her. Every thing being then arranged, the
servant who stood at the horse's head was bid in an
important voice " to let him go," and off they went in
the quietest manner imaginable, without a plunge or
a caper, or any thing like one. Catherine, delighted at
so happy an escape, spoke her pleasure aloud with grateful
surprize ; and her companion immediately made the
matter perfectly simple by assuring her that it was
entirely owing to the peculiarly judicious manner in
which he had then held the reins, and the singular discernment and dexterity with which he had directed his
whip. Catherine, though she could not help wondering
                                                    that

that with such perfect command of his horse, he should
think it necessary to alarm her with a relation of its tricks,
congratulated herself sincerely on being under the care
of so excellent a coachman; and perceiving that the
animal continued to go on in the same quiet manner,
without shewing the smallest propensity towards any
unpleasant vivacity, and (considering its inevitable pace
was ten miles an hour) by no means alarmingly fast, gave
herself up to all the enjoyment of air and exercise of the
most invigorating kind, in a fine mild day of February,
with the consciousness of safety. A silence of several
minutes succeeded their first short dialogue;—it was
broken by Thorpe's saying very abruptly, " Old Allen is
as rich as a Jew—is not he ? " Catherine did not understand him—and he repeated his question, adding in
explanation, " Old Allen, the man you are with."

" Oh ! Mr. Allen, you mean. Yes, I believe, he is very
rich."

" And no children at all ? "

" No—not any."

" A famous thing for his next heirs. He is *your* godfather, is not he ? "

" My godfather !—no."

" But you are always very much with them."

" Yes, very much."

" Aye, that is what I meant. He seems a good kind of
old fellow enough, and has lived very well in his time,
I dare say ; he is not gouty for nothing. Does he drink
his bottle a-day now ? "

" His bottle a-day !—no. Why should you think of
such a thing ? He is a very temperate man, and you
could not fancy him in liquor last night ? "

" Lord help you !—You women are always thinking of
men's being in liquor. Why you do not suppose a man
is overset by a bottle ? I am sure of *this*—that if every
body was to drink their bottle a-day, there would not be
half the disorders in the world there are now. It would
be a famous good thing for us all."

" I can-

" I cannot believe it."

" Oh ! lord, it would be the saving of thousands. There is not the hundredth part of the wine consumed in this kingdom, that there ought to be. Our foggy climate wants help."

" And yet I have heard that there is a great deal of wine drank in Oxford."

" Oxford ! There is no drinking at Oxford now, I assure you. Nobody drinks there. You would hardly meet with a man who goes beyond his four pints at the utmost. Now, for instance, it was reckoned a remarkable thing at the last party in my rooms, that upon an average we cleared about five pints a head. It was looked upon as something out of the common way. *Mine* is famous good stuff to be sure. You would not often meet with any thing like it in Oxford—and that may account for it. But this will just give you a notion of the general rate of drinking there."

" Yes, it does give a notion," said Catherine, warmly, " and that is, that you all drink a great deal more wine than I thought you did. However, I am sure James does not drink so much."

This declaration brought on a loud and overpowering reply, of which no part was very distinct, except the frequent exclamations, amounting almost to oaths, which adorned it, and Catherine was left, when it ended, with rather a strengthened belief of there being a great deal of wine drank in Oxford, and the same happy conviction of her brother's comparative sobriety.

Thorpe's ideas then all reverted to the merits of his own equipage, and she was called on to admire the spirit and freedom with which his horse moved along, and the ease which his paces, as well as the excellence of the springs, gave the motion of the carriage. She followed him in all his admiration as well as she could. To go before, or beyond him was impossible. His knowledge and her ignorance of the subject, his rapidity of expression, and her diffidence of herself put that out of her power ; she

she could strike out nothing new in commendation, but she readily echoed whatever he chose to assert, and it was finally settled between them without any difficulty, that his equipage was altogether the most complete of its kind in England, his carriage the neatest, his horse the best goer, and himself the best coachman.—" You do not really think, Mr. Thorpe," said Catherine, venturing after some time to consider the matter as entirely decided, and to offer some little variation on the subject, " that James's gig will break down ? "

" Break down ! Oh ! lord ! Did you ever see such a little tittuppy thing in your life ? There is not a sound piece of iron about it. The wheels have been fairly worn out these ten years at least—and as for the body ! Upon my soul, you might shake it to pieces yourself with a touch. It is the most devilish little ricketty business I ever beheld !—Thank God ! we have got a better. I would not be bound to go two miles in it for fifty thousand pounds."

" Good heavens ! " cried Catherine, quite frightened, " then pray let us turn back ; they will certainly meet with an accident if we go on. Do let us turn back, Mr. Thorpe ; stop and speak to my brother, and tell him how very unsafe it is."

" Unsafe ! Oh, lord ! what is there in that ? they will only get a roll if it does break down ; and there is plenty of dirt, it will be excellent falling. Oh, curse it ! the carriage is safe enough, if a man knows how to drive it ; a thing of that sort in good hands will last above twenty years after it is fairly worn out. Lord bless you ! I would undertake for five pounds to drive it to York and back again, without losing a nail."

Catherine listened with astonishment ; she knew not how to reconcile two such very different accounts of the same thing ; for she had not been brought up to under-stand the propensities of a rattle, nor to know to how many idle assertions and impudent falsehoods the excess of vanity will lead. Her own family were plain matter-

of-fact people, who seldom aimed at wit of any kind ;
her father, at the utmost, being contented with a pun,
and her mother with a proverb ; they were not in the
habit therefore of telling lies to increase their importance,
or of asserting at one moment what they would contradict
the next. She reflected on the affair for some time in
much perplexity, and was more than once on the point
of requesting from Mr. Thorpe a clearer insight into his
real opinion on the subject ; but she checked herself,
because it appeared to her that he did not excel in giving
those clearer insights, in making those things plain which
he had before made ambiguous ; and, joining to this, the
consideration, that he would not really suffer his sister
and his friend to be exposed to a danger from which he
might easily preserve them, she concluded at last, that
he must know the carriage to be in fact perfectly safe,
and therefore would alarm herself no longer. By him the
whole matter seemed entirely forgotten ; and all the rest
of his conversation, or rather talk, began and ended with
himself and his own concerns. He told her of horses
which he had bought for a trifle and sold for incredible
sums ; of racing matches, in which his judgment had
infallibly foretold the winner ; of shooting parties, in
which he had killed more birds (though without having
one good shot) than all his companions together ; and
described to her some famous day's sport, with the fox-
hounds, in which his foresight and skill in directing the
dogs had repaired the mistakes of the most experienced
huntsman, and in which the boldness of his riding, though
it had never endangered his own life for a moment, had
been constantly leading others into difficulties, which he
calmly concluded had broken the necks of many.

Little as Catherine was in the habit of judging for her
self, and unfixed as were her general notions of what men
ought to be, she could not entirely repress a doubt, while
she bore with the effusions of his endless conceit, of his
being altogether completely agreeable. It was a bold
surmise, for he was Isabella's brother ; and she had been
                                                    assured

assured by James, that his manners would recommend him to all her sex; but in spite of this, the extreme weariness of his company, which crept over her before they had been out an hour, and which continued unceasingly to increase till they stopped in Pulteney-street again, induced her, in some small degree, to resist such high authority, and to distrust his powers of giving universal pleasure.

When they arrived at Mrs. Allen's door, the astonishment of Isabella was hardly to be expressed, on finding that it was too late in the day for them to attend her friend into the house :—" Past three o'clock ! " it was inconceivable, incredible, impossible ! and she would neither believe her own watch, nor her brother's, nor the servant's ; she would believe no assurance of it founded on reason or reality, till Morland produced his watch, and ascertained the fact ; to have doubted a moment longer *then*, would have been equally inconceivable, incredible, and impossible ; and she could only protest, over and over again, that no two hours and a half had ever gone off so swiftly before, as Catherine was called on to confirm ; Catherine could not tell a falsehood even to please Isabella ; but the latter was spared the misery of her friend's dissenting voice, by not waiting for her answer. Her own feelings entirely engrossed her ; her wretchedness was most acute on finding herself obliged to go directly home.—It was ages since she had had a moment's conversation with her dearest Catherine ; and, though she had such thousands of things to say to her, it appeared as if they were never to be together again ; so, with smiles of most exquisite misery, and the laughing eye of utter despondency, she bade her friend adieu and went on.

Catherine found Mrs. Allen just returned from all the busy idleness of the morning, and was immediately greeted with, " Well, my dear, here you are ; " a truth which she had no greater inclination than power to dispute ; " and I hope you have had a pleasant airing ? "

" Yes,

" Yes, ma'am, I thank you ; we could not have had a nicer day."

" So Mrs. Thorpe said ; she was vastly pleased at your all going."

" You have seen Mrs. Thorpe then ? "

" Yes, I went to the Pump-room as soon as you were gone, and there I met her, and we had a great deal of talk together. She says there was hardly any veal to be got at market this morning, it is so uncommonly scarce."

" Did you see any body else of our acquaintance ? "

" Yes ; we agreed to take a turn in the Crescent, and there we met Mrs. Hughes, and Mr. and Miss Tilney walking with her."

" Did you indeed ? and did they speak to you ? "

" Yes, we walked along the Crescent together for half an hour. They seem very agreeable people. Miss Tilney was in a very pretty spotted muslin, and I fancy, by what I can learn, that she always dresses very handsomely. Mrs. Hughes talked to me a great deal about the family."

" And what did she tell you of them ? "

" Oh ! a vast deal indeed ; she hardly talked of any thing else."

" Did she tell you what part of Gloucestershire they come from ? "

" Yes, she did ; but I cannot recollect now. But they are very good kind of people, and very rich. Mrs. Tilney was a Miss Drummond, and she and Mrs. Hughes were school-fellows ; and Miss Drummond had a very large fortune ; and, when she married, her father gave her twenty thousand pounds, and five hundred to buy wedding-clothes. Mrs. Hughes saw all the clothes after they came from the warehouse."

" And are Mr. and Mrs. Tilney in Bath ? "

" Yes, I fancy they are, but I am not quite certain. Upon recollection, however, I have a notion they are both dead ; at least the mother is ; yes, I am sure Mrs. Tilney is dead, because Mrs. Hughes told me there was a very beautiful set of pearls that Mr. Drummond gave his
daughter

daughter on her wedding-day and that Miss Tilney has
got now, for they were put by for her when her mother
died."

" And is Mr. Tilney, my partner, the only son ? "

" I cannot be quite positive about that, my dear ;
I have some idea he is ; but, however, he is a very fine
young man Mrs. Hughes says, and likely to do very
well."

Catherine inquired no further ; she had heard enough
to feel that Mrs. Allen had no real intelligence to give,
and that she was most particularly unfortunate herself
in having missed such a meeting with both brother and
sister. Could she have foreseen such a circumstance,
nothing should have persuaded her to go out with the
others ; and, as it was, she could only lament her ill-luck,
and think over what she had lost, till it was clear to her,
that the drive had by no means been very pleasant and
that John Thorpe himself was quite disagreeable.

CHAP-

CHAPTER X.

THE Allens, Thorpes, and Morlands, all met in the
evening at the theatre ; and, as Catherine and Isabella
sat together, there was then an opportunity for the latter
to utter some few of the many thousand things which
had been collecting within her for communication, in the
immeasurable length of time which had divided them.—
" Oh, heavens ! my beloved Catherine, have I got you at
last ? " was her address on Catherine's entering the box
and sitting by her. " Now, Mr. Morland," for he was
close to her on the other side, " I shall not speak another
word to you all the rest of the evening ; so I charge you
not to expect it. My sweetest Catherine, how have you
been this long age ? but I need not ask you, for you look
delightfully. You really have done your hair in a more
heavenly style than ever : you mischievous creature, do
you want to attract every body ? I assure you, my
brother is quite in love with you already ; and as for
Mr. Tilney—but *that* is a settled thing—even *your* modesty
cannot doubt his attachment now ; his coming back to
Bath makes it too plain. Oh ! what would not I give to
see him ! I really am quite wild with impatience. My
mother says he is the most delightful young man in the
world ; she saw him this morning you know : you must
introduce him to me. Is he in the house now ?—Look
about for heaven's sake ! I assure you, I can hardly
exist till I see him."

" No," said Catherine, " he is not here ; I cannot see
him any where."

" Oh, horrid ! am I never to be acquainted with him ?
How do you like my gown ? I think it does not look
amiss ; the sleeves were entirely my own thought. Do
you know I get so immoderately sick of Bath ; your
brother and I were agreeing this morning that, though it

is

is vastly well to be here for a few weeks, we would not
live here for millions. We soon found out that our tastes
were exactly alike in preferring the country to every
other place; really, our opinions were so exactly the
same, it was quite ridiculous! There was not a single
point in which we differed; I would not have had you
by for the world; you are such a sly thing, I am sure
you would have made some droll remark or other about it."

"No, indeed I should not."

"Oh, yes you would indeed; I know you better than
you know yourself. You would have told us that we
seemed born for each other, or some nonsense of that
kind, which would have distressed me beyond conception;
my cheeks would have been as red as your roses; I would
not have had you by for the world."

"Indeed you do me injustice; I would not have made
so improper a remark upon any account; and besides,
I am sure it would never have entered my head."

Isabella smiled incredulously, and talked the rest of
the evening to James.

Catherine's resolution of endeavouring to meet Miss
Tilney again continued in full force the next morning;
and till the usual moment of going to the Pump-room,
she felt some alarm from the dread of a second prevention.
But nothing of that kind occurred, no visitors appeared
to delay them, and they all three set off in good time for
the Pump-room, where the ordinary course of events and
conversation took place; Mr. Allen, after drinking his
glass of water, joined some gentlemen to talk over the
politics of the day and compare the accounts of their
newspapers; and the ladies walked about together,
noticing every new face, and almost every new bonnet in
the room. The female part of the Thorpe family, attended
by James Morland, appeared among the crowd in less
than a quarter of an hour, and Catherine immediately
took her usual place by the side of her friend. James,
who was now in constant attendance, maintained a similar
position, and separating themselves from the rest of their
party,

party, they walked in that manner for some time, till
Catherine began to doubt the happiness of a situation
which confining her entirely to her friend and brother,
gave her very little share in the notice of either. They
were always engaged in some sentimental discussion or
lively dispute, but their sentiment was conveyed in such
whispering voices, and their vivacity attended with so
much laughter, that though Catherine's supporting opinion
was not unfrequently called for by one or the other, she
was never able to give any, from not having heard a word
of the subject. At length however she was empowered to
disengage herself from her friend, by the avowed necessity
of speaking to Miss Tilney, whom she most joyfully saw
just entering the room with Mrs. Hughes, and whom she
instantly joined, with a firmer determination to be
acquainted, than she might have had courage to command, had she not been urged by the disappointment of
the day before. Miss Tilney met her with great civility,
returned her advances with equal good will, and they
continued talking together as long as both parties remained in the room ; and though in all probability not
an observation was made, nor an expression used by
either which had not been made and used some thousands
of times before, under that roof, in every Bath season,
yet the merit of their being spoken with simplicity and
truth, and without personal conceit, might be something
uncommon.—

" How well your brother dances ! " was an artless
exclamation of Catherine's towards the close of their conversation, which at once surprized and amused her
companion.

" Henry ! " she replied with a smile. " Yes, he does
dance very well."

" He must have thought it very odd to hear me say
I was engaged the other evening, when he saw me sitting
down. But I really had been engaged the whole day to
Mr. Thorpe." Miss Tilney could only bow. " You
cannot think," added Catherine after a moment's silence,
" how

" how surprized I was to see him again. I felt so sure
of his being quite gone away."

" When Henry had the pleasure of seeing you before,
he was in Bath but for a couple of days. He came only
to engage lodgings for us."

" *That* never occurred to me ; and of course, not seeing
him any where, I thought he must be gone. Was not the
young lady he danced with on Monday a Miss Smith ? "

" Yes, an acquaintance of Mrs. Hughes."

" I dare say she was very glad to dance. Do you think
her pretty ? "

" Not very."

" He never comes to the Pump-room, I suppose ? "

" Yes, sometimes ; but he has rid out this morning
with my father."

Mrs. Hughes now joined them, and asked Miss Tilney
if she was ready to go. " I hope I shall have the pleasure
of seeing you again soon," said Catherine. " Shall you
be at the cotillion ball to-morrow ? "

" Perhaps we—— yes, I think we certainly shall."

" I am glad of it, for we shall all be there."—This
civility was duly returned ; and they parted—on Miss
Tilney's side with some knowledge of her new acquaintance's feelings, and on Catherine's, without the smallest
consciousness of having explained them.

She went home very happy. The morning had answered
all her hopes, and the evening of the following day was
now the object of expectation, the future good. What
gown and what head-dress she should wear on the occasion
became her chief concern. She cannot be justified in it.
Dress is at all times a frivolous distinction, and excessive
solicitude about it often destroys its own aim. Catherine
knew all this very well ; her great aunt had read her
a lecture on the subject only the Christmas before ; and
yet she lay awake ten minutes on Wednesday night
debating between her spotted and her tamboured muslin,
and nothing but the shortness of the time prevented her
buying a new one for the evening. This would have been

an

an error in judgment, great though not uncommon, from
which one of the other sex rather than her own, a brother
rather than a great aunt might have warned her, for man
only can be aware of the insensibility of man towards
a new gown. It would be mortifying to the feelings of
many ladies, could they be made to understand how little
the heart of man is affected by what is costly or new in
their attire ; how little it is biassed by the texture of their
muslin, and how unsusceptible of peculiar tenderness
towards the spotted, the sprigged, the mull or the jackonet.
Woman is fine for her own satisfaction alone. No man
will admire her the more, no woman will like her the
better for it. Neatness and fashion are enough for the
former, and a something of shabbiness or impropriety
will be most endearing to the latter.—But not one of
these grave reflections troubled the tranquillity of
Catherine.

She entered the rooms on Thursday evening with feelings very different from what had attended her thither
the Monday before. She had then been exulting in her
engagement to Thorpe, and was now chiefly anxious to
avoid his sight, lest he should engage her again ; for
though she could not, dared not expect that Mr. Tilney
should ask her a third time to dance, her wishes, hopes
and plans all centered in nothing less. Every young lady
may feel for my heroine in this critical moment, for every
young lady has at some time or other known the same
agitation. All have been, or at least all have believed
themselves to be, in danger from the pursuit of some one
whom they wished to avoid ; and all have been anxious
for the attentions of some one whom they wished to
please. As soon as they were joined by the Thorpes,
Catherine's agony began ; she fidgetted about if John
Thorpe came towards her, hid herself as much as possible
from his view, and when he spoke to her pretended not
to hear him. The cotillions were over, the country-
dancing beginning, and she saw nothing of the Tilneys.
" Do not be frightened, my dear Catherine," whispered
Isabella,

Isabella, "but I am really going to dance with your brother again. I declare positively it is quite shocking. I tell him he ought to be ashamed of himself, but you and John must keep us in countenance. Make haste, my dear creature, and come to us. John is just walked off, but he will be back in a moment."

Catherine had neither time nor inclination to answer. The others walked away, John Thorpe was still in view, and she gave herself up for lost. That she might not appear, however, to observe or expect him, she kept her eyes intently fixed on her fan ; and a self-condemnation for her folly, in supposing that among such a crowd they should even meet with the Tilneys in any reasonable time, had just passed through her mind, when she suddenly found herself addressed and again solicited to dance, by Mr. Tilney himself. With what sparkling eyes and ready motion she granted his request, and with how pleasing a flutter of heart she went with him to the set, may be easily imagined. To escape, and, as she believed, so narrowly escape John Thorpe, and to be asked, so immediately on his joining her, asked by Mr. Tilney, as if he had sought her on purpose !—it did not appear to her that life could supply any greater felicity.

Scarcely had they worked themselves into the quiet possession of a place, however, when her attention was claimed by John Thorpe, who stood behind her. "Heyday, Miss Morland !" said he, "what is the meaning of this ?—I thought you and I were to dance together."

"I wonder you should think so, for you never asked me." "That is a good one, by Jove !—I asked you as soon as I came into the room, and I was just going to ask you again, but when I turned round, you were gone ! —this is a cursed shabby trick ! I only came for the sake of dancing with *you*, and I firmly believe you were engaged to me ever since Monday. Yes ; I remember, I asked you while you were waiting in the lobby for your cloak. And here have I been telling all my acquaintance that I was going to dance with the prettiest girl in the room ;

room ; and when they see you standing up with somebody else, they will quiz me famously."

" Oh, no ; they will never think of *me*, after such a description as that."

" By heavens, if they do not, I will kick them out of the room for blockheads. What chap have you there ? " Catherine satisfied his curiosity. " Tilney," he repeated, " Hum—I do not know him. A good figure of a man ; well put together.—Does he want a horse ?—Here is a friend of mine, Sam Fletcher, has got one to sell that would suit any body. A famous clever animal for the road—only forty guineas. I had fifty minds to buy it myself, for it is one of my maxims always to buy a good horse when I meet with one ; but it would not answer my purpose, it would not do for the field. I would give any money for a real good hunter. I have three now, the best that ever were back'd. I would not take eight hundred guineas for them. Fletcher and I mean to get a house in Leicestershire, against the next season. It is so d—— uncomfortable, living at an inn."

This was the last sentence by which he could weary Catherine's attention, for he was just then born off by the resistless pressure of a long string of passing ladies. Her partner now drew near, and said, " That gentleman would have put me out of patience, had he staid with you half a minute longer. He has no business to withdraw the attention of my partner from me. We have entered into a contract of mutual agreeableness for the space of an evening, and all our agreeableness belongs solely to each other for that time. Nobody can fasten themselves on the notice of one, without injuring the rights of the other. I consider a country-dance as an emblem of marriage. Fidelity and complaisance are the principal duties of both ; and those men who do not chuse to dance or marry themselves, have no business with the partners or wives of their neighbours."

" But they are such very different things !— "

" —That

" —That you think they cannot be compared together."

" To be sure not. People that marry can never part, but must go and keep house together. People that dance, only stand opposite each other in a long room for half an hour."

" And such is your definition of matrimony and dancing. Taken in that light certainly, their resemblance is not striking ; but I think I could place them in such a view.—You will allow, that in both, man has the advantage of choice, woman only the power of refusal ; that in both, it is an engagement between man and woman, formed for the advantage of each ; and that when once entered into, they belong exclusively to each other till the moment of its dissolution ; that it is their duty, each to endeavour to give the other no cause for wishing that he or she had bestowed themselves elsewhere, and their best interest to keep their own imaginations from wandering towards the perfections of their neighbours, or fancying that they should have been better off with any one else. You will allow all this ? "

" Yes, to be sure, as you state it, all this sounds very well ; but still they are so very different.—I cannot look upon them at all in the same light, nor think the same duties belong to them."

" In one respect, there certainly is a difference. In marriage, the man is supposed to provide for the support of the woman ; the woman to make the home agreeable to the man ; he is to purvey, and she is to smile. But in dancing, their duties are exactly changed ; the agreeableness, the compliance are expected from him, while she furnishes the fan and the lavender water. *That*, I suppose, was the difference of duties which struck you, as rendering the conditions incapable of comparison."

" No, indeed, I never thought of that."

" Then I am quite at a loss. One thing, however, I must observe. This disposition on your side is rather alarming. You totally disallow any similarity in the
obligations ;

obligations ; and may I not thence infer, that your
notions of the duties of the dancing state are not so strict
as your partner might wish ? Have I not reason to fear,
that if the gentleman who spoke to you just now were to
return, or if any other gentleman were to address you,
there would be nothing to restrain you from conversing
with him as long as you chose ? "

" Mr. Thorpe is such a very particular friend of my
brother's, that if he talks to me, I must talk to him
again ; but there are hardly three young men in the room
besides him, that I have any acquaintance with."

" And is that to be my only security ? alas, alas ! "

" Nay, I am sure you cannot have a better ; for if I do
not know any body, it is impossible for me to talk to
them ; and, besides, I do not *want* to talk to any body."

" Now you have given me a security worth having ;
and I shall proceed with courage. Do you find Bath as
agreeable as when I had the honour of making the inquiry
before ? "

" Yes, quite—more so, indeed."

" More so !—Take care, or you will forget to be tired
of it at the proper time.—You ought to be tired at the
end of six weeks."

" I do not think I should be tired, if I were to stay here
six months."

" Bath, compared with London, has little variety, and
so every body finds out every year. ' For six weeks,
I allow Bath is pleasant enough ; but beyond *that*, it is
the most tiresome place in the world.' You would be
told so by people of all descriptions, who come regularly
every winter, lengthen their six weeks into ten or twelve,
and go away at last because they can afford to stay no
longer."

" Well, other people must judge for themselves, and
those who go to London may think nothing of Bath.
But I, who live in a small retired village in the country,
can never find greater sameness in such a place as this,
than in my own home ; for here are a variety of amusements,

ments, a variety of things to be seen and done all day long, which I can know nothing of there."

" You are not fond of the country."

" Yes, I am. I have always lived there, and always been very happy. But certainly there is much more sameness in a country life than in a Bath life. One day in the country is exactly like another."

" But then you spend your time so much more rationally in the country."

" Do I ? "

" Do you not ? "

" I do not believe there is much difference."

" Here you are in pursuit only of amusement all day long."

" And so I am at home—only I do not find so much of it. I walk about here, and so I do there ;—but here I see a variety of people in every street, and there I can only go and call on Mrs. Allen."

Mr. Tilney was very much amused. " Only go and call on Mrs. Allen ! " he repeated. " What a picture of intellectual poverty ! However, when you sink into this abyss again, you will have more to say. You will be able to talk of Bath, and of all that you did here."

" Oh ! yes. I shall never be in want of something to talk of again to Mrs. Allen, or any body else. I really believe I shall always be talking of Bath, when I am at home again—I *do* like it so very much. If I could but have papa and mamma, and the rest of them here, I suppose I should be too happy ! James's coming (my eldest brother) is quite delightful—and especially as it turns out, that the very family we are just got so intimate with, are his intimate friends already. Oh ! who can ever be tired of Bath ? "

" Not those who bring such fresh feelings of every sort to it, as you do. But papas and mammas, and brothers and intimate friends are a good deal gone by, to most of the frequenters of Bath—and the honest relish of balls and plays, and every-day sights, is past with them."

Here

Here their conversation closed; the demands of the dance becoming now too importunate for a divided attention.

Soon after their reaching the bottom of the set, Catherine perceived herself to be earnestly regarded by a gentleman who stood among the lookers-on, immediately behind her partner. He was a very handsome man, of a commanding aspect, past the bloom, but not past the vigour of life; and with his eye still directed towards her, she saw him presently address Mr. Tilney in a familiar whisper. Confused by his notice, and blushing from the fear of its being excited by something wrong in her appearance, she turned away her head. But while she did so, the gentleman retreated, and her partner coming nearer, said, " I see that you guess what I have just been asked. That gentleman knows your name, and you have a right to know his. It is General Tilney, my father."

Catherine's answer was only " Oh ! "—but it was an " Oh ! " expressing every thing needful; attention to his words, and perfect reliance on their truth. With real interest and strong admiration did her eye now follow the General, as he moved through the crowd, and " How handsome a family they are ! " was her secret remark.

In chatting with Miss Tilney before the evening concluded, a new source of felicity arose to her. She had never taken a country walk since her arrival in Bath. Miss Tilney, to whom all the commonly-frequented environs were familiar, spoke of them in terms which made her all eagerness to know them too; and on her openly fearing that she might find nobody to go with her, it was proposed by the brother and sister that they should join in a walk, some morning or other. "I shall like it," she cried, " beyond any thing in the world; and do not let us put it off—let us go to-morrow." This was readily agreed to, with only a proviso of Miss Tilney's, that it did not rain, which Catherine was sure it would not. At twelve o'clock, they were to call for her in Pulteney-street—and " remember—twelve o'clock," was

her

her parting speech to her new friend. Of her other, her older, her more established friend, Isabella, of whose fidelity and worth she had enjoyed a fortnight's experience, she scarcely saw any thing during the evening. Yet, though longing to make her acquainted with her happiness, she cheerfully submitted to the wish of Mr. Allen, which took them rather early away, and her spirits danced within her, as she danced in her chair all the way home.

CHAPTER XI.

THE morrow brought a very sober looking morning ; the sun making only a few efforts to appear; and Catherine augured from it, every thing most favourable to her wishes. A bright morning so early in the year, she allowed would generally turn to rain, but a cloudy one foretold improvement as the day advanced. She applied to Mr. Allen for confirmation of her hopes, but Mr. Allen not having his own skies and barometer about him, declined giving any absolute promise of sunshine. She applied to Mrs. Allen, and Mrs. Allen's opinion was more positive. " She had no doubt in the world of its being a very fine day, if the clouds would only go off, and the sun keep out."

At about eleven o'clock however, a few specks of small rain upon the windows caught Catherine's watchful eye, and " Oh ! dear, I do believe it will be wet," broke from her in a most desponding tone.

" I thought how it would be," said Mrs. Allen.

" No walk for me to-day," sighed Catherine ;—" but perhaps it may come to nothing, or it may hold up before twelve."

" Perhaps it may, but then, my dear, it will be so dirty."

" Oh ! that will not signify ; I never mind dirt."

" No," replied her friend very placidly, " I know you never mind dirt."

After a short pause, " It comes on faster and faster ! " said Catherine, as she stood watching at a window.

" So it does indeed. If it keeps raining, the streets will be very wet."

" There are four umbrellas up already. How I hate the sight of an umbrella ! "

" They

" They are disagreeable things to carry. I would much rather take a chair at any time."

" It was such a nice looking morning ! I felt so convinced it would be dry ! "

" Any body would have thought so indeed. There will be very few people in the Pump-room, if it rains all the morning. I hope Mr. Allen will put on his great coat when he goes, but I dare say he will not, for he had rather do any thing in the world than walk out in a great coat ; I wonder he should dislike it, it must be so comfortable."

The rain continued—fast, though not heavy. Catherine went every five minutes to the clock, threatening on each return that, if it still kept on raining another five minutes, she would give up the matter as hopeless. The clock struck twelve, and it still rained.—" You will not be able to go, my dear."

" I do not quite despair yet. I shall not give it up till a quarter after twelve. This is just the time of day for it to clear up, and I do think it looks a little lighter. There, it is twenty minutes after twelve, and now I *shall* give it up entirely. Oh ! that we had such weather here as they had at Udolpho, or at least in Tuscany and the South of France !—the night that poor St. Aubin died !— such beautiful weather ! "

At half past twelve, when Catherine's anxious attention to the weather was over, and she could no longer claim any merit from its amendment, the sky began voluntarily to clear. A gleam of sunshine took her quite by surprize ; she looked round ; the clouds were parting, and she instantly returned to the window to watch over and encourage the happy appearance. Ten minutes more made it certain that a bright afternoon would succeed, and justified the opinion of Mrs. Allen, who had " always thought it would clear up." But whether Catherine might still expect her friends, whether there had not been too much rain for Miss Tilney to venture, must yet be a question.

G 2

It

It was too dirty for Mrs. Allen to accompany her husband to the Pump-room; he accordingly set off by himself, and Catherine had barely watched him down the street, when her notice was claimed by the approach of the same two open carriages, containing the same three people that had surprized her so much a few mornings back.

"Isabella, my brother, and Mr. Thorpe, I declare! They are coming for me perhaps—but I shall not go— I cannot go indeed, for you know Miss Tilney may still call." Mrs. Allen agreed to it. John Thorpe was soon with them, and his voice was with them yet sooner, for on the stairs he was calling out to Miss Morland to be quick. "Make haste! make haste!" as he threw open the door—"put on your hat this moment—there is no time to be lost—we are going to Bristol.—How d'ye do, Mrs. Allen?"

"To Bristol! Is not that a great way off?—But, how-ever, I cannot go with you to-day, because I am engaged; I expect some friends every moment." This was of course vehemently talked down as no reason at all; Mrs. Allen was called on to second him, and the two others walked in, to give their assistance. "My sweetest Catherine, is not this delightful? We shall have a most heavenly drive. You are to thank your brother and me for the scheme; it darted into our heads at breakfast-time, I verily believe at the same instant; and we should have been off two hours ago if it had not been for this detestable rain. But it does not signify, the nights are moonlight, and we shall do delightfully. Oh! I am in such extasies at the thoughts of a little country air and quiet!—so much better than going to the Lower Rooms. We shall drive directly to Clifton and dine there; and, as soon as dinner is over, if there is time for it, go on to Kingsweston."

"I doubt our being able to do so much," said Morland.

"You croaking fellow!" cried Thorpe, "we shall be able to do ten times more. Kingsweston! aye, and Blaize Castle

Castle too, and any thing else we can hear of ; but here is your sister says she will not go."

" Blaize Castle ! " cried Catherine ; " what is that ? "

" The finest place in England—worth going fifty miles at any time to see."

" What, is it really a castle, an old castle ? "

" The oldest in the kingdom."

" But is it like what one reads of ? "

" Exactly—the very same."

" But now really—are there towers and long galleries ? "

" By dozens."

" Then I should like to see it ; but I cannot——I cannot go."

" Not go !—my beloved creature, what do you mean ? "

" I cannot go, because "——(looking down as she spoke, fearful of Isabella's smile) " I expect Miss Tilney and her brother to call on me to take a country walk. They promised to come at twelve, only it rained ; but now, as it is so fine, I dare say they will be here soon."

" Not they indeed," cried Thorpe ; " for, as we turned into Broad-street, I saw them—does he not drive a phaeton with bright chesnuts ? "

" I do not know indeed."

" Yes, I know he does ; I saw him. You are talking of the man you danced with last night, are not you ? "

" Yes."

" Well, I saw him at that moment turn up the Lansdown Road,—driving a smart-looking girl."

" Did you indeed ? "

" Did upon my soul ; knew him again directly, and he seemed to have got some very pretty cattle too."

" It is very odd ! but I suppose they thought it would be too dirty for a walk."

" And well they might, for I never saw so much dirt in my life. Walk ! you could no more walk than you could fly ! it has not been so dirty the whole winter ; it is ancle-deep every where."

Isabella

Isabella corroborated it :—" My dearest Catherine, you cannot form an idea of the dirt ; come, you must go ; you cannot refuse going now."

" I should like to see the castle ; but may we go all over it ? may we go up every staircase, and into every suite of rooms ? "

" Yes, yes, every hole and corner."

" But then,—if they should only be gone out for an hour till it is drier, and call by and bye ? "

" Make yourself easy, there is no danger of that, for I heard Tilney hallooing to a man who was just passing by on horseback, that they were going as far as Wick Rocks."

" Then I will. Shall I go, Mrs. Allen ? "

" Just as you please, my dear."

" Mrs. Allen, you must persuade her to go," was the general cry. Mrs. Allen was not inattentive to it :— " Well, my dear," said she, " suppose you go."—And in two minutes they were off.

Catherine's feelings, as she got into the carriage, were in a very unsettled state ; divided between regret for the loss of one great pleasure, and the hope of soon enjoying another, almost its equal in degree, however unlike in kind. She could not think the Tilneys had acted quite well by her, in so readily giving up their engagement, without sending her any message of excuse. It was now but an hour later than the time fixed on for the beginning of their walk ; and, in spite of what she had heard of the prodigious accumulation of dirt in the course of that hour, she could not from her own observation help thinking, that they might have gone with very little inconvenience. To feel herself slighted by them was very painful. On the other hand, the delight of exploring an edifice like Udolpho, as her fancy represented Blaize Castle to be, was such a counterpoise of good, as might console her for almost any thing.

They passed briskly down Pulteney-street, and through Laura-place, without the exchange of many words. Thorpe

Thorpe talked to his horse, and she meditated, by turns,
on broken promises and broken arches, phaetons and
false hangings, Tilneys and trap-doors. As they entered
Argyle-buildings, however, she was roused by this address
from her companion, " Who is that girl who looked at
you so hard as she went by ? "

" Who ?—where ? "

" On the right-hand pavement—she must be almost
out of sight now." Catherine looked round and saw Miss
Tilney leaning on her brother's arm, walking slowly down
the street. She saw them both looking back at her.
" Stop, stop, Mr. Thorpe, she impatiently cried, it is
Miss Tilney ; it is indeed.—How could you tell me they
were gone ?—Stop, stop, I will get out this moment and
go to them." But to what purpose did she speak ?—
Thorpe only lashed his horse into a brisker trot ; the
Tilneys, who had soon ceased to look after her, were in
a moment out of sight round the corner of Laura-place,
and in another moment she was herself whisked into the
Market-place. Still, however, and during the length of
another street, she intreated him to stop. " Pray, pray
stop, Mr. Thorpe.—I cannot go on.—I will not go on.—
I must go back to Miss Tilney." But Mr. Thorpe only
laughed, smacked his whip, encouraged his horse, made
odd noises, and drove on ; and Catherine, angry and
vexed as she was, having no power of getting away, was
obliged to give up the point and submit. Her reproaches,
however, were not spared. " How could you deceive me
so, Mr. Thorpe ?—How could you say, that you saw
them driving up the Lansdown-road ?—I would not have
had it happen so for the world.—They must think it so
strange ; so rude of me ! to go by them, too, without
saying a word ! You do not know how vexed I am.—
I shall have no pleasure at Clifton, nor in any thing else.
I had rather, ten thousand times rather get out now, and
walk back to them. How could you say, you saw them
driving out in a phaeton ? " Thorpe defended himself
very stoutly, declared he had never seen two men so
much

much alike in his life, and would hardly give up the point
of its having been Tilney himself.

Their drive, even when this subject was over, was not
likely to be very agreeable. Catherine's complaisance
was no longer what it had been in their former airing.
She listened reluctantly, and her replies were short.
Blaize Castle remained her only comfort ; towards *that*,
she still looked at intervals with pleasure ; though rather
than be disappointed of the promised walk, and especially
rather than be thought ill of by the Tilneys, she would
willingly have given up all the happiness which its walls
could supply—the happiness of a progress through a long
suite of lofty rooms, exhibiting the remains of magnificent
furniture, though now for many years deserted—the
happiness of being stopped in their way along narrow,
winding vaults, by a low, grated door ; or even of having
their lamp, their only lamp, extinguished by a sudden
gust of wind, and of being left in total darkness. In the
meanwhile, they proceeded on their journey without any
mischance ; and were within view of the town of Keyn-
sham, when a halloo from Morland, who was behind
them, made his friend pull up, to know what was the
matter. The others then came close enough for conversation, and Morland said, " We had better go back,
Thorpe ; it is too late to go on to-day ; your sister thinks
so as well as I. We have been exactly an hour coming
from Pulteney-street, very little more than seven miles ;
and, I suppose, we have at least eight more to go. It
will never do. We set out a great deal too late. We had
much better put it off till another day, and turn round."

" It is all one to me," replied Thorpe rather angrily ;
and instantly turning his horse, they were on their way
back to Bath.

" If your brother had not got such a d—— beast to
drive," said he soon afterwards, " we might have done it
very well. My horse would have trotted to Clifton within
the hour, if left to himself, and I have almost broke my
arm with pulling him in to that cursed broken-winded
jade's

jade's pace. Morland is a fool for not keeping a horse and gig of his own."

" No, he is not," said Catherine warmly, " for I am sure he could not afford it."

" And why cannot he afford it ? "

" Because he has not money enough."

" And whose fault is that ? "

" Nobody's, that I know of." Thorpe then said something in the loud, incoherent way to which he had often recourse, about its being a d—— thing to be miserly ; and that if people who rolled in money could not afford things, he did not know who could ; which Catherine did not even endeavour to understand. Disappointed of what was to have been the consolation for her first disappointment, she was less and less disposed either to be agreeable herself, or to find her companion so ; and they returned to Pulteney-street without her speaking twenty words.

As she entered the house, the footman told her, that a gentleman and lady had called and inquired for her a few minutes after her setting off ; that, when he told them she was gone out with Mr. Thorpe, the lady had asked whether any message had been left for her ; and on his saying no, had felt for a card, but said she had none about her, and went away. Pondering over these heart-rending tidings, Catherine walked slowly up stairs. At the head of them she was met by Mr. Allen, who, on hearing the reason of their speedy return, said, " I am glad your brother had so much sense ; I am glad you are come back. It was a strange, wild scheme."

They all spent the evening together at Thorpe's. Catherine was disturbed and out of spirits ; but Isabella seemed to find a pool of commerce, in the fate of which she shared, by private partnership with Morland, a very good equivalent for the quiet and country air of an inn at Clifton. Her satisfaction, too, in not being at the Lower Rooms, was spoken more than once. " How I pity the poor creatures that are going there ! How
glad

glad I am that I am not amongst them! I wonder
whether it will be a full ball or not! They have not
begun dancing yet. I would not be there for all the world.
It is so delightful to have an evening now and then to
oneself. I dare say it will not be a very good ball. I know
the Mitchells will not be there. I am sure I pity every
body that is. But I dare say, Mr. Morland, you long to
be at it, do not you? I am sure you do. Well, pray
do not let any body here be a restraint on you. I dare
say we could do very well without you; but you men
think yourselves of such consequence."

Catherine could almost have accused Isabella of being
wanting in tenderness towards herself and her sorrows;
so very little did they appear to dwell on her mind, and
so very inadequate was the comfort she offered. "Do
not be so dull, my dearest creature," she whispered.
"You will quite break my heart. It was amazingly
shocking to be sure; but the Tilneys were entirely to
blame. Why were not they more punctual? It was
dirty, indeed, but what did that signify? I am sure
John and I should not have minded it. I never mind
going through any thing, where a friend is concerned;
that is my disposition, and John is just the same; he has
amazing strong feelings. Good heavens! what a delightful hand you have got! Kings, I vow! I never was so
happy in my life! I would fifty times rather you should
have them than myself."

And now I may dismiss my heroine to the sleepless
couch, which is the true heroine's portion; to a pillow
strewed with thorns and wet with tears. And lucky may
she think herself, if she get another good night's rest in
the course of the next three months.

CHAP-

CHAPTER XII.

" MRS. ALLEN," said Catherine the next morning, " will there be any harm in my calling on Miss Tilney to-day ? I shall not be easy till I have explained every thing."

" Go by all means, my dear ; only put on a white gown ; Miss Tilney always wears white."

Catherine cheerfully complied ; and being properly equipped, was more impatient than ever to be at the Pump-room, that she might inform herself of General Tilney's lodgings, for though she believed they were in Milsom-street, she was not certain of the house, and Mrs. Allen's wavering convictions only made it more doubtful. To Milsom-street she was directed ; and having made herself perfect in the number, hastened away with eager steps and a beating heart to pay her visit, explain her conduct, and be forgiven ; tripping lightly through the church-yard, and resolutely turning away her eyes, that she might not be obliged to see her beloved Isabella and her dear family, who, she had reason to believe, were in a shop hard by. She reached the house without any impediment, looked at the number, knocked at the door, and inquired for Miss Tilney. The man believed Miss Tilney to be at home, but was not quite certain. Would she be pleased to send up her name ? She gave her card. In a few minutes the servant returned, and with a look which did not quite confirm his words, said he had been mistaken, for that Miss Tilney was walked out. Catherine, with a blush of mortification, left the house. She felt almost persuaded that Miss Tilney *was* at home, and too much offended to admit her ; and as she retired down the street, could not withhold one glance at the drawing-room windows, in expectation of seeing her there, but no one appeared at them. At the bottom of the street, however, she looked back again, and

and then, not at a window, but issuing from the door, she
saw Miss Tilney herself. She was followed by a gentleman, whom Catherine believed to be her father, and they
turned up towards Edgar's-buildings. Catherine, in deep
mortification, proceeded on her way. She could almost
be angry herself at such angry incivility ; but she checked
the resentful sensation ; she remembered her own ignorance. She knew not how such an offence as her's might
be classed by the laws of worldly politeness, to what
a degree of unforgivingness it might with propriety lead,
nor to what rigours of rudeness in return it might justly
make her amenable.

Dejected and humbled, she had even some thoughts of
not going with the others to the theatre that night ; but
it must be confessed that they were not of long continuance : for she soon recollected, in the first place, that
she was without any excuse for staying at home ; and,
in the second, that it was a play she wanted very much
to see. To the theatre accordingly they all went ; no
Tilneys appeared to plague or please her ; she feared that,
amongst the many perfections of the family, a fondness
for plays was not to be ranked ; but perhaps it was
because they were habituated to the finer performances
of the London stage, which she knew, on Isabella's
authority, rendered every thing else of the kind " quite
horrid." She was not deceived in her own expectation of
pleasure ; the comedy so well suspended her care, that
no one, observing her during the first four acts, would
have supposed she had any wretchedness about her. On
the beginning of the fifth, however, the sudden view of
Mr. Henry Tilney and his father, joining a party in the
opposite box, recalled her to anxiety and distress. The
stage could no longer excite genuine merriment—no
longer keep her whole attention. Every other look upon
an average was directed towards the opposite box ; and,
for the space of two entire scenes, did she thus watch
Henry Tilney, without being once able to catch his eye.
No longer could he be suspected of indifference for a play ;
his

his notice was never withdrawn from the stage during two whole scenes. At length, however, he did look towards her, and he bowed—but such a bow ! no smile, no continued observance attended it ; his eyes were immediately returned to their former direction. Catherine was restlessly miserable ; she could almost have run round to the box in which he sat, and forced him to hear her explanation. Feelings rather natural than heroic possessed her ; instead of considering her own dignity injured by this ready condemnation—instead of proudly resolving, in conscious innocence, to shew her resentment towards him who could harbour a doubt of it, to leave to him all the trouble of seeking an explanation, and to enlighten him on the past only by avoiding his sight, or flirting with somebody else, she took to herself all the shame of misconduct, or at least of its appearance, and was only eager for an opportunity of explaining its cause.

The play concluded—the curtain fell—Henry Tilney was no longer to be seen where he had hitherto sat, but his father remained, and perhaps he might be now coming round to their box. She was right ; in a few minutes he appeared, and, making his way through the then thinning rows, spoke with like calm politeness to Mrs. Allen and her friend.—Not with such calmness was he answered by the latter : " Oh ! Mr. Tilney, I have been quite wild to speak to you, and make my apologies. You must have thought me so rude ; but indeed it was not my own fault,—was it, Mrs. Allen ? Did not they tell me that Mr. Tilney and his sister were gone out in a phaeton together ? and then what could I do ? But I had ten thousand times rather have been with you ; now had not I, Mrs. Allen ? "

" My dear, you tumble my gown," was Mrs. Allen's reply.

Her assurance, however, standing sole as it did, was not thrown away ; it brought a more cordial, more natural smile into his countenance, and he replied in a tone which retained only a little affected reserve :—
" We

" We were much obliged to you at any rate for wishing
us a pleasant walk after our passing you in Argyle-street :
you were so kind as to look back on purpose."

" But indeed I did not wish you a pleasant walk ;
I never thought of such a thing ; but I begged Mr. Thorpe
so earnestly to stop ; I called out to him as soon as ever
I saw you ; now, Mrs. Allen, did not——Oh ! you were
not there ; but indeed I did ; and, if Mr. Thorpe would
only have stopped, I would have jumped out and run
after you."

Is there a Henry in the world who could be insensible
to such a declaration ? Henry Tilney at least was not.
With a yet sweeter smile, he said every thing that need
be said of his sister's concern, regret, and dependence on
Catherine's honour.—" Oh ! do not say Miss Tilney was
not angry," cried Catherine, " because I know she was ;
for she would not see me this morning when I called ;
I saw her walk out of the house the next minute after
my leaving it ; I was hurt, but I was not affronted.
Perhaps you did not know I had been there."

" I was not within at the time ; but I heard of it from
Eleanor, and she has been wishing ever since to see you,
to explain the reason of such incivility ; but perhaps
I can do it as well. It was nothing more than that my
father——they were just preparing to walk out, and he
being hurried for time, and not caring to have it put off,
made a point of her being denied. That was all, I do
assure you. She was very much vexed, and meant to
make her apology as soon as possible."

Catherine's mind was greatly eased by this information,
yet a something of solicitude remained, from which sprang
the following question, thoroughly artless in itself, though
rather distressing to the gentleman :—" But, Mr. Tilney,
why were *you* less generous than your sister ? If she felt
such confidence in my good intentions, and could suppose
it to be only a mistake, why should *you* be so ready to
take offence ? "

" Me !—I take offence ! "

" Nay,

"Nay, I am sure by your look, when you came into the box, you were angry."

"I angry! I could have no right."

"Well, nobody would have thought you had no right who saw your face." He replied by asking her to make room for him, and talking of the play.

He remained with them some time, and was only too agreeable for Catherine to be contented when he went away. Before they parted, however, it was agreed that the projected walk should be taken as soon as possible; and, setting aside the misery of his quitting their box, she was, upon the whole, left one of the happiest creatures in the world.

While talking to each other, she had observed with some surprize, that John Thorpe, who was never in the same part of the house for ten minutes together, was engaged in conversation with General Tilney; and she felt something more than surprize, when she thought she could perceive herself the object of their attention and discourse. What could they have to say of her? She feared General Tilney did not like her appearance: she found it was implied in his preventing her admittance to his daughter, rather than postpone his own walk a few minutes. "How came Mr. Thorpe to know your father?" was her anxious inquiry, as she pointed them out to her companion. He knew nothing about it; but his father, like every military man, had a very large acquaintance.

When the entertainment was over, Thorpe came to assist them in getting out. Catherine was the immediate object of his gallantry; and, while they waited in the lobby for a chair, he prevented the inquiry which had travelled from her heart almost to the tip of her tongue, by asking, in a consequential manner, whether she had seen him talking with General Tilney:—"He is a fine old fellow, upon my soul!—stout, active,—looks as young as his son. I have a great regard for him, I assure you: a gentleman-like, good sort of fellow as ever lived."

"But how came you to know him?"

"Know

" Know him !—There are few people much about town that I do not know. I have met him for ever at the Bedford ; and I knew his face again to-day the moment he came into the billiard-room. One of the best players we have, by the bye ; and we had a little touch together, though I was almost afraid of him at first : the odds were five to four against me ; and, if I had not made one of the cleanest strokes that perhaps ever was made in this world——I took his ball exactly——but I could not make you understand it without a table ;—however I *did* beat him. A very fine fellow ; as rich as a Jew. I should like to dine with him ; I dare say he gives famous dinners. But what do you think we have been talking of ?—You. Yes, by heavens !—and the General thinks you the finest girl in Bath."

" Oh ! nonsense ! how can you say so ? "

" And what do you think I said ? " (lowering his voice) " Well done, General, said I, I am quite of your mind."

Here, Catherine, who was much less gratified by his admiration than by General Tilney's, was not sorry to be called away by Mr. Allen. Thorpe, however, would see her to her chair, and, till she entered it, continued the same kind of delicate flattery, in spite of her entreating him to have done.

That General Tilney, instead of disliking, should admire her, was very delightful ; and she joyfully thought, that there was not one of the family whom she need now fear to meet.—The evening had done more, much more, for her, than could have been expected.

CHAP-

CHAPTER XIII.

MONDAY, Tuesday, Wednesday, Thursday, Friday and Saturday have now passed in review before the reader; the events of each day, its hopes and fears, mortifications and pleasures have been separately stated, and the pangs of Sunday only now remain to be described, and close the week. The Clifton scheme had been deferred, not relinquished, and on the afternoon's Crescent of this day, it was brought forward again. In a private consultation between Isabella and James, the former of whom had particularly set her heart upon going, and the latter no less anxiously placed his upon pleasing her, it was agreed that, provided the weather were fair, the party should take place on the following morning; and they were to set off very early, in order to be at home in good time. The affair thus determined, and Thorpe's approbation secured, Catherine only remained to be apprized of it. She had left them for a few minutes to speak to Miss Tilney. In that interval the plan was completed, and as soon as she came again, her agreement was demanded; but instead of the gay acquiescence expected by Isabella, Catherine looked grave, was very sorry, but could not go. The engagement which ought to have kept her from joining in the former attempt, would make it impossible for her to accompany them now. She had that moment settled with Miss Tilney to take their promised walk to-morrow; it was quite determined, and she would not, upon any account, retract. But that she *must* and *should* retract, was instantly the eager cry of both the Thorpes; they must go to Clifton to-morrow, they would not go without her, it would be nothing to put off a mere walk for one day longer, and they would not hear of a refusal. Catherine was distressed, but not subdued. "Do not urge me, Isabella. I am engaged to Miss Tilney. I cannot go."

go." This availed nothing. The same arguments assailed her again ; she must go, she should go, and they would not hear of a refusal. " It would be so easy to tell Miss Tilney that you had just been reminded of a prior engagement, and must only beg to put off the walk till Tuesday."

" No, it would not be easy. I could not do it. There has been no prior engagement." But Isabella became only more and more urgent ; calling on her in the most affectionate manner ; addressing her by the most endearing names. She was sure her dearest, sweetest Catherine would not seriously refuse such a trifling request to a friend who loved her so dearly. She knew her beloved Catherine to have so feeling a heart, so sweet a temper, to be so easily persuaded by those she loved. But all in vain ; Catherine felt herself to be in the right, and though pained by such tender, such flattering supplication, could not allow it to influence her. Isabella then tried another method. She reproached her with having more affection for Miss Tilney, though she had known her so little a while, than for her best and oldest friends ; with being grown cold and indifferent, in short, towards herself. " I cannot help being jealous, Catherine, when I see myself slighted for strangers, I, who love you so excessively ! When once my affections are placed, it is not in the power of any thing to change them. But I believe my feelings are stronger than any body's ; I am sure they are too strong for my own peace ; and to see myself supplanted in your friendship by strangers, does cut me to the quick, I own. These Tilneys seem to swallow up every thing else."

Catherine thought this reproach equally strange and unkind. Was it the part of a friend thus to expose her feelings to the notice of others ? Isabella appeared to her ungenerous and selfish, regardless of every thing but her own gratification. These painful ideas crossed her mind, though she said nothing. Isabella, in the meanwhile, had applied her handkerchief to her eyes ; and Morland, miserable at such a sight, could not help saying, " Nay, Catherine.

Catherine. I think you cannot stand out any longer now. The sacrifice is not much ; and to oblige such a friend—I shall think you quite unkind, if you still refuse."

This was the first time of her brother's openly siding against her, and anxious to avoid his displeasure, she proposed a compromise. If they would only put off their scheme till Tuesday, which they might easily do, as it depended only on themselves, she could go with them, and every body might then be satisfied. But " No, no, no ! " was the immediate answer ; " that could not be, for Thorpe did not know that he might not go to town on Tuesday." Catherine was sorry, but could do no more ; and a short silence ensued, which was broken by Isabella ; who in a voice of cold resentment said, " Very well, then there is an end of the party. If Catherine does not go, I cannot. I cannot be the only woman. I would not, upon any account in the world, do so improper a thing."

" Catherine, you must go," said James.

" But why cannot Mr. Thorpe drive one of his other sisters ? I dare say either of them would like to go."

" Thank ye," cried Thorpe, " but I did not come to Bath to drive my sisters about, and look like a fool. No, if you do not go, d—— me if I do. I only go for the sake of driving you."

" That is a compliment which gives me no pleasure." But her words were lost on Thorpe, who had turned abruptly away.

The three others still continued together, walking in a most uncomfortable manner to poor Catherine ; some times not a word was said, sometimes she was again attacked with supplications or reproaches, and her arm was still linked within Isabella's, though their hearts were at war. At one moment she was softened, at another irritated ; always distressed, but always steady.

" I did not think you had been so obstinate, Catherine," said James ; " you were not used to be so hard to per-

H 2   suade ;

suade ; you once were the kindest, best-tempered of my sisters."

" I hope I am not less so now," she replied, very feelingly ; " but indeed I cannot go. If I am wrong, I am doing what I believe to be right."

" I suspect," said Isabella, in a low voice, " there is no great struggle."

Catherine's heart swelled ; she drew away her arm, and Isabella made no opposition. Thus passed a long ten minutes, till they were again joined by Thorpe, who coming to them with a gayer look, said, " Well, I have settled the matter, and now we may all go to-morrow with a safe conscience. I have been to Miss Tilney, and made your excuses."

" You have not ! " cried Catherine.

" I have, upon my soul. Left her this moment. Told her you had sent me to say, that having just recollected a prior engagement of going to Clifton with us to-morrow, you could not have the pleasure of walking with her till Tuesday. She said very well, Tuesday was just as convenient to her ; so there is an end of all our difficulties.— A pretty good thought of mine—hey ? "

Isabella's countenance was once more all smiles and good-humour, and James too looked happy again.

" A most heavenly thought indeed ! Now, my sweet Catherine, all our distresses are over ; you are honourably acquitted, and we shall have a most delightful party."

" This will not do," said Catherine ; " I cannot submit to this. I must run after Miss Tilney directly and set her right."

Isabella, however, caught hold of one hand ; Thorpe of the other ; and remonstrances poured in from all three. Even James was quite angry. When every thing was settled, when Miss Tilney herself said that Tuesday would suit her as well, it was quite ridiculous, quite absurd to make any further objection.

" I do not care. Mr. Thorpe had no business to invent any such message. If I had thought it right to put it off,
I could

I could have spoken to Miss Tilney myself. This is only doing it in a ruder way; and how do I know that Mr. Thorpe has——he may be mistaken again perhaps; he led me into one act of rudeness by his mistake on Friday. Let me go, Mr. Thorpe; Isabella, do not hold me."

Thorpe told her it would be in vain to go after the Tilneys; they were turning the corner into Brock-street, when he had overtaken them, and were at home by this time.

" Then I will go after them," said Catherine; " wherever they are I will go after them. It does not signify talking. If I could not be persuaded into doing what I thought wrong, I never will be tricked into it." And with these words she broke away and hurried off. Thorpe would have darted after her, but Morland withheld him. " Let her go, let her go, if she will go."

" She is as obstinate as—— "

Thorpe never finished the simile, for it could hardly have been a proper one.

Away walked Catherine in great agitation, as fast as the crowd would permit her, fearful of being pursued, yet determined to persevere. As she walked, she reflected on what had passed. It was painful to her to disappoint and displease them, particularly to displease her brother; but she could not repent her resistance. Setting her own inclination apart, to have failed a second time in her engagement to Miss Tilney, to have retracted a promise voluntarily made only five minutes before, and on a false pretence too, must have been wrong. She had not been withstanding them on selfish principles alone, she had not consulted merely her own gratification; *that* might have been ensured in some degree by the excursion itself, by seeing Blaize Castle; no, she had attended to what was due to others, and to her own character in their opinion. Her conviction of being right however was not enough to restore her composure, till she had spoken to Miss Tilney she could not be at ease; and quickening her pace when she got clear of the Crescent, she almost

ran

ran over the remaining ground till she gained the top of
Milsom-street. So rapid had been her movements, that
in spite of the Tilneys' advantage in the outset, they were
but just turning into their lodgings as she came within
view of them ; and the servant still remaining at the open
door, she used only the ceremony of saying that she must
speak with Miss Tilney that moment, and hurrying by
him proceeded up stairs. Then, opening the first door
before her, which happened to be the right, she immediately found herself in the drawing-room with General
Tilney, his son and daughter. Her explanation, defective
only in being—from her irritation of nerves and shortness
of breath—no explanation at all, was instantly given.
" I am come in a great hurry—It was all a mistake—
I never promised to go—I told them from the first I could
not go.—I ran away in a great hurry to explain it.—I did
not care what you thought of me.—I would not stay for
the servant."

The business however, though not perfectly elucidated
by this speech, soon ceased to be a puzzle. Catherine
found that John Thorpe *had* given the message ; and
Miss Tilney had no scruple in owning herself greatly
surprized by it. But whether her brother had still
exceeded her in resentment, Catherine, though she in-
stinctively addressed herself as much to one as to the
other in her vindication, had no means of knowing.
Whatever might have been felt before her arrival, her
eager declarations immediately made every look and
sentence as friendly as she could desire.

The affair thus happily settled, she was introduced by
Miss Tilney to her father, and received by him with such
ready, such solicitous politeness as recalled Thorpe's
information to her mind, and made her think with
pleasure that he might be sometimes depended on. To
such anxious attention was the general's civility carried,
that not aware of her extraordinary swiftness in entering
the house, he was quite angry with the servant whose
neglect had reduced her to open the door of the apartment

ment herself. "What did William mean by it ? He should make a point of inquiring into the matter." And if Catherine had not most warmly asserted his innocence, it seemed likely that William would lose the favour of his master for ever, if not his place, by her rapidity.

After sitting with them a quarter of an hour, she rose to take leave, and was then most agreeably surprized by General Tilney's asking her if she would do his daughter the honour of dining and spending the rest of the day with her. Miss Tilney added her own wishes. Catherine was greatly obliged ; but it was quite out of her power. Mr. and Mrs. Allen would expect her back every moment. The general declared he could say no more ; the claims of Mr. and Mrs. Allen were not to be superseded ; but on some other day he trusted, when longer notice could be given, they would not refuse to spare her to her friend. " Oh, no ; Catherine was sure they would not have the least objection, and she should have great pleasure in coming." The general attended her himself to the street-door, saying every thing gallant as they went down stairs, admiring the elasticity of her walk, which corresponded exactly with the spirit of her dancing, and making her one of the most graceful bows she had ever beheld, when they parted.

Catherine, delighted by all that had passed, proceeded gaily to Pulteney-street ; walking, as she concluded, with great elasticity, though she had never thought of it before. She reached home without seeing any thing more of the offended party ; and now that she had been triumphant throughout, had carried her point and was secure of her walk, she began (as the flutter of her spirits subsided) to doubt whether she had been perfectly right. A sacrifice was always noble ; and if she had given way to their entreaties, she should have been spared the distressing idea of a friend displeased, a brother angry, and a scheme of great happiness to both destroyed, perhaps through her means. To ease her mind, and ascertain by the opinion of an unprejudiced person what her own conduct had

had really been, she took occasion to mention before Mr.
Allen the half-settled scheme of her brother and the
Thorpes for the following day. Mr. Allen caught at it
directly. " Well," said he, " and do you think of going
too ? "

" No ; I had just engaged myself to walk with Miss
Tilney before they told me of it ; and therefore you know
I could not go with them, could I ? "

" No, certainly not ; and I am glad you do not think
of it. These schemes are not at all the thing. Young
men and women driving about the country in open
carriages ! Now and then it is very well ; but going to
inns and public places together ! It is not right ; and
I wonder Mrs. Thorpe should allow it. I am glad you do
not think of going ; I am sure Mrs. Morland would not
be pleased. Mrs. Allen, are not you of my way of thinking ? Do not you think these kind of projects objectionable ? "

" Yes, very much so indeed. Open carriages are nasty
things. A clean gown is not five minutes wear in them.
You are splashed getting in and getting out ; and the
wind takes your hair and your bonnet in every direction.
I hate an open carriage myself."

" I know you do ; but that is not the question. Do
not you think it has an odd appearance, if young ladies
are frequently driven about in them by young men, to
whom they are not even related ? "

" Yes, my dear, a very odd appearance indeed. I cannot
bear to see it."

" Dear madam," cried Catherine, " then why did not
you tell me so before ? I am sure if I had known it to
be improper, I would not have gone with Mr. Thorpe at
all ; but I always hoped you would tell me, if you thought
I was doing wrong."

" And so I should, my dear, you may depend on it ;
for as I told Mrs. Morland at parting, I would always do
the best for you in my power. But one must not be over
particular. Young people *will* be young people, as your
good

good mother says herself. You know I wanted you, when we first came, not to buy that sprigged muslin, but you would. Young people do not like to be always thwarted."

"But this was something of real consequence; and I do not think you would have found me hard to persuade."

"As far as it has gone hitherto, there is no harm done," said Mr. Allen; "and I would only advise you, my dear, not to go out with Mr. Thorpe any more."

"That is just what I was going to say," added his wife.

Catherine, relieved for herself, felt uneasy for Isabella; and after a moment's thought, asked Mr. Allen whether it would not be both proper and kind in her to write to Miss Thorpe, and explain the indecorum of which she must be as insensible as herself; for she considered that Isabella might otherwise perhaps be going to Clifton the next day, in spite of what had passed. Mr. Allen however discouraged her from doing any such thing. "You had better leave her alone, my dear, she is old enough to know what she is about; and if not, has a mother to advise her. Mrs. Thorpe is too indulgent beyond a doubt; but however you had better not interfere. She and your brother chuse to go, and you will be only getting ill-will."

Catherine submitted; and though sorry to think that Isabella should be doing wrong, felt greatly relieved by Mr. Allen's approbation of her own conduct, and truly rejoiced to be preserved by his advice from the danger of falling into such an error herself. Her escape from being one of the party to Clifton was now an escape indeed; for what would the Tilneys have thought of her, if she had broken her promise to them in order to do what was wrong in itself? if she had been guilty of one breach of propriety, only to enable her to be guilty of another?

CHAP-

CHAPTER XIV.

THE next morning was fair, and Catherine almost expected another attack from the assembled party. With Mr. Allen to support her, she felt no dread of the event : but she would gladly be spared a contest, where victory itself was painful ; and was heartily rejoiced therefore at neither seeing nor hearing any thing of them. The Tilneys called for her at the appointed time ; and no new difficulty arising, no sudden recollection, no unexpected summons, no impertinent intrusion to disconcert their measures, my heroine was most unnaturally able to fulfil her engagement, though it was made with the hero himself. They determined on walking round Beechen Cliff, that noble hill, whose beautiful verdure and hanging coppice render it so striking an object from almost every opening in Bath.

" I never look at it," said Catherine, as they walked along the side of the river, " without thinking of the south of France."

" You have been abroad then ? " said Henry, a little surprized.

" Oh ! no, I only mean what I have read about. It always puts me in mind of the country that Emily and her father travelled through, in the ' Mysteries of Udolpho.' But you never read novels, I dare say ? "

" Why not ? "

" Because they are not clever enough for you—gentlemen read better books."

" The person, be it gentleman or lady, who has not pleasure in a good novel, must be intolerably stupid. I have read all Mrs. Radcliffe's works, and most of them with great pleasure. The Mysteries of Udolpho, when I had once begun it, I could not lay down again ;—I remember finishing it in two days—my hair standing on end the whole time."

" Yes,"

" Yes," added Miss Tilney, " and I remember that you undertook to read it aloud to me, and that when I was called away for only five minutes to answer a note, instead of waiting for me, you took the volume into the Hermitage-walk, and I was obliged to stay till you had finished it."

" Thank you, Eleanor ;—a most honourable testimony. You see, Miss Morland, the injustice of your suspicions. Here was I, in my eagerness to get on, refusing to wait only five minutes for my sister ; breaking the promise I had made of reading it aloud, and keeping her in suspense at a most interesting part, by running away with the volume, which, you are to observe, was her own, par-ticularly her own. I am proud when I reflect on it, and I think it must establish me in your good opinion."

" I am very glad to hear it indeed, and now I shall never be ashamed of liking Udolpho myself. But I really thought before, young men despised novels amazingly."

" It is *amazingly;* it may well suggest *amazement* if they do—for they read nearly as many as women. I myself have read hundreds and hundreds. Do not imagine that you can cope with me in a knowledge of Julias and Louisas. If we proceed to particulars, and engage in the never-ceasing inquiry of ' Have you read this ? ' and ' Have you read that ? ' I shall soon leave you as far behind me as—what shall I say ?—I want an appropriate simile ;—as far as your friend Emily herself left poor Valancourt when she went with her aunt into Italy. Consider how many years I have had the start of you. I had entered on my studies at Oxford, while you were a good little girl working your sampler at home ! "

" Not very good I am afraid. But now really, do not you think Udolpho the nicest book in the world ? "

" The nicest ;—by which I suppose you mean the neatest. That must depend upon the binding."

" Henry," said Miss Tilney, " you are very impertinent. Miss Morland, he is treating you exactly as he does his sister. He is for ever finding fault with me, for some incorrectness of language, and now he is taking the same
liberty

liberty with you. The word ' nicest,' as you used it, did not suit him ; and you had better change it as soon as you can, or we shall be overpowered with Johnson and Blair all the rest of the way."

" I am sure," cried Catherine, " I did not mean to say any thing wrong ; but it *is* a nice book, and why should not I call it so ? "

" Very true," said Henry, " and this is a very nice day, and we are taking a very nice walk, and you are two very nice young ladies. Oh ! it is a very nice word indeed !— it does for every thing. Originally perhaps it was applied only to express neatness, propriety, delicacy, or refinement ;—people were nice in their dress, in their sentiments, or their choice. But now every commendation on every subject is comprised in that one word."

" While, in fact," cried his sister, " it ought only to be applied to you, without any commendation at all. You are more nice than wise. Come, Miss Morland, let us leave him to meditate over our faults in the utmost propriety of diction, while we praise Udolpho in whatever terms we like best. It is a most interesting work. You are fond of that kind of reading ? "

" To say the truth, I do not much like any other."

" Indeed ! "

" That is, I can read poetry and plays, and things of that sort, and do not dislike travels. But history, real solemn history, I cannot be interested in. Can you ? "

" Yes, I am fond of history."

" I wish I were too. I read it a little as a duty, but it tells me nothing that does not either vex or weary me. The quarrels of popes and kings, with wars or pestilences, in every page ; the men all so good for nothing, and hardly any women at all—it is very tiresome : and yet I often think it odd that it should be so dull, for a great deal of it must be invention. The speeches that are put into the heroes' mouths, their thoughts and designs—the chief of all this must be invention, and invention is what delights me in other books."

" Historians,

" Historians, you think," said Miss Tilney, " are not happy in their flights of fancy. They display imagination without raising interest. I am fond of history—and am very well contented to take the false with the true. In the principal facts they have sources of intelligence in former histories and records, which may be as much depended on, I conclude, as any thing that does not actually pass under one's own observation ; and as for the little embellishments you speak of, they are embellishments, and I like them as such. If a speech be well drawn up, I read it with pleasure, by whomsoever it may be made—and probably with much greater, if the production of Mr. Hume or Mr. Robertson, than if the genuine words of Caractacus, Agricola, or Alfred the Great."

" You are fond of history !—and so are Mr. Allen and my father ; and I have two brothers who do not dislike it. So many instances within my small circle of friends is remarkable ! At this rate, I shall not pity the writers of history any longer. If people like to read their books, it is all very well, but to be at so much trouble in filling great volumes, which, as I used to think, nobody would willingly ever look into, to be labouring only for the torment of little boys and girls, always struck me as a hard fate ; and though I know it is all very right and necessary, I have often wondered at the person's courage that could sit down on purpose to do it."

" That little boys and girls should be tormented," said Henry, " is what no one at all acquainted with human nature in a civilized state can deny ; but in behalf of our most distinguished historians, I must observe, that they might well be offended at being supposed to have no higher aim ; and that by their method and style, they are perfectly well qualified to torment readers of the most advanced reason and mature time of life. I use the verb ' to torment,' as I observed to be your own method, instead of ' to instruct,' supposing them to be now admitted as synonimous."

" You think me foolish to call instruction a torment, but

but if you had been as much used as myself to hear poor little children first learning their letters and then learning to spell, if you had ever seen how stupid they can be for a whole morning together, and how tired my poor mother is at the end of it, as I am in the habit of seeing almost every day of my life at home, you would allow that to *torment* and to *instruct* might sometimes be used as synonimous words."

" Very probably. But historians are not accountable for the difficulty of learning to read ; and even you your-self, who do not altogether seem particularly friendly to very severe, very intense application, may perhaps be brought to acknowledge that it is very well worth while to be tormented for two or three years of one's life, for the sake of being able to read all the rest of it. Consider— if reading had not been taught, Mrs. Radcliffe would have written in vain—or perhaps might not have written at all."

Catherine assented—and a very warm panegyric from her on that lady's merits, closed the subject.—The Tilneys were soon engaged in another on which she had nothing to say. They were viewing the country with the eyes of persons accustomed to drawing, and decided on its capability of being formed into pictures, with all the eagerness of real taste. Here Catherine was quite lost. She knew nothing of drawing—nothing of taste :—and she listened to them with an attention which brought her little profit, for they talked in phrases which conveyed scarcely any idea to her. The little which she could understand however appeared to contradict the very few notions she had entertained on the matter before. It seemed as if a good view were no longer to be taken from the top of an high hill, and that a clear blue sky was no longer a proof of a fine day. She was heartily ashamed of her ignorance. A misplaced shame. Where people wish to attach, they should always be ignorant. To come with a well-informed mind, is to come with an inability of administering to the vanity of others, which

a sensible

a sensible person would always wish to avoid. A woman especially, if she have the misfortune of knowing any thing, should conceal it as well as she can.

The advantages of natural folly in a beautiful girl have been already set forth by the capital pen of a sister author;—and to her treatment of the subject I will only add in justice to men, that though to the larger and more trifling part of the sex, imbecility in females is a great enhancement of their personal charms, there is a portion of them too reasonable and too well informed themselves to desire any thing more in woman than ignorance. But Catherine did not know her own advantages—did not know that a good-looking girl, with an affectionate heart and a very ignorant mind, cannot fail of attracting a clever young man, unless circumstances are particularly untoward. In the present instance, she confessed and lamented her want of knowledge; declared that she would give any thing in the world to be able to draw; and a lecture on the picturesque immediately followed, in which his instructions were so clear that she soon began to see beauty in every thing admired by him, and her attention was so earnest, that he became perfectly satisfied of her having a great deal of natural taste. He talked of fore-grounds, distances, and second distances—side-screens and perspectives—lights and shades;—and Catherine was so hopeful a scholar, that when they gained the top of Beechen Cliff, she voluntarily rejected the whole city of Bath, as unworthy to make part of a landscape. Delighted with her progress, and fearful of wearying her with too much wisdom at once, Henry suffered the subject to decline, and by an easy transition from a piece of rocky fragment and the withered oak which he had placed near its summit, to oaks in general, to forests, the inclosure of them, waste lands, crown lands and government, he shortly found himself arrived at politics; and from politics, it was an easy step to silence. The general pause which succeeded his short disquisition on the state of the nation, was put an end to by Catherine, who, in rather

a solemn

a solemn tone of voice, uttered these words, " I have heard that something very shocking indeed, will soon come out in London."

Miss Tilney, to whom this was chiefly addressed, was startled, and hastily replied, " Indeed !—and of what nature ? "

" That I do not know, nor who is the author. I have only heard that it is to be more horrible than any thing we have met with yet."

" Good heaven !—Where could you hear of such a thing ? "

" A particular friend of mine had an account of it in a letter from London yesterday. It is to be uncommonly dreadful. I shall expect murder and every thing of the kind."

" You speak with astonishing composure ! But I hope your friend's accounts have been exaggerated ;—and if such a design is known beforehand, proper measures will undoubtedly be taken by government to prevent its coming to effect."

" Government," said Henry, endeavouring not to smile, " neither desires nor dares to interfere in such matters. There must be murder ; and government cares not how much."

The ladies stared. He laughed, and added, " Come, shall I make you understand each other, or leave you to puzzle out an explanation as you can ? No—I will be noble. I will prove myself a man, no less by the generosity of my soul than the clearness of my head. I have no patience with such of my sex as disdain to let themselves sometimes down to the comprehension of yours. Perhaps the abilities of women are neither sound nor acute— neither vigorous nor keen. Perhaps they may want observation, discernment, judgment, fire, genius, and wit."

" Miss Morland, do not mind what he says ;—but have the goodness to satisfy me as to this dreadful riot."

" Riot !—what riot ? "

" My

" My dear Eleanor, the riot is only in your own brain.
The confusion there is scandalous. Miss Morland has
been talking of nothing more dreadful than a new publication which is shortly to come out, in three duodecimo
volumes, two hundred and seventy-six pages in each,
with a frontispiece to the first, of two tombstones and
a lantern—do you understand ?—And you, Miss Morland
—my stupid sister has mistaken all your clearest expressions. You talked of expected horrors in London—and
instead of instantly conceiving, as any rational creature
would have done, that such words could relate only to
a circulating library, she immediately pictured to herself
a mob of three thousand men assembling in St. George's
Fields ; the Bank attacked, the Tower threatened, the
streets of London flowing with blood, a detachment of the
12th Light Dragoons, (the hopes of the nation,) called up
from Northampton to quell the insurgents, and the
gallant Capt. Frederick Tilney, in the moment of charging
at the head of his troop, knocked off his horse by a brickbat
from an upper window. Forgive her stupidity. The fears
of the sister have added to the weakness of the woman ;
but she is by no means a simpleton in general."

Catherine looked grave. " And now, Henry," said
Miss Tilney, " that you have made us understand each
other, you may as well make Miss Morland understand
yourself—unless you mean to have her think you intolerably rude to your sister, and a great brute in your
opinion of women in general. Miss Morland is not used
to your odd ways."

" I shall be most happy to make her better acquainted
with them."

" No doubt ;—but that is no explanation of the
present."

" What am I to do ? "

" You know what you ought to do. Clear your character
handsomely before her. Tell her that you think very
highly of the understanding of women."

" Miss Morland, I think very highly of the understanding of all the women in the world—especially of those—whoever they may be—with whom I happen to be in company."

" That is not enough. Be more serious."

" Miss Morland, no one can think more highly of the understanding of women than I do. In my opinion, nature has given them so much, that they never find it necessary to use more than half."

" We shall get nothing more serious from him now, Miss Morland. He is not in a sober mood. But I do assure you that he must be entirely misunderstood, if he can ever appear to say an unjust thing of any woman at all, or an unkind one of me."

It was no effort to Catherine to believe that Henry Tilney could never be wrong. His manner might sometimes surprize, but his meaning must always be just :—and what she did not understand, she was almost as ready to admire, as what she did. The whole walk was delightful, and though it ended too soon, its conclusion was delightful too ;—her friends attended her into the house, and Miss Tilney, before they parted, addressing herself with respectful form, as much to Mrs. Allen as to Catherine, petitioned for the pleasure of her company to dinner on the day after the next. No difficulty was made on Mrs. Allen's side—and the only difficulty on Catherine's was in concealing the excess of her pleasure.

The morning had passed away so charmingly as to banish all her friendship and natural affection ; for no thought of Isabella or James had crossed her during their walk. When the Tilneys were gone, she became amiable again, but she was amiable for some time to little effect ; Mrs. Allen had no intelligence to give that could relieve her anxiety, she had heard nothing of any of them. Towards the end of the morning however, Catherine having occasion for some indispensable yard of ribbon which must be bought without a moment's delay, walked out into the town, and in Bond-street overtook the second Miss Thorpe, as she was loitering towards
Edgar's

Edgar's Buildings between two of the sweetest girls in the world, who had been her dear friends all the morning. From her, she soon learned that the party to Clifton had taken place. "They set off at eight this morning," said Miss Anne, "and I am sure I do not envy them their drive. I think you and I are very well off to be out of the scrape.—It must be the dullest thing in the world, for there is not a soul at Clifton at this time of year. Belle went with your brother, and John drove Maria."

Catherine spoke the pleasure she really felt on hearing this part of the arrangement.

"Oh! yes," rejoined the other, "Maria is gone. She was quite wild to go. She thought it would be something very fine. I cannot say I admire her taste; and for my part I was determined from the first not to go, if they pressed me ever so much."

Catherine, a little doubtful of this, could not help answering, "I wish you could have gone too. It is a pity you could not all go."

"Thank you; but it is quite a matter of indifference to me. Indeed, I would not have gone on any account. I was saying so to Emily and Sophia when you over-took us."

Catherine was still unconvinced; but glad that Anne should have the friendship of an Emily and a Sophia to console her, she bade her adieu without much uneasiness, and returned home, pleased that the party had not been prevented by her refusing to join it, and very heartily wishing that it might be too pleasant to allow either James or Isabella to resent her resistance any longer.

CHAP-

CHAPTER XV.

EARLY the next day, a note from Isabella, speaking peace and tenderness in every line, and entreating the immediate presence of her friend on a matter of the utmost importance, hastened Catherine, in the happiest state of confidence and curiosity, to Edgar's Buildings.— The two youngest Miss Thorpes were by themselves in the parlour; and, on Anne's quitting it to call her sister, Catherine took the opportunity of asking the other for some particulars of their yesterday's party. Maria desired no greater pleasure than to speak of it; and Catherine immediately learnt that it had been altogether the most delightful scheme in the world; that nobody could imagine how charming it had been, and that it had been more delightful than any body could conceive. Such was the information of the first five minutes; the second unfolded thus much in detail,—that they had driven directly to the York Hotel, ate some soup, and bespoke an early dinner, walked down to the Pump-room, tasted the water, and laid out some shillings in purses and spars; thence adjourned to eat ice at a pastry-cook's, and hurrying back to the Hotel, swallowed their dinner in haste, to prevent being in the dark; and then had a delightful drive back, only the moon was not up, and it rained a little, and Mr. Morland's horse was so tired he could hardly get it along.

Catherine listened with heartfelt satisfaction. It appeared that Blaize Castle had never been thought of; and, as for all the rest, there was nothing to regret for half an instant.—Maria's intelligence concluded with a tender effusion of pity for her sister Anne, whom she represented as insupportably cross, from being excluded the party.

" She will never forgive me, I am sure; but, you know, how

how could I help it ? John would have me go, for he vowed he would not drive her, because she had such thick ancles. I dare say she will not be in good humour again this month ; but I am determined I will not be cross ; it is not a little matter that puts me out of temper."

Isabella now entered the room with so eager a step, and a look of such happy importance, as engaged all her friend's notice. Maria was without ceremony sent away, and Isabella, embracing Catherine, thus began :—" Yes, my dear Catherine, it is so indeed ; your penetration has not deceived you.—Oh ! that arch eye of yours !—It sees through every thing."

Catherine replied only by a look of wondering ignorance.

" Nay, my beloved, sweetest friend," continued the other, " compose yourself.—I am amazingly agitated, as you perceive. Let us sit down and talk in comfort. Well, and so you guessed it the moment you had my note ?— Sly creature !—Oh ! my dear Catherine, you alone who know my heart can judge of my present happiness. Your brother is the most charming of men. I only wish I were more worthy of him.—But what will your excellent father and mother say ?—Oh ! heavens ! when I think of them I am so agitated ! "

Catherine's understanding began to awake : an idea of the truth suddenly darted into her mind ; and, with the natural blush of so new an emotion, she cried out, " Good heaven !—my dear Isabella, what do you mean ? Can you—can you really be in love with James ? "

This bold surmise, however, she soon learnt comprehended but half the fact. The anxious affection, which she was accused of having continually watched in Isabella's every look and action, had, in the course of their yesterday's party, received the delightful confession of an equal love. Her heart and faith were alike engaged to James.— Never had Catherine listened to any thing so full of interest, wonder, and joy. Her brother and her friend engaged !—New to such circumstances, the importance of it appeared unspeakably great, and she contemplated it

as

as one of those grand events, of which the ordinary course of life can hardly afford a return. The strength of her feelings she could not express; the nature of them, however, contented her friend. The happiness of having such a sister was their first effusion, and the fair ladies mingled in embraces and tears of joy.

Delighting, however, as Catherine sincerely did in the prospect of the connexion, it must be acknowledged that Isabella far surpassed her in tender anticipations.—" You will be so infinitely dearer to me, my Catherine, than either Anne or Maria : I feel that I shall be so much more attached to my dear Morland's family than to my own."

This was a pitch of friendship beyond Catherine.

" You are so like your dear brother," continued Isabella, " that I quite doated on you the first moment I saw you. But so it always is with me ; the first moment settles every thing. The very first day that Morland came to us last Christmas—the very first moment I beheld him—my heart was irrecoverably gone. I remember I wore my yellow gown, with my hair done up in braids ; and when I came into the drawing-room, and John introduced him, I thought I never saw any body so handsome before."

Here Catherine secretly acknowledged the power of love ; for, though exceedingly fond of her brother, and partial to all his endowments, she had never in her life thought him handsome.

" I remember too, Miss Andrews drank tea with us that evening, and wore her puce-coloured sarsenet ; and she looked so heavenly, that I thought your brother must certainly fall in love with her ; I could not sleep a wink all night for thinking of it. Oh ! Catherine, the many sleepless nights I have had on your brother's account !— I would not have you suffer half what I have done ! I am grown wretchedly thin I know ; but I will not pain you by describing my anxiety ; you have seen enough of it. I feel that I have betrayed myself perpetually ;—so unguarded in speaking of my partiality for the church !— But my secret I was always sure would be safe with *you*."

Catherine

Catherine felt that nothing could have been safer ; but ashamed of an ignorance little expected, she dared no longer contest the point, nor refuse to have been as full of arch penetration and affectionate sympathy as Isabella chose to consider her. Her brother she found was preparing to set off with all speed to Fullerton, to make known his situation and ask consent ; and here was a source of some real agitation to the mind of Isabella. Catherine endeavoured to persuade her, as she was herself persuaded, that her father and mother would never oppose their son's wishes.—" It is impossible," said she, " for parents to be more kind, or more desirous of their children's happiness ; I have no doubt of their consenting immediately."

" Morland says exactly the same," replied Isabella ; " and yet I dare not expect it ; my fortune will be so small ; they never can consent to it. Your brother, who might marry any body ! "

Here Catherine again discerned the force of love.

" Indeed, Isabella, you are too humble.—The difference of fortune can be nothing to signify."

" Oh ! my sweet Catherine, in *your* generous heart I know it would signify nothing ; but we must not expect such disinterestedness in many. As for myself, I am sure I only wish our situations were reversed. Had I the command of millions, were I mistress of the whole world, your brother would be my only choice."

This charming sentiment, recommended as much by sense as novelty, gave Catherine a most pleasing remembrance of all the heroines of her acquaintance ; and she thought her friend never looked more lovely than in uttering the grand idea.—" I am sure they will consent," was her frequent declaration ; " I am sure they will be delighted with you."

" For my own part," said Isabella, " my wishes are so moderate, that the smallest income in nature would be enough for me. Where people are really attached, poverty itself is wealth : grandeur I detest : I would not

not settle in London for the universe. A cottage in some
retired village would be extasy. There are some charming
little villas about Richmond."

" Richmond ! " cried Catherine.—" You must settle
near Fullerton. You must be near us."

" I am sure I shall be miserable if we do not. If I can
but be near *you*, I shall be satisfied. But this is idle
talking ! I will not allow myself to think of such things,
till we have your father's answer. Morland says that by
sending it to-night to Salisbury, we may have it to-
morrow.—To-morrow ?—I know I shall never have
courage to open the letter. I know it will be the death
of me."

A reverie succeeded this conviction—and when Isabella
spoke again, it was to resolve on the quality of her
wedding-gown.

Their conference was put an end to by the anxious
young lover himself, who came to breathe his parting
sigh before he set off for Wiltshire. Catherine wished to
congratulate him, but knew not what to say, and her
eloquence was only in her eyes. From them however the
eight parts of speech shone out most expressively, and
James could combine them with ease. Impatient for the
realization of all that he hoped at home, his adieus were
not long ; and they would have been yet shorter, had he
not been frequently detained by the urgent entreaties
of his fair one that he would go. Twice was he called
almost from the door by her eagerness to have him gone.
" Indeed, Morland, I must drive you away. Consider
how far you have to ride. I cannot bear to see you linger
so. For Heaven's sake, waste no more time. There, go,
go—I insist on it."

The two friends, with hearts now more united than
ever, were inseparable for the day ; and in schemes of
sisterly happiness the hours flew along. Mrs. Thorpe and
her son, who were acquainted with every thing, and who
seemed only to want Mr. Morland's consent, to consider
Isabella's engagement as the most fortunate circumstance
imaginable

imaginable for their family, were allowed to join their counsels, and add their quota of significant looks and mysterious expressions to fill up the measure of curiosity to be raised in the unprivileged younger sisters. To Catherine's simple feelings, this odd sort of reserve seemed neither kindly meant, nor consistently supported ; and its unkindness she would hardly have forborn pointing out, had its inconsistency been less their friend ;—but Anne and Maria soon set her heart at ease by the sagacity of their " I know what ; " and the evening was spent in a sort of war of wit, a display of family ingenuity ; on one side in the mystery of an affected secret, on the other of undefined discovery, all equally acute.

Catherine was with her friend again the next day, endeavouring to support her spirits, and while away the many tedious hours before the delivery of the letters ; a needful exertion, for as the time of reasonable expectation drew near, Isabella became more and more desponding, and before the letter arrived, had worked herself into a state of real distress. But when it did come, where could distress be found ? " I have had no difficulty in gaining the consent of my kind parents, and am promised that every thing in their power shall be done to forward my happiness," were the first three lines, and in one moment all was joyful security. The brightest glow was instantly spread over Isabella's features, all care and anxiety seemed removed, her spirits became almost too high for controul, and she called herself without scruple the happiest of mortals.

Mrs. Thorpe, with tears of joy, embraced her daughter, her son, her visitor, and could have embraced half the inhabitants of Bath with satisfaction. Her heart was overflowing with tenderness. It was " dear John," and " dear Catherine " at every word ;—" dear Anne and dear Maria " must immediately be made sharers in their felicity ; and two " dears " at once before the name of Isabella were not more than that beloved child had now well earned. John himself was no skulker in joy. He

not

not only bestowed on Mr. Morland the high commendation of being one of the finest fellows in the world, but
swore off many sentences in his praise.

The letter, whence sprang all this felicity, was short,
containing little more than this assurance of success;
and every particular was deferred till James could write
again. But for particulars Isabella could well afford to
wait. The needful was comprised in Mr. Morland's
promise; his honour was pledged to make every thing
easy; and by what means their income was to be formed,
whether landed property were to be resigned, or funded
money made over, was a matter in which her disinterested spirit took no concern. She knew enough to feel
secure of an honourable and speedy establishment, and
her imagination took a rapid flight over its attendant
felicities. She saw herself at the end of a few weeks,
the gaze and admiration of every new acquaintance at
Fullerton, the envy of every valued old friend in Putney,
with a carriage at her command, a new name on her
tickets, and a brilliant exhibition of hoop rings on her
finger.

When the contents of the letter were ascertained, John
Thorpe, who had only waited its arrival to begin his
journey to London, prepared to set off. " Well, Miss
Morland," said he, on finding her alone in the parlour,
" I am come to bid you good bye." Catherine wished
him a good journey. Without appearing to hear her, he
walked to the window, fidgetted about, hummed a tune,
and seemed wholly self-occupied.

" Shall not you be late at Devizes ? " said Catherine.
He made no answer; but after a minute's silence burst
out with, " A famous good thing this marrying scheme,
upon my soul ! A clever fancy of Morland's and Belle's.
What do you think of it, Miss Morland ? *I* say it is no
bad notion."

" I am sure I think it a very good one."

" Do you ?—that's honest, by heavens ! I am glad
you are no enemy to matrimony however. Did you ever
hear

hear the old song, 'Going to one wedding brings on another?' I say, you will come to Belle's wedding, I hope."

"Yes; I have promised your sister to be with her, if possible."

"And then you know"—twisting himself about and forcing a foolish laugh—"I say, then you know, we may try the truth of this same old song."

"May we?—but I never sing. Well, I wish you a good journey. I dine with Miss Tilney to-day, and must now be going home."

"Nay, but there is no such confounded hurry.—Who knows when we may be together again?—Not but that I shall be down again by the end of a fortnight, and a devilish long fortnight it will appear to me."

"Then why do you stay away so long?" replied Catherine—finding that he waited for an answer.

"That is kind of you, however—kind and good-natured.—I shall not forget it in a hurry.—But you have more good-nature and all that, than any body living I believe. A monstrous deal of good-nature, and it is not only good-nature, but you have so much, so much of every thing; and then you have such—upon my soul I do not know any body like you."

"Oh! dear, there are a great many people like me, I dare say, only a great deal better. Good morning to you."

"But I say, Miss Morland, I shall come and pay my respects at Fullerton before it is long, if not disagreeable."

"Pray do.—My father and mother will be very glad to see you."

"And I hope—I hope, Miss Morland, *you* will not be sorry to see me."

"Oh! dear, not at all. There are very few people I am sorry to see. Company is always cheerful."

"That is just my way of thinking. Give me but a little cheerful company, let me only have the company
of

of the people I love, let me only be where I like and with
whom I like, and the devil take the rest, say I.—And
I am heartily glad to hear you say the same. But I have
a notion, Miss Morland, you and I think pretty much
alike upon most matters."

" Perhaps we may ; but it is more than I ever thought
of. And as to *most matters*, to say the truth, there are
not many that I know my own mind about."

" By Jove, no more do I. It is not my way to bother
my brains with what does not concern me. My notion
of things is simple enough. Let me only have the girl
I like, say I, with a comfortable house over my head, and
what care I for all the rest ? Fortune is nothing. I am
sure of a good income of my own ; and if she had not
a penny, why so much the better."

" Very true. I think like you there. If there is a good
fortune on one side, there can be no occasion for any on
the other. No matter which has it, so that there is enough.
I hate the idea of one great fortune looking out for another.
And to marry for money I think the wickedest thing in
existence.—Good day.—We shall be very glad to see you
at Fullerton, whenever it is convenient." And away she
went. It was not in the power of all his gallantry to
detain her longer. With such news to communicate, and
such a visit to prepare for, her departure was not to be
delayed by any thing in his nature to urge ; and she
hurried away, leaving him to the undivided consciousness
of his own happy address, and her explicit encouragement.

The agitation which she had herself experienced on
first learning her brother's engagement, made her expect
to raise no inconsiderable emotion in Mr. and Mrs. Allen,
by the communication of the wonderful event. How
great was her disappointment ! The important affair,
which many words of preparation ushered in, had been
foreseen by them both ever since her brother's arrival ;
and all that they felt on the occasion was comprehended
in a wish for the young people's happiness, with a remark,

on

on the gentleman's side, in favour of Isabella's beauty, and on the lady's, of her great good luck. It was to Catherine the most surprizing insensibility. The disclosure however of the great secret of James's going to Fullerton the day before, did raise some emotion in Mrs. Allen. She could not listen to that with perfect calmness ; but repeatedly regretted the necessity of its concealment, wished she could have known his intention, wished she could have seen him before he went, as she should certainly have troubled him with her best regards to his father and mother, and her kind compliments to all the Skinners.

END OF VOL. I.

VOLUME TWO

short. Ten to one but he guesses the reason, and that
is exactly what I want to avoid, so I shall insist on his
keeping his conjecture to himself."

Isabella's opinion of the Tilneys did not influence her
friend ; she was sure there had been no insolence in the
manners either of brother or sister ; and she did not
credit there being any pride in their hearts. The evening
rewarded her confidence ; she was met by one with the
same kindness, and by the other with the same attention
as heretofore : Miss Tilney took pains to be near her,
and Henry asked her to dance.

Having heard the day before in Milsom-street, that
their elder brother, Captain Tilney, was expected almost
every hour, she was at no loss for the name of a very
fashionable-looking, handsome young man, whom she had
never seen before, and who now evidently belonged to
their party. She looked at him with great admiration,
and even supposed it possible, that some people might
think him handsomer than his brother, though, in her
eyes, his air was more assuming, and his countenance
less prepossessing. His taste and manners were beyond
a doubt decidedly inferior ; for, within her hearing, he
not only protested against every thought of dancing
himself, but even laughed openly at Henry for finding it
possible. From the latter circumstance it may be pre-
sumed, that, whatever might be our heroine's opinion of
him, his admiration of her was not of a very dangerous
kind ; not likely to produce animosities between the
brothers, nor persecutions to the lady. *He* cannot be the
instigator of the three villains in horsemen's great coats,
by whom she will hereafter be forced into a travelling-
chaise and four, which will drive off with incredible speed.
Catherine, meanwhile, undisturbed by presentiments of
such an evil, or of any evil at all, except that of having
but a short set to dance down, enjoyed her usual happiness
with Henry Tilney, listening with sparkling eyes to every
thing he said ; and, in finding him irresistible, becoming
so herself.

At

At the end of the first dance, Captain Tilney came towards them again, and, much to Catherine's dissatisfaction, pulled his brother away. They retired whispering together; and, though her delicate sensibility did not take immediate alarm, and lay it down as fact, that Captain Tilney must have heard some malevolent misrepresentation of her, which he now hastened to communicate to his brother, in the hope of separating them for ever, she could not have her partner conveyed from her sight without very uneasy sensations. Her suspense was of full five minutes' duration; and she was beginning to think it a very long quarter of an hour, when they both returned, and an explanation was given, by Henry's requesting to know, if she thought her friend, Miss Thorpe, would have any objection to dancing, as his brother would be most happy to be introduced to her. Catherine, without hesitation, replied, that she was very sure Miss Thorpe did not mean to dance at all. The cruel reply was passed on to the other, and he immediately walked away.

" Your brother will not mind it I know," said she, " because I heard him say before, that he hated dancing; but it was very good-natured in him to think of it. I suppose he saw Isabella sitting down, and fancied she might wish for a partner; but he is quite mistaken, for she would not dance upon any account in the world."

Henry smiled, and said, " How very little trouble it can give you to understand the motive of other people's actions."

" Why ?—What do you mean ? "

" With you, it is not, How is such a one likely to be influenced ? What is the inducement most likely to act upon such a person's feelings, age, situation, and probable habits of life considered ?—but, how should *I* be influenced, what would be *my* inducement in acting so and so ? "

" I do not understand you."

" Then we are on very unequal terms, for I understand you perfectly well."

" Me ?

" Me ?—yes ; I cannot speak well enough to be unintelligible."

" Bravo !—an excellent satire on modern language."

" But pray tell me what you mean."

" Shall I indeed ?—Do you really desire it ?—But you
are not aware of the consequences ; it will involve you
in a very cruel embarrassment, and certainly bring on
a disagreement between us."

" No, no ; it shall not do either ; I am not afraid."

" Well then, I only meant that your attributing my
brother's wish of dancing with Miss Thorpe to good-
nature alone, convinced me of your being superior in
good-nature yourself to all the rest of the world."

Catherine blushed and disclaimed, and the gentleman's
predictions were verified. There was a something, however, in his words which repaid her for the pain of confusion ; and that something occupied her mind so much,
that she drew back for some time, forgetting to speak
or to listen, and almost forgetting where she was ; till,
roused by the voice of Isabella, she looked up and saw
her with Captain Tilney preparing to give them hands
across.

Isabella shrugged her shoulders and smiled, the only
explanation of this extraordinary change which could at
that time be given ; but as it was not quite enough for
Catherine's comprehension, she spoke her astonishment
in very plain terms to her partner.

" I cannot think how it could happen ! Isabella was so
determined not to dance."

" And did Isabella never change her mind before ? "

" Oh ! but, because——and your brother !—After what
you told him from me, how could he think of going to
ask her ? "

" I cannot take surprize to myself on that head. You
bid me be surprized on your friend's account, and therefore I am ; but as for my brother, his conduct in the
business, I must own, has been no more than I believed
him perfectly equal to. The fairness of your friend was
an

an open attraction ; her firmness, you know, could only be understood by yourself."

"You are laughing ; but, I assure you, Isabella is very firm in general."

"It is as much as should be said of any one. To be always firm must be to be often obstinate. When properly to relax is the trial of judgment ; and, without reference to my brother, I really think Miss Thorpe has by no means chosen ill in fixing on the present hour."

The friends were not able to get together for any confidential discourse till all the dancing was over ; but then, as they walked about the room arm in arm, Isabella thus explained herself :—" I do not wonder at your surprize ; and I am really fatigued to death. He is such a rattle !—Amusing enough, if my mind had been disengaged ; but I would have given the world to sit still."

" Then why did not you ? "

" Oh ! my dear ! it would have looked so particular ; and you know how I abhor doing that. I refused him as long as I possibly could, but he would take no denial. You have no idea how he pressed me. I begged him to excuse me, and get some other partner—but no, not he ; after aspiring to my hand, there was nobody else in the room he could bear to think of ; and it was not that he wanted merely to dance, he wanted to be with *me*. Oh ! such nonsense !—I told him he had taken a very unlikely way to prevail upon me ; for, of all things in the world, I hated fine speeches and compliments ;—and so—— and so then I found there would be no peace if I did not stand up. Besides, I thought Mrs. Hughes, who introduced him, might take it ill if I did not : and your dear brother, I am sure he would have been miserable if I had sat down the whole evening. I am so glad it is over ! My spirits are quite jaded with listening to his nonsense : and then,—being such a smart young fellow, I saw every eye was upon us."

" He is very handsome indeed."

" Handsome !

" Handsome !—Yes, I suppose he may. I dare say people would admire him in general ; but he is not at all in my style of beauty. I hate a florid complexion and dark eyes in a man. However, he is very well. Amazingly conceited, I am sure. I took him down several times you know in my way."

When the young ladies next met, they had a far more interesting subject to discuss. James Morland's second letter was then received, and the kind intentions of his father fully explained. A living, of which Mr. Morland was himself patron and incumbent, of about four hundred pounds yearly value, was to be resigned to his son as soon as he should be old enough to take it ; no trifling deduction from the family income, no niggardly assignment to one of ten children. An estate of at least equal value, moreover, was assured as his future inheritance.

James expressed himself on the occasion with becoming gratitude ; and the necessity of waiting between two and three years before they could marry, being, however unwelcome, no more than he had expected, was born by him without discontent. Catherine, whose expectations had been as unfixed as her ideas of her father's income, and whose judgment was now entirely led by her brother, felt equally well satisfied, and heartily congratulated Isabella on having every thing so pleasantly settled.

" It is very charming indeed," said Isabella, with a grave face. " Mr. Morland has behaved vastly handsome indeed," said the gentle Mrs. Thorpe, looking anxiously at her daughter. "I only wish I could do as much. One could not expect more from him you know. If he finds he *can* do more by and bye, I dare say he will, for I am sure he must be an excellent good hearted man. Four hundred is but a small income to begin on indeed, but your wishes, my dear Isabella, are so moderate, you do not consider how little you ever want, my dear."

" It is not on my own account I wish for more ; but
I cannot

I cannot bear to be the means of injuring my dear Morland,
making him sit down upon an income hardly enough to
find one in the common necessaries of life. For myself,
it is nothing; I never think of myself."

" I know you never do, my dear; and you will always
find your reward in the affection it makes every body
feel for you. There never was a young woman so beloved
as you are by every body that knows you; and I dare say
when Mr. Morland sees you, my dear child—but do not
let us distress our dear Catherine by talking of such
things. Mr. Morland has behaved so very handsome you
know. I always heard he was a most excellent man;
and you know, my dear, we are not to suppose but what,
if you had had a suitable fortune, he would have come
down with something more, for I am sure he must be
a most liberal-minded man."

" Nobody can think better of Mr. Morland than I do,
I am sure. But every body has their failing you know,
and every body has a right to do what they like with
their own money." Catherine was hurt by these insinua-
tions. " I am very sure," said she, " that my father has
promised to do as much as he can afford."

Isabella recollected herself. " As to that, my sweet
Catherine, there cannot be a doubt, and you know me
well enough to be sure that a much smaller income would
satisfy me. It is not the want of more money that makes
me just at present a little out of spirits; I hate money;
and if our union could take place now upon only fifty
pounds a year, I should not have a wish unsatisfied. Ah!
my Catherine, you have found me out. There's the sting.
The long, long, endless two years and half that are to pass
before your brother can hold the living."

" Yes, yes, my darling Isabella," said Mrs. Thorpe,
" we perfectly see into your heart. You have no disguise.
We perfectly understand the present vexation; and
every body must love you the better for such a noble
honest affection."

Catherine's uncomfortable feelings began to lessen.
She

She endeavoured to believe that the delay of the marriage was the only source of Isabella's regret ; and when she saw her at their next interview as cheerful and amiable as ever, endeavoured to forget that she had for a minute thought otherwise. James soon followed his letter, and was received with the most gratifying kindness.

CHAP-

CHAPTER II.

THE Allens had now entered on the sixth week of their stay in Bath ; and whether it should be the last, was for some time a question, to which Catherine listened with a beating heart. To have her acquaintance with the Tilneys end so soon, was an evil which nothing could counterbalance. Her whole happiness seemed at stake, while the affair was in suspense, and every thing secured when it was determined that the lodgings should be taken for another fortnight. What this additional fortnight was to produce to her beyond the pleasure of sometimes seeing Henry Tilney, made but a small part of Catherine's speculation. Once or twice indeed, since James's engagement had taught her what *could* be done, she had got so far as to indulge in a secret " perhaps," but in general the felicity of being with him for the present bounded her views : the present was now comprised in another three weeks, and her happiness being certain for that period, the rest of her life was at such a distance as to excite but little interest. In the course of the morning which saw this business arranged, she visited Miss Tilney, and poured forth her joyful feelings. It was doomed to be a day of trial. No sooner had she expressed her delight in Mr. Allen's lengthened stay, than Miss Tilney told her of her father's having just determined upon quitting Bath by the end of another week. Here was a blow ! The past suspense of the morning had been ease and quiet to the present disappointment. Catherine's countenance fell, and in a voice of most sincere concern she echoed Miss Tilney's concluding words, " By the end of another week ! "

" Yes, my father can seldom be prevailed on to give the waters what I think a fair trial. He has been disappointed of some friends' arrival whom he expected to

meet

meet here, and as he is now pretty well, is in a hurry to
get home."

" I am very sorry for it," said Catherine dejectedly,
" if I had known this before—"

" Perhaps," said Miss Tilney in an embarrassed manner,
" you would be so good—it would make me very happy
if— "

The entrance of her father put a stop to the civility,
which Catherine was beginning to hope might introduce
a desire of their corresponding. After addressing her
with his usual politeness, he turned to his daughter and
said, " Well, Eleanor, may I congratulate you on being
successful in your application to your fair friend ? "

" I was just beginning to make the request, sir, as you
came in."

" Well, proceed by all means. I know how much your
heart is in it. My daughter, Miss Morland," he continued,
without leaving his daughter time to speak, " has been
forming a very bold wish. We leave Bath, as she has
perhaps told you, on Saturday se'nnight. A letter from
my steward tells me that my presence is wanted at home ;
and being disappointed in my hope of seeing the Marquis
of Longtown and General Courteney here, some of my
very old friends, there is nothing to detain me longer in
Bath. And could we carry our selfish point with you,
we should leave it without a single regret. Can you, in
short, be prevailed on to quit this scene of public triumph
and oblige your friend Eleanor with your company in
Gloucestershire ? I am almost ashamed to make the
request, though its presumption would certainly appear
greater to every creature in Bath than yourself. Modesty
such as your's—but not for the world would I pain it by
open praise. If you can be induced to honour us with
a visit, you will make us happy beyond expression.
'Tis true, we can offer you nothing like the gaieties of this
lively place ; we can tempt you neither by amusement
nor splendour, for our mode of living, as you see, is plain
and unpretending ; yet no endeavours shall be wanting
on

on our side to make Northanger Abbey not wholly disagreeable."

Northanger Abbey!—These were thrilling words, and wound up Catherine's feelings to the highest point of extasy. Her grateful and gratified heart could hardly restrain its expressions within the language of tolerable calmness. To receive so flattering an invitation! To have her company so warmly solicited! Every thing honourable and soothing, every present enjoyment, and every future hope was contained in it ; and her acceptance, with only the saving clause of papa and mamma's approbation, was eagerly given.—" I will write home directly," said she, " and if they do not object, as I dare say they will not "—

General Tilney was not less sanguine, having already waited on her excellent friends in Pulteney-street, and obtained their sanction of his wishes. " Since they can consent to part with you," said he, " we may expect philosophy from all the world."

Miss Tilney was earnest, though gentle, in her secondary civilities, and the affair became in a few minutes as nearly settled, as this necessary reference to Fullerton would allow.

The circumstances of the morning had led Catherine's feelings through the varieties of suspense, security, and disappointment ; but they were now safely lodged in perfect bliss ; and with spirits elated to rapture, with Henry at her heart, and Northanger Abbey on her lips, she hurried home to write her letter. Mr. and Mrs. Morland, relying on the discretion of the friends to whom they had already entrusted their daughter, felt no doubt of the propriety of an acquaintance which had been formed under their eye, and sent therefore by return of post their ready consent to her visit in Gloucestershire. This indulgence, though not more than Catherine had hoped for, completed her conviction of being favoured beyond every other human creature, in friends and fortune, circumstance and chance. Every thing seemed

to

to co-operate for her advantage. By the kindness of her
first friends the Allens, she had been introduced into
scenes, where pleasures of every kind had met her. Her
feelings, her preferences had each known the happiness
of a return. Wherever she felt attachment, she had been
able to create it. The affection of Isabella was to be
secured to her in a sister. The Tilneys, they, by whom
above all, she desired to be favourably thought of,
outstripped even her wishes in the flattering measures by
which their intimacy was to be continued. She was to
be their chosen visitor, she was to be for weeks under
the same roof with the person whose society she mostly
prized—and, in addition to all the rest, this roof was to
be the roof of an abbey !—Her passion for ancient edifices
was next in degree to her passion for Henry Tilney—and
castles and abbies made usually the charm of those
reveries which his image did not fill. To see and explore
either the ramparts and keep of the one, or the cloisters
of the other, had been for many weeks a darling wish,
though to be more than the visitor of an hour, had seemed
too nearly impossible for desire. And yet, this was to
happen. With all the chances against her of house, hall,
place, park, court, and cottage, Northanger turned up an
abbey, and she was to be its inhabitant. Its long, damp
passages, its narrow cells and ruined chapel, were to be
within her daily reach, and she could not entirely subdue
the hope of some traditional legends, some awful memorials
of an injured and ill-fated nun.

It was wonderful that her friends should seem so little
elated by the possession of such a home ; that the consciousness of it should be so meekly born. The power of
early habit only could account for it. A distinction to
which they had been born gave no pride. Their superiority
of abode was no more to them than their superiority of
person.

Many were the inquiries she was eager to make of
Miss Tilney ; but so active were her thoughts, that when
these inquiries were answered, she_was hardly more
                                                    assured

assured than before, of Northanger Abbey having been a richly-endowed convent at the time of the Reformation, of its having fallen into the hands of an ancestor of the Tilneys on its dissolution, of a large portion of the ancient building still making a part of the present dwelling although the rest was decayed, or of its standing low in a valley, sheltered from the north and east by rising woods of oak.

CHAP-

CHAPTER III.

WITH a mind thus full of happiness, Catherine was hardly aware that two or three days had passed away, without her seeing Isabella for more than a few minutes together. She began first to be sensible of this, and to sigh for her conversation, as she walked along the Pump-room one morning, by Mrs. Allen's side, without any thing to say or to hear; and scarcely had she felt a five minutes' longing of friendship, before the object of it appeared, and inviting her to a secret conference, led the way to a seat. " This is my favourite place," said she, as they sat down on a bench between the doors, which commanded a tolerable view of every body entering at either, " it is so out of the way."

Catherine, observing that Isabella's eyes were continually bent towards one door or the other, as in eager expectation, and remembering how often she had been falsely accused of being arch, thought the present a fine opportunity for being really so; and therefore gaily said, " Do not be uneasy, Isabella. James will soon be here."

" Psha! my dear creature," she replied, " do not think me such a simpleton as to be always wanting to confine him to my elbow. It would be hideous to be always together; we should be the jest of the place. And so you are going to Northanger!—I am amazingly glad of it. It is one of the finest old places in England, I understand. I shall depend upon a most particular description of it."

" You shall certainly have the best in my power to give. But who are you looking for? Are your sisters coming? "

" I am not looking for any body. One's eyes must be somewhere, and you know what a foolish trick I have of fixing mine, when my thoughts are an hundred miles off.

I am

I am amazingly absent ; I believe I am the most absent
creature in the world. Tilney says it is always the case
with minds of a certain stamp."

" But I thought, Isabella, you had something in
particular to tell me ? "

" Oh ! yes, and so I have. But here is a proof of what
I was saying. My poor head ! I had quite forgot it.
Well, the thing is this, I have just had a letter from
John ;—you can guess the contents."

" No, indeed, I cannot."

" My sweet love, do not be so abominably affected.
What can he write about, but yourself ? You know he
is over head and ears in love with you."

" With *me*, dear Isabella ! "

" Nay, my sweetest Catherine, this is being quite
absurd ! Modesty, and all that, is very well in its way,
but really a little common honesty is sometimes quite as
becoming. I have no idea of being so overstrained !
It is fishing for compliments. His attentions were such
as a child must have noticed. And it was but half an
hour before he left Bath, that you gave him the most
positive encouragement. He says so in this letter, says
that he as good as made you an offer, and that you
received his advances in the kindest way ; and now he
wants me to urge his suit, and say all manner of pretty
things to you. So it is in vain to affect ignorance."

Catherine, with all the earnestness of truth, expressed
her astonishment at such a charge, protesting her innocence of every thought of Mr. Thorpe's being in love with
her, and the consequent impossibility of her having ever
intended to encourage him. " As to any attentions on
his side, I do declare, upon my honour, I never was
sensible of them for a moment—except just his asking me
to dance the first day of his coming. And as to making
me an offer, or any thing like it, there must be some
unaccountable mistake. I could not have misunderstood
a thing of that kind, you know !—and, as I ever wish to
be believed, I solemnly protest that no syllable of such
a nature

a nature ever passed between us. The last half hour
before he went away !—It must be all and completely
a mistake—for I did not see him once that whole morning."

"But *that* you certainly did, for you spent the whole
morning in Edgar's Buildings—it was the day your
father's consent came—and I am pretty sure that you
and John were alone in the parlour, some time before you
left the house."

"Are you ?—Well, if you say it, it was so, I dare say—
but for the life of me, I cannot recollect it.—I *do* remember
now being with you, and seeing him as well as the rest—but
that we were ever alone for five minutes—However, it is
not worth arguing about, for whatever might pass on his
side, you must be convinced, by my having no recollection
of it, that I never thought, nor expected, nor wished for
any thing of the kind from him. I am excessively concerned that he should have any regard for me—but
indeed it has been quite unintentional on my side, I never
had the smallest idea of it. Pray undeceive him as soon
as you can, and tell him I beg his pardon—that is—I do
not know what I ought to say—but make him understand
what I mean, in the properest way. I would not speak
disrespectfully of a brother of your's, Isabella, I am sure ;
but you know very well that if I could think of one man
more than another—*he* is not the person." Isabella was
silent. " My dear friend, you must not be angry with
me. I cannot suppose your brother cares so very much
about me. And, you know, we shall still be sisters."

" Yes, yes," (with a blush) " there are more ways than
one of our being sisters.—But where am I wandering
to ?—Well, my dear Catherine, the case seems to be, that
you are determined against poor John—is not it so ? "

" I certainly cannot return his affection, and as certainly never meant to encourage it."

" Since that is the case, I am sure I shall not tease you
any further. John desired me to speak to you on the
subject, and therefore I have. But I confess, as soon as
I read his letter, I thought it a very foolish, imprudent

business, and not likely to promote the good of either ;
for what were you to live upon, supposing you came
together ?   You have both of you something to be sure,
but it is not a trifle that will support a family now-a-days ;
and after all that romancers may say, there is no doing
without money.   I only wonder John could think of
it ; he could not have received my last."

" You *do* acquit me then of any thing wrong ?—You
are convinced that I never meant to deceive your brother,
never suspected him of liking me till this moment ? "

" Oh ! as to that," answered Isabella laughingly, " I do
not pretend to determine what your thoughts and designs
in time past may have been.   All that is best known to
yourself.   A little harmless flirtation or so will occur,
and one is often drawn on to give more encouragement
than one wishes to stand by.   But you may be assured
that I am the last person in the world to judge you
severely.   All those things should be allowed for in
youth and high spirits.   What one means one day, you
know, one may not mean the next.   Circumstances
change, opinions alter."

" But my opinion of your brother never did alter ;
it was always the same.   You are describing what never
happened."

" My dearest Catherine," continued the other without
at all listening to her, " I would not for all the world be
the means of hurrying you into an engagement before
you knew what you were about.   I do not think any
thing would justify me in wishing you to sacrifice all your
happiness merely to oblige my brother, because he is my
brother, and who perhaps after all, you know, might be
just as happy without you, for people seldom know what
they would be at, young men especially, they are so
amazingly changeable and inconstant.   What I say is,
why should a brother's happiness be dearer to me than
a friend's ?   You know I carry my notions of friendship
pretty high.   But, above all things, my dear Catherine,
do not be in a hurry.   Take my word for it, that if you

are

are in too great a hurry, you will certainly live to repent
it. Tilney says, there is nothing people are so often
deceived in, as the state of their own affections, and
I believe he is very right. Ah! here he comes; never
mind, he will not see us, I am sure."

Catherine, looking up, perceived Captain Tilney; and
Isabella, earnestly fixing her eye on him as she spoke,
soon caught his notice. He approached immediately,
and took the seat to which her movements invited him.
His first address made Catherine start. Though spoken
low, she could distinguish, "What! always to be watched,
in person or by proxy!"

"Psha, nonsense!" was Isabella's answer in the same
half whisper. "Why do you put such things into my
head? If I could believe it—my spirit, you know, is
pretty independent."

"I wish your heart were independent. That would
be enough for me."

"My heart, indeed! What can you have to do with
hearts? You men have none of you any hearts."

"If we have not hearts, we have eyes; and they give
us torment enough."

"Do they? I am sorry for it; I am sorry they find
any thing so disagreeable in me. I will look another way.
I hope this pleases you, (turning her back on him,) I hope
your eyes are not tormented now."

"Never more so; for the edge of a blooming cheek is
still in view—at once too much and too little."

Catherine heard all this, and quite out of countenance
could listen no longer. Amazed that Isabella could
endure it, and jealous for her brother, she rose up, and
saying she should join Mrs. Allen, proposed their walking.
But for this Isabella shewed no inclination. She was so
amazingly tired, and it was so odious to parade about
the Pump-room; and if she moved from her seat she
should miss her sisters, she was expecting her sisters
every moment; so that her dearest Catherine must
excuse her, and must sit quietly down again. But

L 2   Catherine

Catherine could be stubborn too ; and Mrs. Allen just then coming up to propose their returning home, she joined her and walked out of the Pump-room, leaving Isabella still sitting with Captain Tilney. With much uneasiness did she thus leave them. It seemed to her that Captain Tilney was falling in love with Isabella, and Isabella unconsciously encouraging him ; unconsciously it must be, for Isabella's attachment to James was as certain and well acknowledged as her engagement. To doubt her truth or good intentions was impossible ; and yet, during the whole of their conversation her manner had been odd. She wished Isabella had talked more like her usual self, and not so much about money ; and had not looked so well pleased at the sight of Captain Tilney. How strange that she should not perceive his admiration ! Catherine longed to give her a hint of it, to put her on her guard, and prevent all the pain which her too lively behaviour might otherwise create both for him and her brother.

The compliment of John Thorpe's affection did not make amends for this thoughtlessness in his sister. She was almost as far from believing as from wishing it to be sincere ; for she had not forgotten that he could mistake, and his assertion of the offer and of her encouragement convinced her that his mistakes could sometimes be very egregious. In vanity therefore she gained but little, her chief profit was in wonder. That he should think it worth his while to fancy himself in love with her, was a matter of lively astonishment. Isabella talked of his attentions ; *she* had never been sensible of any ; but Isabella had said many things which she hoped had been spoken in haste, and would never be said again ; and upon this she was glad to rest altogether for present ease and comfort.

CHAP-

CHAPTER IV.

A FEW days passed away, and Catherine, though not allowing herself to suspect her friend, could not help watching her closely. The result of her observations was not agreeable. Isabella seemed an altered creature. When she saw her indeed surrounded only by their immediate friends in Edgar's Buildings or Pulteney-street, her change of manners was so trifling that, had it gone no farther, it might have passed unnoticed. A something of languid indifference, or of that boasted absence of mind which Catherine had never heard of before, would occasionally come across her; but had nothing worse appeared, *that* might only have spread a new grace and inspired a warmer interest. But when Catherine saw her in public, admitting Captain Tilney's attentions as readily as they were offered, and allowing him almost an equal share with James in her notice and smiles, the alteration became too positive to be past over. What could be meant by such unsteady conduct, what her friend could be at, was beyond her comprehension. Isabella could not be aware of the pain she was inflicting; but it was a degree of wilful thoughtlessness which Catherine could not but resent. James was the sufferer. She saw him grave and uneasy; and however careless of his present comfort the woman might be who had given him her heart, to *her* it was always an object. For poor Captain Tilney too she was greatly concerned. Though his looks did not please her, his name was a passport to her good will, and she thought with sincere compassion of his approaching disappointment; for, in spite of what she had believed herself to overhear in the Pump-room, his behaviour was so incompatible with a knowledge of Isabella's engagement, that she could not, upon reflection, imagine him aware of it. He might be jealous of her

brother

brother as a rival, but if more had seemed implied, the fault must have been in her misapprehension. She wished, by a gentle remonstrance, to remind Isabella of her situation, and make her aware of this double unkindness ; but for remonstrance, either opportunity or comprehension was always against her. If able to suggest a hint, Isabella could never understand it. In this distress, the intended departure of the Tilney family became her chief consolation ; their journey into Gloucestershire was to take place within a few days, and Captain Tilney's removal would at least restore peace to every heart but his own. But Captain Tilney had at present no intention of removing ; he was not to be of the party to Northanger, he was to continue at Bath. When Catherine knew this, her resolution was directly made. She spoke to Henry Tilney on the subject, regretting his brother's evident partiality for Miss Thorpe, and entreating him to make known her prior engagement.

" My brother does know it," was Henry's answer.

" Does he ?—then why does he stay here ? "

He made no reply, and was beginning to talk of something else ; but she eagerly continued, " Why do not you persuade him to go away ? The longer he stays, the worse it will be for him at last. Pray advise him for his own sake, and for every body's sake, to leave Bath directly. Absence will in time make him comfortable again ; but he can have no hope here, and it is only staying to be miserable." Henry smiled and said, " I am sure my brother would not wish to do that."

" Then you will persuade him to go away ? "

" Persuasion is not at command ; but pardon me, if I cannot even endeavour to persuade him. I have myself told him that Miss Thorpe is engaged. He knows what he is about, and must be his own master."

" No, he does not know what he is about," cried Catherine ; " he does not know the pain he is giving my brother. Not that James has ever told me so, but I am sure he is very uncomfortable."

" And

" And are you sure it is my brother's doing ? "

" Yes, very sure."

" Is it my brother's attentions to Miss Thorpe, or Miss Thorpe's admission of them, that gives the pain ? "

" Is not it the same thing ? "

" I think Mr. Morland would acknowledge a difference. No man is offended by another man's admiration of the woman he loves ; it is the woman only who can make it a torment."

Catherine blushed for her friend, and said, " Isabella is wrong. But I am sure she cannot mean to torment, for she is very much attached to my brother. She has been in love with him ever since they first met, and while my father's consent was uncertain, she fretted herself almost into a fever. You know she must be attached to him."

" I understand : she is in love with James, and flirts with Frederick."

" Oh ! no, not flirts. A woman in love with one man cannot flirt with another."

" It is probable that she will neither love so well, nor flirt so well, as she might do either singly. The gentlemen must each give up a little."

After a short pause, Catherine resumed with " Then you do not believe Isabella so very much attached to my brother ? "

" I can have no opinion on that subject."

" But what can your brother mean ? If he knows her engagement, what can he mean by his behaviour ? "

" You are a very close questioner."

" Am I ?—I only ask what I want to be told."

" But do you only ask what I can be expected to tell ? "

" Yes, I think so ; for you must know your brother's heart."

" My brother's heart, as you term it, on the present occasion, I assure you I can only guess at."

" Well ? "

" Well !—Nay, if it is to be guess-work, let us all guess
for

for ourselves. To be guided by second-hand conjecture
is pitiful. The premises are before you. My brother is
a lively, and perhaps sometimes a thoughtless young man;
he has had about a week's acquaintance with your friend,
and he has known her engagement almost as long as he
has known her."

" Well," said Catherine, after some moments' consideration, " *you* may be able to guess at your brother's
intentions from all this ; but I am sure I cannot. But is
not your father uncomfortable about it ?—Does not he
want Captain Tilney to go away ?—Sure, if your father
were to speak to him, he would go."

" My dear Miss Morland," said Henry, " in this amiable
solicitude for your brother's comfort, may you not be
a little mistaken ? Are you not carried a little too far ?
Would he thank you, either on his own account or Miss
Thorpe's, for supposing that her affection, or at least her
good-behaviour, is only to be secured by her seeing nothing
of Captain Tilney ? Is he safe only in solitude ?—or,
is her heart constant to him only when unsolicited by
any one else ?—He cannot think this—and you may be
sure that he would not have you think it. I will not say,
' Do not be uneasy,' because I know that you are so, at
this moment ; but be as little uneasy as you can. You
have no doubt of the mutual attachment of your brother
and your friend ; depend upon it therefore, that real
jealousy never can exist between them ; depend upon it
that no disagreement between them can be of any duration. Their hearts are open to each other, as neither
heart can be to you ; they know exactly what is required
and what can be borne ; and you may be certain, that
one will never tease the other beyond what is known to
be pleasant."

Perceiving her still to look doubtful and grave, he
added, " Though Frederick does not leave Bath with us,
he will probably remain but a very short time, perhaps
only a few days behind us. His leave of absence will soon
expire, and he must return to his regiment.—And what
will

will then be their acquaintance ?—The mess-room will drink Isabella Thorpe for a fortnight, and she will laugh with your brother over poor Tilney's passion for a month."

Catherine would contend no longer against comfort. She had resisted its approaches during the whole length of a speech, but it now carried her captive. Henry Tilney must know best. She blamed herself for the extent of her fears, and resolved never to think so seriously on the subject again.

Her resolution was supported by Isabella's behaviour in their parting interview. The Thorpes spent the last evening of Catherine's stay in Pulteney-street, and nothing passed between the lovers to excite her uneasiness, or make her quit them in apprehension. James was in excellent spirits, and Isabella most engagingly placid. Her tenderness for her friend seemed rather the first feeling of her heart ; but that at such a moment was allowable ; and once she gave her lover a flat contradiction, and once she drew back her hand ; but Catherine remembered Henry's instructions, and placed it all to judicious affection. The embraces, tears, and promises of the parting fair ones may be fancied.

CHAP-

CHAPTER V.

MR. and Mrs. Allen were sorry to lose their young friend, whose good-humour and cheerfulness had made her a valuable companion, and in the promotion of whose enjoyment their own had been gently increased. Her happiness in going with Miss Tilney, however, prevented their wishing it otherwise ; and, as they were to remain only one more week in Bath themselves, her quitting them now would not long be felt. Mr. Allen attended her to Milsom-street, where she was to breakfast, and saw her seated with the kindest welcome among her new friends ; but so great was her agitation in finding herself as one of the family, and so fearful was she of not doing exactly what was right, and of not being able to preserve their good opinion, that, in the embarrassment of the first five minutes, she could almost have wished to return with him to Pulteney-street.

Miss Tilney's manners and Henry's smile soon did away some of her unpleasant feelings ; but still she was far from being at ease ; nor could the incessant attentions of the General himself entirely reassure her. Nay, perverse as it seemed, she doubted whether she might not have felt less, had she been less attended to. His anxiety for her comfort—his continual solicitations that she would eat, and his often-expressed fears of her seeing nothing to her taste—though never in her life before had she beheld half such variety on a breakfast-table—made it impossible for her to forget for a moment that she was a visitor. She felt utterly unworthy of such respect, and knew not how to reply to it. Her tranquillity was not improved by the General's impatience for the appearance of his eldest son, nor by the displeasure he expressed at his laziness when Captain Tilney at last came down. She was quite pained by the severity of his father's reproof,

reproof, which seemed disproportionate to the offence ;
and much was her concern increased, when she found
herself the principal cause of the lecture ; and that his
tardiness was chiefly resented from being disrespectful
to her. This was placing her in a very uncomfortable
situation, and she felt great compassion for Captain
Tilney, without being able to hope for his good-will.

He listened to his father in silence, and attempted
not any defence, which confirmed her in fearing, that the
inquietude of his mind, on Isabella's account, might, by
keeping him long sleepless, have been the real cause of
his rising late.—It was the first time of her being decidedly
in his company, and she had hoped to be now able to
form her opinion of him ; but she scarcely heard his voice
while his father remained in the room ; and even afterwards, so much were his spirits affected, she could
distinguish nothing but these words, in a whisper to
Eleanor, " How glad I shall be when you are all off."

The bustle of going was not pleasant.—The clock struck
ten while the trunks were carrying down, and the General
had fixed to be out of Milsom-street by that hour. His
great coat, instead of being brought for him to put on
directly, was spread out in the curricle in which he was
to accompany his son. The middle seat of the chaise
was not drawn out, though there were three people to go
in it, and his daughter's maid had so crowded it with
parcels, that Miss Morland would not have room to sit ;
and, so much was he influenced by this apprehension
when he handed her in, that she had some difficulty in
saving her own new writing-desk from being thrown out
into the street.—At last, however, the door was closed
upon the three females, and they set off at the sober pace
in which the handsome, highly-fed four horses of a gentleman usually perform a journey of thirty miles : such was
the distance of Northanger from Bath, to be now divided
into two equal stages. Catherine's spirits revived as they
drove from the door ; for with Miss Tilney she felt no
restraint ; and, with the interest of a road entirely new

to

to her, of an abbey before, and a curricle behind, she
caught the last view of Bath without any regret, and
met with every mile-stone before she expected it. The
tediousness of a two hours' bait at Petty-France, in which
there was nothing to be done but to eat without being
hungry, and loiter about without any thing to see, next
followed—and her admiration of the style in which they
travelled, of the fashionable chaise-and-four—postilions
handsomely liveried, rising so regularly in their stirrups,
and numerous out-riders properly mounted, sunk a little
under this consequent inconvenience. Had their party
been perfectly agreeable, the delay would have been
nothing ; but General Tilney, though so charming a man,
seemed always a check upon his children's spirits, and
scarcely any thing was said but by himself ; the observation of which, with his discontent at whatever the inn
afforded, and his angry impatience at the waiters, made
Catherine grow every moment more in awe of him, and
appeared to lengthen the two hours into four.—At last,
however, the order of release was given ; and much was
Catherine then surprized by the General's proposal of her
taking his place in his son's curricle for the rest of the
journey :—" the day was fine, and he was anxious for her
seeing as much of the country as possible."

The remembrance of Mr. Allen's opinion, respecting
young men's open carriages, made her blush at the mention of such a plan, and her first thought was to decline
it ; but her second was of greater deference for General
Tilney's judgment ; he could not propose any thing
improper for her ; and, in the course of a few minutes,
she found herself with Henry in the curricle, as happy
a being as ever existed. A very short trial convinced
her that a curricle was the prettiest equipage in the world ;
the chaise-and-four wheeled off with some grandeur, to be
sure, but it was a heavy and troublesome business, and
she could not easily forget its having stopped two hours
at Petty-France. Half the time would have been enough
for the curricle, and so nimbly were the light horses
disposed

disposed to move, that, had not the General chosen to
have his own carriage lead the way, they could have
passed it with ease in half a minute. But the merit of
the curricle did not all belong to the horses ;—Henry
drove so well,—so quietly—without making any disturbance, without parading to her, or swearing at them ; so
different from the only gentleman-coachman whom it
was in her power to compare him with !—And then his
hat sat so well, and the innumerable capes of his great
coat looked so becomingly important !—To be driven by
him, next to being dancing with him, was certainly the
greatest happiness in the world. In addition to every
other delight, she had now that of listening to her own
praise ; of being thanked at least, on his sister's account,
for her kindness in thus becoming her visitor ; of hearing
it ranked as real friendship, and described as creating
real gratitude. His sister, he said, was uncomfortably
circumstanced—she had no female companion—and, in
the frequent absence of her father, was sometimes without
any companion at all.

" But how can that be ? " said Catherine, " are not
you with her ? "

" Northanger is not more than half my home ; I have
an establishment at my own house in Woodston, which is
nearly twenty miles from my father's, and some of my
time is necessarily spent there."

" How sorry you must be for that ! "

" I am always sorry to leave Eleanor."

" Yes ; but besides your affection for her, you must
be so fond of the abbey !—After being used to such
a home as the abbey, an ordinary parsonage-house must
be very disagreeable."

He smiled, and said, " You have formed a very favourable idea of the abbey."

" To be sure I have. Is not it a fine old place, just like
what one reads about ? "

" And are you prepared to encounter all the horrors
that a building such as ' what one reads about ' may
produce ?

produce ?—Have you a stout heart ?—Nerves fit for sliding pannels and tapestry ? "

" Oh ! yes—I do not think I should be easily frightened, because there would be so many people in the house— and besides, it has never been uninhabited and left deserted for years, and then the family come back to it unawares, without giving any notice, as generally happens."

" No, certainly.—We shall not have to explore our way into a hall dimly lighted by the expiring embers of a wood fire—nor be obliged to spread our beds on the floor of a room without windows, doors, or furniture. But you must be aware that when a young lady is (by whatever means) introduced into a dwelling of this kind, she is always lodged apart from the rest of the family. While they snugly repair to their own end of the house, she is formally conducted by Dorothy the ancient housekeeper up a different staircase, and along many gloomy passages, into an apartment never used since some cousin or kin died in it about twenty years before. Can you stand such a ceremony as this ? Will not your mind misgive you, when you find yourself in this gloomy chamber—too lofty and extensive for you, with only the feeble rays of a single lamp to take in its size—its walls hung with tapestry exhibiting figures as large as life, and the bed, of dark green stuff or purple velvet, presenting even a funereal appearance. Will not your heart sink within you ? "

" Oh ! but this will not happen to me, I am sure."

" How fearfully will you examine the furniture of your apartment !—And what will you discern ?—Not tables, toilettes, wardrobes, or drawers, but on one side perhaps the remains of a broken lute, on the other a ponderous chest which no efforts can open, and over the fire-place the portrait of some handsome warrior, whose features will so incomprehensibly strike you, that you will not be able to withdraw your eyes from it. Dorothy meanwhile, no less struck by your appearance, gazes on you in great agitation, and drops a few unintelligible hints. To raise
your

your spirits, moreover, she gives you reason to suppose that the part of the abbey you inhabit is undoubtedly haunted, and informs you that you will not have a single domestic within call. With this parting cordial she curtseys off—you listen to the sound of her receding footsteps as long as the last echo can reach you—and when, with fainting spirits, you attempt to fasten your door, you discover, with increased alarm, that it has no lock."

"Oh! Mr. Tilney, how frightful!—This is just like a book!—But it cannot really happen to me. I am sure your housekeeper is not really Dorothy.—Well, what then?"

"Nothing further to alarm perhaps may occur the first night. After surmounting your *unconquerable* horror of the bed, you will retire to rest, and get a few hours' unquiet slumber. But on the second, or at farthest the *third* night after your arrival, you will probably have a violent storm. Peals of thunder so loud as to seem to shake the edifice to its foundation will roll round the neighbouring mountains—and during the frightful gusts of wind which accompany it, you will probably think you discern (for your lamp is not extinguished) one part of the hanging more violently agitated than the rest. Unable of course to repress your curiosity in so favourable a moment for indulging it, you will instantly arise, and throwing your dressing-gown around you, proceed to examine this mystery. After a very short search, you will discover a division in the tapestry so artfully constructed as to defy the minutest inspection, and on opening it, a door will immediately appear—which door being only secured by massy bars and a padlock, you will, after a few efforts, succeed in opening,—and, with your lamp in your hand, will pass through it into a small vaulted room."

"No, indeed; I should be too much frightened to do any such thing."

"What! not when Dorothy has given you to understand that there is a secret subterraneous communication between your apartment and the chapel of St. Anthony, scarcely

scarcely two miles off—Could you shrink from so simple an adventure ? No, no, you will proceed into this small vaulted room, and through this into several others, without perceiving any thing very remarkable in either. In one perhaps there may be a dagger, in another a few drops of blood, and in a third the remains of some instrument of torture ; but there being nothing in all this out of the common way, and your lamp being nearly exhausted, you will return towards your own apartment. In repassing through the small vaulted room, however, your eyes will be attracted towards a large, old-fashioned cabinet of ebony and gold, which, though narrowly examining the furniture before, you had passed unnoticed. Impelled by an irresistible presentiment, you will eagerly advance to it, unlock its folding doors, and search into every drawer ; —but for some time without discovering any thing of importance—perhaps nothing but a considerable hoard of diamonds. At last, however, by touching a secret spring, an inner compartment will open—a roll of paper appears :—you seize it—it contains many sheets of manuscript—you hasten with the precious treasure into your own chamber, but scarcely have you been able to decipher 'Oh ! thou—whomsoever thou mayst be, into whose hands these memoirs of the wretched Matilda may fall '—when your lamp suddenly expires in the socket, and leaves you in total darkness.'

"Oh ! no, no—do not say so. Well, go on."

But Henry was too much amused by the interest he had raised, to be able to carry it farther ; he could no longer command solemnity either of subject or voice, and was obliged to entreat her to use her own fancy in the perusal of Matilda's woes. Catherine, recollecting herself, grew ashamed of her eagerness, and began earnestly to assure him that her attention had been fixed without the smallest apprehension of really meeting with what he related. "Miss Tilney, she was sure, would never put her into such a chamber as he had described !—She was not at all afraid."

As

As they drew near the end of their journey, her impatience for a sight of the abbey—for some time suspended by his conversation on subjects very different—returned in full force, and every bend in the road was expected with solemn awe to afford a glimpse of its massy walls of grey stone, rising amidst a grove of ancient oaks, with the last beams of the sun playing in beautiful splendour on its high Gothic windows. But so low did the building stand, that she found herself passing through the great gates of the lodge into the very grounds of Northanger, without having discerned even an antique chimney.

She knew not that she had any right to be surprized, but there was a something in this mode of approach which she certainly had not expected. To pass between lodges of a modern appearance, to find herself with such ease in the very precincts of the abbey, and driven so rapidly along a smooth, level road of fine gravel, without obstacle, alarm or solemnity of any kind, struck her as odd and inconsistent. She was not long at leisure however for such considerations. A sudden scud of rain driving full in her face, made it impossible for her to observe any thing further, and fixed all her thoughts on the welfare of her new straw bonnet :—and she was actually under the Abbey walls, was springing, with Henry's assistance, from the carriage, was beneath the shelter of the old porch, and had even passed on to the hall, where her friend and the General were waiting to welcome her, without feeling one aweful foreboding of future misery to herself, or one moment's suspicion of any past scenes of horror being acted within the solemn edifice. The breeze had not seemed to waft the sighs of the murdered to her ; it had wafted nothing worse than a thick mizzling rain ; and having given a good shake to her habit, she was ready to be shewn into the common drawing-room, and capable of considering where she was.

An abbey !—yes, it was delightful to be really in an abbey !—but she doubted, as she looked round the room, whether any thing within her observation, would have given her the consciousness. The furniture was in all the profusion and elegance of modern taste. The fire-place, where she had expected the ample width and ponderous carving of former times, was contracted to a Rumford, with slabs of plain though handsome marble, and ornaments over it of the prettiest English china. The windows, to which she looked with peculiar dependence, from having heard the General talk of his preserving them in their Gothic form with reverential care, were yet less what her fancy had portrayed. To be sure, the pointed arch was preserved—the form of them was Gothic—they might be even casements—but every pane was so large, so clear, so light! To an imagination which had hoped for the smallest divisions, and the heaviest stone-work, for painted glass, dirt and cobwebs, the difference was very distressing.

The General, perceiving how her eye was employed, began to talk of the smallness of the room and simplicity of the furniture, where every thing being for daily use, pretended only to comfort, &c. ; flattering himself however that there were some apartments in the Abbey not unworthy her notice—and was proceeding to mention the costly gilding of one in particular, when taking out his watch, he stopped short to pronounce it with surprize within twenty minutes of five ! This seemed the word of separation, and Catherine found herself hurried away by Miss Tilney in such a manner as convinced her that the strictest punctuality to the family hours would be expected at Northanger.

Returning through the large and lofty hall, they ascended a broad staircase of shining oak, which, after many flights and many landing-places, brought them upon a long wide gallery. On one side it had a range of doors, and it was lighted on the other by windows which Catherine had only time to discover looked into a quadrangle, before Miss Tilney led the way into a chamber, and scarcely staying to hope she would find it comfortable, left her with an anxious entreaty that she would make as little alteration as possible in her dress.

CHAP-

CHAPTER VI.

A MOMENT's glance was enough to satisfy Catherine
that her apartment was very unlike the one which Henry
had endeavoured to alarm her by the description of.—It
was by no means unreasonably large, and contained
neither tapestry nor velvet.—The walls were papered,
the floor was carpeted ; the windows were neither less
perfect, nor more dim than those of the drawing-room
below ; the furniture, though not of the latest fashion,
was handsome and comfortable, and the air of the room
altogether far from uncheerful. Her heart instantane-
ously at ease on this point, she resolved to lose no time
in particular examination of any thing, as she greatly
dreaded disobliging the General by any delay. Her habit
therefore was thrown off with all possible haste, and she
was preparing to unpin the linen package, which the
chaise-seat had conveyed for her immediate accommodation, when her eye suddenly fell on a large high chest,
standing back in a deep recess on one side of the fire-
place. The sight of it made her start ; and, forgetting
every thing else, she stood gazing on it in motionless
wonder, while these thoughts crossed her :—

" This is strange indeed ! I did not expect such a sight
as this !—An immense heavy chest !—What can it hold?—
Why should it be placed here ?—Pushed back too, as if
meant to be out of sight !—I will look into it—cost me
what it may, I will look into it—and directly too—by
day-light.—If I stay till evening my candle may go out."
She advanced and examined it closely : it was of cedar,
curiously inlaid with some darker wood, and raised, about
a foot from the ground, on a carved stand of the same.
The lock was silver, though tarnished from age ; at each
end were the imperfect remains of handles also of silver,
broken perhaps prematurely by some strange violence ;

and,

and, on the centre of the lid, was a mysterious cypher, in the same metal. Catherine bent over it intently, but without being able to distinguish any thing with certainty. She could not, in whatever direction she took it, believe the last letter to be a *T;* and yet that it should be any thing else in that house was a circumstance to raise no common degree of astonishment. If not originally their's, by what strange events could it have fallen into the Tilney family ?

Her fearful curiosity was every moment growing greater ; and seizing, with trembling hands, the hasp of the lock, she resolved at all hazards to satisfy herself at least as to its contents. With difficulty, for something seemed to resist her efforts, she raised the lid a few inches ; but at that moment a sudden knocking at the door of the room made her, starting, quit her hold, and the lid closed with alarming violence. This ill-timed intruder was Miss Tilney's maid, sent by her mistress to be of use to Miss Morland ; and though Catherine immediately dismissed her, it recalled her to the sense of what she ought to be doing, and forced her, in spite of her anxious desire to penetrate this mystery, to proceed in her dressing without further delay. Her progress was not quick, for her thoughts and her eyes were still bent on the object so well calculated to interest and alarm ; and though she dared not waste a moment upon a second attempt, she could not remain many paces from the chest. At length, however, having slipped one arm into her gown, her toilette seemed so nearly finished, that the impatience of her curiosity might safely be indulged. One moment surely might be spared ; and, so desperate should be the exertion of her strength, that, unless secured by supernatural means, the lid in one moment should be thrown back. With this spirit she sprang forward, and her confidence did not deceive her. Her resolute effort threw back the lid, and gave to her astonished eyes the view of a white cotton counterpane, properly folded, reposing at one end of the chest in undisputed possession !

She

She was gazing on it with the first blush of surprize, when Miss Tilney, anxious for her friend's being ready, entered the room, and to the rising shame of having harboured for some minutes an absurd expectation, was then added the shame of being caught in so idle a search. " That is a curious old chest, is not it ? " said Miss Tilney, as Catherine hastily closed it and turned away to the glass. " It is impossible to say how many generations it has been here. How it came to be first put in this room I know not, but I have not had it moved, because I thought it might sometimes be of use in holding hats and bonnets. The worst of it is that its weight makes it difficult to open. In that corner, however, it is at least out of the way."

Catherine had no leisure for speech, being at once blushing, tying her gown, and forming wise resolutions with the most violent dispatch. Miss Tilney gently hinted her fear of being late ; and in half a minute they ran down stairs together, in an alarm not wholly un- founded, for General Tilney was pacing the drawing-room, his watch in his hand, and having, on the very instant of their entering, pulled the bell with violence, ordered " Dinner to be on table *directly !* "

Catherine trembled at the emphasis with which he spoke, and sat pale and breathless, in a most humble mood, concerned for his children, and detesting old chests ; and the General recovering his politeness as he looked at her, spent the rest of his time in scolding his daughter, for so foolishly hurrying her fair friend, who was abso- lutely out of breath from haste, when there was not the least occasion for hurry in the world : but Catherine could not at all get over the double distress of having involved her friend in a lecture and been a great simpleton herself, till they were happily seated at the dinner-table, when the General's complacent smiles, and a good appetite of her own, restored her to peace. The dining- parlour was a noble room, suitable in its dimensions to a much larger drawing-room than the one in common use,
and

and fitted up in a style of luxury and expense which was
almost lost on the unpractised eye of Catherine, who saw
little more than its spaciousness and the number of their
attendants. Of the former, she spoke aloud her admiration ; and the General, with a very gracious countenance,
acknowledged that it was by no means an ill-sized room ;
and further confessed, that, though as careless on such
subjects as most people, he did look upon a tolerably
large eating-room as one of the necessaries of life ; he
supposed, however, " that she must have been used to
much better sized apartments at Mr. Allen's ? "

" No, indeed," was Catherine's honest assurance ; " Mr.
Allen's dining-parlour was not more than half as large : "
and she had never seen so large a room as this in her life.
The General's good-humour increased.—Why, as he *had*
such rooms, he thought it would be simple not to make
use of them ; but, upon his honour, he believed there
might be more comfort in rooms of only half their size.
Mr. Allen's house, he was sure, must be exactly of the
true size for rational happiness.

The evening passed without any further disturbance,
and, in the occasional absence of General Tilney, with
much positive cheerfulness. It was only in his presence
that Catherine felt the smallest fatigue from her journey ;
and even then, even in moments of languor or restraint,
a sense of general happiness preponderated, and she could
think of her friends in Bath without one wish of being
with them.

The night was stormy ; the wind had been rising at
intervals the whole afternoon ; and by the time the party
broke up, it blew and rained violently. Catherine, as she
crossed the hall, listened to the tempest with sensations
of awe ; and, when she heard it rage round a corner of
the ancient building and close with sudden fury a distant
door, felt for the first time that she was really in an
Abbey.—Yes, these were characteristic sounds ;—they
brought to her recollection a countless variety of dreadful
situations and horrid scenes, which such buildings had
witnessed,

witnessed, and such storms ushered in ; and most heartily
did she rejoice in the happier circumstances attending her
entrance within walls so solemn !—*She* had nothing to
dread from midnight assassins or drunken gallants.
Henry had certainly been only in jest in what he had
told her that morning. In a house so furnished, and so
guarded, she could have nothing to explore or to suffer ;
and might go to her bedroom as securely as if it had been
her own chamber at Fullerton. Thus wisely fortifying
her mind, as she proceeded up stairs, she was enabled,
especially on perceiving that Miss Tilney slept only two
doors from her, to enter her room with a tolerably stout
heart ; and her spirits were immediately assisted by the
cheerful blaze of a wood fire. " How much better is this,"
said she, as she walked to the fender—" how much better
to find a fire ready lit, than to have to wait shivering in
the cold till all the family are in bed, as so many poor
girls have been obliged to do, and then to have a faithful
old servant frightening one by coming in with a faggot !
How glad I am that Northanger is what it is ! If it had
been like some other places, I do not know that, in such
a night as this, I could have answered for my courage :—
but now, to be sure, there is nothing to alarm one."

She looked round the room. The window curtains
seemed in motion. It could be nothing but the violence
of the wind penetrating through the divisions of the
shutters ; and she stept boldly forward, carelessly
humming a tune, to assure herself of its being so, peeped
courageously behind each curtain, saw nothing on either
low window seat to scare her, and on placing a hand
against the shutter, felt the strongest conviction of the
wind's force. A glance at the old chest, as she turned
away from this examination, was not without its use ;
she scorned the causeless fears of an idle fancy, and began
with a most happy indifference to prepare herself for bed.
" She should take her time ; she should not hurry herself ; she did not care if she were the last person up in the
house. But she would not make up her fire ; *that* would
seem

seem cowardly, as if she wished for the protection of light
after she were in bed." The fire therefore died away, and
Catherine, having spent the best part of an hour in her
arrangements, was beginning to think of stepping into
bed, when, on giving a parting glance round the room,
she was struck by the appearance of a high, old-fashioned
black cabinet, which, though in a situation conspicuous
enough, had never caught her notice before. Henry's
words, his description of the ebony cabinet which was to
escape her observation at first, immediately rushed across
her ; and though there could be nothing really in it, there
was something whimsical, it was certainly a very remarkable coincidence ! She took her candle and looked closely
at the cabinet. It was not absolutely ebony and gold ;
but it was Japan, black and yellow Japan of the handsomest kind ; and as she held her candle, the yellow had
very much the effect of gold. The key was in the door,
and she had a strange fancy to look into it ; not however
with the smallest expectation of finding any thing, but
it was so very odd, after what Henry had said. In short,
she could not sleep till she had examined it. So, placing
the candle with great caution on a chair, she seized the
key with a very tremulous hand and tried to turn it ;
but it resisted her utmost strength. Alarmed, but not
discouraged, she tried it another way ; a bolt flew, and
she believed herself successful ; but how strangely
mysterious !—the door was still immoveable. She paused
a moment in breathless wonder. The wind roared down
the chimney, the rain beat in torrents against the windows,
and every thing seemed to speak the awfulness of her
situation. To retire to bed, however, unsatisfied on such
a point, would be vain, since sleep must be impossible
with the consciousness of a cabinet so mysteriously closed
in her immediate vicinity. Again therefore she applied
herself to the key, and after moving it in every possible
way for some instants with the determined celerity of
hope's last effort, the door suddenly yielded to her hand :
her heart leaped with exultation at such a victory, and
having

having thrown open each folding door, the second being
secured only by bolts of less wonderful construction than
the lock, though in that her eye could not discern any
thing unusual, a double range of small drawers appeared
in view, with some larger drawers above and below them ;
and in the centre, a small door, closed also with a lock
and key, secured in all probability a cavity of importance.

Catherine's heart beat quick, but her courage did not
fail her. With a cheek flushed by hope, and an eye
straining with curiosity, her fingers grasped the handle
of a drawer and drew it forth. It was entirely empty.
With less alarm and greater eagerness she seized a second,
a third, a fourth ; each was equally empty. Not one
was left unsearched, and in not one was any thing found.
Well read in the art of concealing a treasure, the possibility of false linings to the drawers did not escape her,
and she felt round each with anxious acuteness in vain.
The place in the middle alone remained now unexplored ;
and though she had " never from the first had the smallest
idea of finding any thing in any part of the cabinet, and
was not in the least disappointed at her ill success thus
far, it would be foolish not to examine it thoroughly
while she was about it." It was some time however
before she could unfasten the door, the same difficulty
occurring in the management of this inner lock as of the
outer ; but at length it did open ; and not vain, as
hitherto, was her search ; her quick eyes directly fell on
a roll of paper pushed back into the further part of the
cavity, apparently for concealment, and her feelings at
that moment were indescribable. Her heart fluttered,
her knees trembled, and her cheeks grew pale. She
seized, with an unsteady hand, the precious manuscript,
for half a glance sufficed to ascertain written characters ;
and while she acknowledged with awful sensations this
striking exemplification of what Henry had foretold,
resolved instantly to peruse every line before she attempted
to rest.

The dimness of the light her candle emitted made her
turn

turn to it with alarm ; but there was no danger of its
sudden extinction, it had yet some hours to burn ; and
that she might not have any greater difficulty in distin-
guishing the writing than what its ancient date might
occasion, she hastily snuffed it. Alas ! it was snuffed
and extinguished in one. A lamp could not have expired
with more awful effect. Catherine, for a few moments,
was motionless with horror. It was done completely ;
not a remnant of light in the wick could give hope to
the rekindling breath. Darkness impenetrable and immoveable filled the room. A violent gust of wind, rising
with sudden fury, added fresh horror to the moment.
Catherine trembled from head to foot. In the pause
which succeeded, a sound like receding footsteps and the
closing of a distant door struck on her affrighted ear.
Human nature could support no more. A cold sweat
stood on her forehead, the manuscript fell from her hand,
and groping her way to the bed, she jumped hastily in,
and sought some suspension of agony by creeping far
underneath the clothes. To close her eyes in sleep that
night, she felt must be entirely out of the question.
With a curiosity so justly awakened, and feelings in every
way so agitated, repose must be absolutely impossible.
The storm too abroad so dreadful !—She had not been
used to feel alarm from wind, but now every blast seemed
fraught with awful intelligence. The manuscript so
wonderfully found, so wonderfully accomplishing the
morning's prediction, how was it to be accounted for ?—
What could it contain ?—to whom could it relate ?—by
what means could it have been so long concealed ?—and
how singularly strange that it should fall to her lot to
discover it ! Till she had made herself mistress of its
contents, however, she could have neither repose nor
comfort ; and with the sun's first rays she was determined
to peruse it. But many were the tedious hours which
must yet intervene. She shuddered, tossed about in her
bed, and envied every quiet sleeper. The storm still
raged, and various were the noises, more terrific even
than

than the wind, which struck at intervals on her startled ear. The very curtains of her bed seemed at one moment in motion, and at another the lock of her door was agitated, as if by the attempt of somebody to enter. Hollow murmurs seemed to creep along the gallery, and more than once her blood was chilled by the sound of distant moans. Hour after hour passed away, and the wearied Catherine had heard three proclaimed by all the clocks in the house, before the tempest subsided, or she unknowingly fell fast asleep.

CHAP-

CHAPTER VII.

THE housemaid's folding back her window-shutters at
eight o'clock the next day, was the sound which first
roused Catherine ; and she opened her eyes, wondering
that they could ever have been closed, on objects of
cheerfulness ; her fire was already burning, and a bright
morning had succeeded the tempest of the night.   Instan-
taneously with the consciousness of existence, returned
her recollection of the manuscript ; and springing from
the bed in the very moment of the maid's going away,
she eagerly collected every scattered sheet which had
burst from the roll on its falling to the ground, and flew
back to enjoy the luxury of their perusal on her pillow.
She now plainly saw that she must not expect a manuscript of equal length with the generality of what she had
shuddered over in books, for the roll, seeming to consist
entirely of small disjointed sheets, was altogether but of
trifling size, and much less than she had supposed it to
be at first.

Her greedy eye glanced rapidly over a page.   She
started at its import.   Could it be possible, or did not her
senses play her false ?—An inventory of linen, in coarse
and modern characters, seemed all that was before her !
If the evidence of sight might be trusted, she held a
washing-bill in her hand.   She seized another sheet, and
saw the same articles with little variation ; a third,
a fourth, and a fifth presented nothing new.   Shirts,
stockings, cravats and waistcoats faced her in each.
Two others, penned by the same hand, marked an expendi-
ture scarcely more interesting, in letters, hair-powder,
shoe-string and breeches-ball.   And the larger sheet,
which had inclosed the rest, seemed by its first cramp
line, " To poultice chesnut mare,"—a farrier's bill !   Such
was the collection of papers, (left perhaps, as she could
then

then suppose, by the negligence of a servant in the place whence she had taken them,) which had filled her with expectation and alarm, and robbed her of half her night's rest! She felt humbled to the dust. Could not the adventure of the chest have taught her wisdom? A corner of it catching her eye as she lay, seemed to rise up in judgment against her. Nothing could now be clearer than the absurdity of her recent fancies. To suppose that a manuscript of many generations back could have remained undiscovered in a room such as that, so modern, so habitable!—or that she should be the first to possess the skill of unlocking a cabinet, the key of which was open to all!

How could she have so imposed on herself?—Heaven forbid that Henry Tilney should ever know her folly! And it was in a great measure his own doing, for had not the cabinet appeared so exactly to agree with his description of her adventures, she should never have felt the smallest curiosity about it. This was the only comfort that occurred. Impatient to get rid of those hateful evidences of her folly, those detestable papers then scattered over the bed, she rose directly, and folding them up as nearly as possible in the same shape as before, returned them to the same spot within the cabinet, with a very hearty wish that no untoward accident might ever bring them forward again, to disgrace her even with herself.

Why the locks should have been so difficult to open however, was still something remarkable, for she could now manage them with perfect ease. In this there was surely something mysterious, and she indulged in the flattering suggestion for half a minute, till the possibility of the door's having been at first unlocked, and of being herself its fastener, darted into her head, and cost her another blush.

She got away as soon as she could from a room in which her conduct produced such unpleasant reflections, and found her way with all speed to the breakfast-parlour,

as

as it had been pointed out to her by Miss Tilney the evening before. Henry was alone in it ; and his immediate hope of her having been undisturbed by the tempest, with an arch reference to the character of the building they inhabited, was rather distressing. For the world would she not have her weakness suspected ; and yet, unequal to an absolute falsehood, was constrained to acknowledge that the wind had kept her awake a little. " But we have a charming morning after it," she added, desiring to get rid of the subject ; " and storms and sleeplessness are nothing when they are over. What beautiful hyacinths !—I have just learnt to love a hyacinth."

" And how might you learn ?—By accident or argument ? "

" Your sister taught me ; I cannot tell how. Mrs. Allen used to take pains, year after year, to make me like them ; but I never could, till I saw them the other day in Milsom-street ; I am naturally indifferent about flowers."

" But now you love a hyacinth. So much the better. You have gained a new source of enjoyment, and it is well to have as many holds upon happiness as possible. Besides, a taste for flowers is always desirable in your sex, as a means of getting you out of doors, and tempting you to more frequent exercise than you would otherwise take. And though the love of a hyacinth may be rather domestic, who can tell, the sentiment once raised, but you may in time come to love a rose ? "

" But I do not want any such pursuit to get me out of doors. The pleasure of walking and breathing fresh air is enough for me, and in fine weather I am out more than half my time.—Mamma says, I am never within."

" At any rate, however, I am pleased that you have learnt to love a hyacinth. The mere habit of learning to love is the thing ; and a teachableness of disposition in a young lady is a great blessing.—Has my sister a pleasant mode of instruction ? "

Catherine

Catherine was saved the embarrassment of attempting an answer, by the entrance of the General, whose smiling compliments announced a happy state of mind, but whose gentle hint of sympathetic early rising did not advance her composure.

The elegance of the breakfast set forced itself on Catherine's notice when they were seated at table ; and, luckily, it had been the General's choice. He was enchanted by her approbation of his taste, confessed it to be neat and simple, thought it right to encourage the manufacture of his country ; and for his part, to his uncritical palate, the tea was as well flavoured from the clay of Staffordshire, as from that of Dresden or Sève. But this was quite an old set, purchased two years ago. The manufacture was much improved since that time ; he had seen some beautiful specimens when last in town, and had he not been perfectly without vanity of that kind, might have been tempted to order a new set. He trusted, however, that an opportunity might ere long occur of selecting one—though not for himself. Catherine was probably the only one of the party who did not understand him.

Shortly after breakfast Henry left them for Woodston, where business required and would keep him two or three days. They all attended in the hall to see him mount his horse, and immediately on re-entering the breakfast room, Catherine walked to a window in the hope of catching another glimpse of his figure. " This is a somewhat heavy call upon your brother's fortitude," observed the General to Eleanor. " Woodston will make but a sombre appearance to-day."

" Is it a pretty place ? " asked Catherine.

" What say you, Eleanor ?—speak your opinion, for ladies can best tell the taste of ladies in regard to places as well as men. I think it would be acknowledged by the most impartial eye to have many recommendations. The house stands among fine meadows facing the south-east, with an excellent kitchen-garden in the same aspect ;
the

the walls surrounding which I built and stocked myself about ten years ago, for the benefit of my son. It is a family living, Miss Morland ; and the property in the place being chiefly my own, you may believe I take care that it shall not be a bad one. Did Henry's income depend solely on this living, he would not be ill provided for. Perhaps it may seem odd, that with only two younger children, I should think any profession necessary for him ; and certainly there are moments when we could all wish him disengaged from every tie of business. But though I may not exactly make converts of you young ladies, I am sure your father, Miss Morland, would agree with me in thinking it expedient to give every young man some employment. The money is nothing, it is not an object, but employment is the thing. Even Frederick, my eldest son, you see, who will perhaps inherit as considerable a landed property as any private man in the county, has his profession."

The imposing effect of this last argument was equal to his wishes. The silence of the lady proved it to be unanswerable.

Something had been said the evening before of her being shewn over the house, and he now offered himself as her conductor ; and though Catherine had hoped to explore it accompanied only by his daughter, it was a proposal of too much happiness in itself, under any circumstances, not to be gladly accepted ; for she had been already eighteen hours in the Abbey, and had seen only a few of its rooms. The netting-box, just leisurely drawn forth, was closed with joyful haste, and she was ready to attend him in a moment. " And when they had gone over the house, he promised himself moreover the pleasure of accompanying her into the shrubberies and garden." She curtsied her acquiescence. " But perhaps it might be more agreeable to her to make those her first object. The weather was at present favourable, and at this time of year the uncertainty was very great of its continuing so.—Which would she prefer ? He was
equally

equally at her service.—Which did his daughter think would most accord with her fair friend's wishes ?—But he thought he could discern.—Yes, he certainly read in Miss Morland's eyes a judicious desire of making use of the present smiling weather.—But when did she judge amiss ?—The Abbey would be always safe and dry.—He yielded implicitly, and would fetch his hat and attend them in a moment." He left the room, and Catherine, with a disappointed, anxious face, began to speak of her unwillingness that he should be taking them out of doors against his own inclination, under a mistaken idea of pleasing her ; but she was stopt by Miss Tilney's saying, with a little confusion, "I believe it will be wisest to take the morning while it is so fine ; and do not be uneasy on my father's account, he always walks out at this time of day."

Catherine did not exactly know how this was to be understood. Why was Miss Tilney embarrassed ? Could there be any unwillingness on the General's side to shew her over the Abbey ? The proposal was his own. And was not it odd that he should *always* take his walk so early ? Neither her father nor Mr. Allen did so. It was certainly very provoking. She was all impatience to see the house, and had scarcely any curiosity about the grounds. If Henry had been with them indeed !— but now she should not know what was picturesque when she saw it. Such were her thoughts, but she kept them to herself, and put on her bonnet in patient discontent.

She was struck however, beyond her expectation, by the grandeur of the Abbey, as she saw it for the first time from the lawn. The whole building enclosed a large court ; and two sides of the quadrangle, rich in Gothic ornaments, stood forward for admiration. The remainder was shut off by knolls of old trees, or luxuriant planta- tions, and the steep woody hills rising behind to give it shelter, were beautiful even in the leafless month of March. Catherine had seen nothing to compare with it ; and her feelings of delight were so strong, that without waiting for any better authority, she boldly burst forth

in

in wonder and praise. The General listened with assent-
ing gratitude ; and it seemed as if his own estimation of
Northanger had waited unfixed till that hour.

The kitchen-garden was to be next admired, and he
led the way to it across a small portion of the park.

The number of acres contained in this garden was such
as Catherine could not listen to without dismay, being
more than double the extent of all Mr. Allen's, as well as
her father's, including church-yard and orchard. The
walls seemed countless in number, endless in length ;
a village of hot-houses seemed to arise among them, and
a whole parish to be at work within the inclosure. The
General was flattered by her looks of surprize, which told
him almost as plainly, as he soon forced her to tell him
in words, that she had never seen any gardens at all
equal to them before ;—and he then modestly owned that,
" without any ambition of that sort himself—without
any solicitude about it,—he did believe them to be
unrivalled in the kingdom. If he had a hobby-horse, it
was *that*. He loved a garden. Though careless enough
in most matters of eating, he loved good fruit—or if he
did not, his friends and children did. There were great
vexations however attending such a garden as his. The
utmost care could not always secure the most valuable
fruits. The pinery had yielded only one hundred in the
last year. Mr. Allen, he supposed, must feel these
inconveniences as well as himself."

" No, not at all. Mr. Allen did not care about the
garden, and never went into it."

With a triumphant smile of self-satisfaction, the
General wished he could do the same, for he never entered
his, without being vexed in some way or other, by its
falling short of his plan.

" How were Mr. Allen's succession-houses worked ? "
describing the nature of his own as they entered them.

" Mr. Allen had only one small hot-house, which Mrs.
Allen had the use of for her plants in winter, and there
was a fire in it now and then."

" He

" He is a happy man ! " said the General, with a look of very happy contempt.

Having taken her into every division, and led her under every wall, till she was heartily weary of seeing and wondering, he suffered the girls at last to seize the advantage of an outer door, and then expressing his wish to examine the effect of some recent alterations about the tea-house, proposed it as no unpleasant extension of their walk, if Miss Morland were not tired. " But where are you going, Eleanor ?—Why do you chuse that cold, damp path to it ? Miss Morland will get wet. Our best way is across the park."

" This is so favourite a walk of mine," said Miss Tilney, " that I always think it the best and nearest way. But perhaps it may be damp."

It was a narrow winding path through a thick grove of old Scotch firs ; and Catherine, struck by its gloomy aspect, and eager to enter it, could not, even by the General's disapprobation, be kept from stepping forward. He perceived her inclination, and having again urged the plea of health in vain, was too polite to make further opposition. He excused himself however from attending them :—" The rays of the sun were not too cheerful for him, and he would meet them by another course." He turned away ; and Catherine was shocked to find how much her spirits were relieved by the separation. The shock however being less real than the relief, offered it no injury ; and she began to talk with easy gaiety of the delightful melancholy which such a grove inspired.

" I am particularly fond of this spot," said her companion, with a sigh. " It was my mother's favourite walk."

Catherine had never heard Mrs. Tilney mentioned in the family before, and the interest excited by this tender remembrance, shewed itself directly in her altered countenance, and in the attentive pause with which she waited for something more.

" I used to walk here so often with her!" added Eleanor;

" though

" though I never loved it then, as I have loved it since. At that time indeed I used to wonder at her choice. But her memory endears it now."

" And ought it not," reflected Catherine, " to endear it to her husband ? Yet the General would not enter it." Miss Tilney continuing silent, she ventured to say, " Her death must have been a great affliction ! "

" A great and increasing one," replied the other, in a low voice. " I was only thirteen when it happened ; and though I felt my loss perhaps as strongly as one so young could feel it, I did not, I could not then know what a loss it was." She stopped for a moment, and then added, with great firmness, " I have no sister, you know —and though Henry—though my brothers are very affectionate, and Henry is a great deal here, which I am most thankful for, it is impossible for me not to be often solitary."

" To be sure you must miss him very much."

" A mother would have been always present. A mother would have been a constant friend ; her influence would have been beyond all other."

" Was she a very charming woman ? Was she handsome ? Was there any picture of her in the Abbey ? And why had she been so partial to that grove ? Was it from dejection of spirits ? "—were questions now eagerly poured forth ;—the first three received a ready affirmative, the two others were passed by ; and Catherine's interest in the deceased Mrs. Tilney augmented with every question, whether answered or not. Of her unhappiness in marriage, she felt persuaded. The General certainly had been an unkind husband. He did not love her walk : —could he therefore have loved her ? And besides, handsome as he was, there was a something in the turn of his features which spoke his not having behaved well to her.

" Her picture, I suppose," blushing at the consummate art of her own question, " hangs in your father's room ? "

" No ;—it was intended for the drawing-room ; but my father was dissatisfied with the painting, and for some time

time it had no place. Soon after her death I obtained it for my own, and hung it in my bed-chamber—where I shall be happy to shew it you ;—it is very like."—Here was another proof. A portrait—very like—of a departed wife, not valued by the husband !—He must have been dreadfully cruel to her !

Catherine attempted no longer to hide from herself the nature of the feelings which, in spite of all his attentions, he had previously excited ; and what had been terror and dislike before, was now absolute aversion. Yes, aversion ! His cruelty to such a charming woman made him odious to her. She had often read of such characters ; characters, which Mr. Allen had been used to call unnatural and overdrawn ; but here was proof positive of the contrary.

She had just settled this point, when the end of the path brought them directly upon the General ; and in spite of all her virtuous indignation, she found herself again obliged to walk with him, listen to him, and even to smile when he smiled. Being no longer able however to receive pleasure from the surrounding objects, she soon began to walk with lassitude ; the General perceived it, and with a concern for her health, which seemed to reproach her for her opinion of him, was most urgent for returning with his daughter to the house. He would follow them in a quarter of an hour. Again they parted— but Eleanor was called back in half a minute to receive a strict charge against taking her friend round the Abbey till his return. This second instance of his anxiety to delay what she so much wished for, struck Catherine as very remarkable.

CHAP-

CHAPTER VIII.

An hour passed away before the General came in,
spent, on the part of his young guest, in no very favourable
consideration of his character.—"This lengthened absence,
these solitary rambles, did not speak a mind at ease, or
a conscience void of reproach."—At length he appeared;
and, whatever might have been the gloom of his meditations, he could still smile with *them.* Miss Tilney, understanding in part her friend's curiosity to see the house,
soon revived the subject; and her father being, contrary
to Catherine's expectations, unprovided with any pretence
for further delay, beyond that of stopping five minutes
to order refreshments to be in the room by their return,
was at last ready to escort them.

They set forward; and, with a grandeur of air, a dignified step, which caught the eye, but could not shake the
doubts of the well-read Catherine, he led the way across
the hall, through the common drawing-room and one
useless anti-chamber, into a room magnificent both in size
and furniture—the real drawing-room, used only with
company of consequence.—It was very noble—very
grand—very charming!—was all that Catherine had to
say, for her indiscriminating eye scarcely discerned the
colour of the satin; and all minuteness of praise, all
praise that had much meaning, was supplied by the
General : the costliness or elegance of any room's fitting-
up could be nothing to her ; she cared for no furniture of
a more modern date than the fifteenth century. When
the General had satisfied his own curiosity, in a close
examination of every well-known ornament, they proceeded into the library, an apartment, in its way, of equal
magnificence, exhibiting a collection of books, on which
an humble man might have looked with pride.—Catherine
heard, admired, and wondered with more genuine feeling
than before—gathered all that she could from this store-
house

house of knowledge, by running over the titles of half
a shelf, and was ready to proceed. But suites of apartments did not spring up with her wishes.—Large as was
the building, she had already visited the greatest part ;
though, on being told that, with the addition of the
kitchen, the six or seven rooms she had now seen surrounded three sides of the court, she could scarcely
believe it, or overcome the suspicion of there being many
chambers secreted. It was some relief, however, that they
were to return to the rooms in common use, by passing
through a few of less importance, looking into the court,
which, with occasional passages, not wholly unintricate,
connected the different sides ;—and she was further
soothed in her progress, by being told, that she was
treading what had once been a cloister, having traces of
cells pointed out, and observing several doors, that were
neither opened nor explained to her ;—by finding herself
successively in a billiard-room, and in the General's
private apartment, without comprehending their connexion, or being able to turn aright when she left them ;
and lastly, by passing through a dark little room, owning
Henry's authority, and strewed with his litter of books,
guns, and great coats.

From the dining-room of which, though already seen,
and always to be seen at five o'clock, the General could
not forego the pleasure of pacing out the length, for the
more certain information of Miss Morland, as to what
she neither doubted nor cared for, they proceeded by
quick communication to the kitchen—the ancient kitchen
of the convent, rich in the massy walls and smoke of
former days, and in the stoves and hot closets of the
present. The General's improving hand had not loitered
here : every modern invention to facilitate the labour of
the cooks, had been adopted within this, their spacious
theatre ; and, when the genius of others had failed, his
own had often produced the perfection wanted. His
endowments of this spot alone might at any time have
placed him high among the benefactors of the convent.

With

With the walls of the kitchen ended all the antiquity
of the Abbey; the fourth side of the quadrangle having,
on account of its decaying state, been removed by the
General's father, and the present erected in its place.
All that was venerable ceased here. The new building
was not only new, but declared itself to be so; intended
only for offices, and enclosed behind by stable-yards, no
uniformity of architecture had been thought necessary.
Catherine could have raved at the hand which had swept
away what must have been beyond the value of all the
rest, for the purposes of mere domestic economy; and
would willingly have been spared the mortification of
a walk through scenes so fallen, had the General allowed
it; but if he had a vanity, it was in the arrangement of
his offices; and as he was convinced, that, to a mind like
Miss Morland's, a view of the accommodations and com-
forts, by which the labours of her inferiors were softened,
must always be gratifying, he should make no apology
for leading her on. They took a slight survey of all;
and Catherine was impressed, beyond her expectation, by
their multiplicity and their convenience. The purposes
for which a few shapeless pantries and a comfortless
scullery were deemed sufficient at Fullerton, were here
carried on in appropriate divisions, commodious and
roomy. The number of servants continually appearing,
did not strike her less than the number of their offices.
Wherever they went, some pattened girl stopped to
curtsey, or some footman in dishabille sneaked off. Yet
this was an Abbey!—How inexpressibly different in these
domestic arrangements from such as she had read about
—from abbeys and castles, in which, though certainly
larger than Northanger, all the dirty work of the house
was to be done by two pair of female hands at the utmost.
How they could get through it all, had often amazed
Mrs. Allen; and, when Catherine saw what was necessary
here, she began to be amazed herself.

They returned to the hall, that the chief stair-case
might be ascended, and the beauty of its wood, and
ornaments

ornaments of rich carving might be pointed out : having
gained the top, they turned in an opposite direction from
the gallery in which her room lay, and shortly entered
one on the same plan, but superior in length and breadth.
She was here shewn successively into three large bedchambers, with their dressing-rooms, most completely
and handsomely fitted up ; every thing that money and
taste could do, to give comfort and elegance to apartments, had been bestowed on these ; and, being furnished
within the last five years, they were perfect in all that
would be generally pleasing, and wanting in all that could
give pleasure to Catherine. As they were surveying the
last, the General, after slightly naming a few of the
distinguished characters, by whom they had at times been
honoured, turned with a smiling countenance to Catherine,
and ventured to hope, that henceforward some of their
earliest tenants might be " our friends from Fullerton."
She felt the unexpected compliment, and deeply regretted
the impossibility of thinking well of a man so kindly
disposed towards herself, and so full of civility to all her
family.

The gallery was terminated by folding doors, which
Miss Tilney, advancing, had thrown open, and passed
through, and seemed on the point of doing the same by
the first door to the left, in another long reach of gallery,
when the General, coming forwards, called her hastily,
and, as Catherine thought, rather angrily back, demanding
whither she were going ?—And what was there more to
be seen ?—Had not Miss Morland already seen all that
could be worth her notice ?—And did she not suppose
her friend might be glad of some refreshment after so
much exercise ? Miss Tilney drew back directly, and the
heavy doors were closed upon the mortified Catherine,
who, having seen, in a momentary glance beyond them,
a narrower passage, more numerous openings, and symptoms of a winding stair-case, believed herself at last
within the reach of something worth her notice ; and felt,
as she unwillingly paced back the gallery, that she would
rather

rather be allowed to examine that end of the house, than see all the finery of all the rest.—The General's evident desire of preventing such an examination was an additional stimulant. Something was certainly to be concealed ; her fancy, though it had trespassed lately once or twice, could not mislead her here ; and what that something was, a short sentence of Miss Tilney's, as they followed the General at some distance down stairs, seemed to point out :—" I was going to take you into what was my mother's room—the room in which she died—— " were all her words ; but few as they were, they conveyed pages of intelligence to Catherine. It was no wonder that the General should shrink from the sight of such objects as that room must contain ; a room in all probability never entered by him since the dreadful scene had passed, which released his suffering wife, and left him to the stings of conscience.

She ventured, when next alone with Eleanor, to express her wish of being permitted to see it, as well as all the rest of that side of the house ; and Eleanor promised to attend her there, whenever they should have a convenient hour. Catherine understood her :—the General must be watched from home, before that room could be entered. " It remains as it was, I suppose ? " said she, in a tone of feeling.

" Yes, entirely."

" And how long ago may it be that your mother died ? "

" She has been dead these nine years." And nine years, Catherine knew was a trifle of time, compared with what generally elapsed after the death of an injured wife, before her room was put to rights.

" You were with her, I suppose, to the last ? "

" No," said Miss Tilney, sighing ; " I was unfortunately from home.—Her illness was sudden and short ; and, before I arrived it was all over."

Catherine's blood ran cold with the horrid suggestions which naturally sprang from these words. Could it be possible ?—Could Henry's father ?——And yet how many
were

were the examples to justify even the blackest suspicions !
—And, when she saw him in the evening, while she worked
with her friend, slowly pacing the drawing-room for an
hour together in silent thoughtfulness, with downcast eyes
and contracted brow, she felt secure from all possibility
of wronging him. It was the air and attitude of a Montoni !—What could more plainly speak the gloomy work-
ings of a mind not wholly dead to every sense of humanity,
in its fearful review of past scenes of guilt ? Unhappy
man !—And the anxiousness of her spirits directed her
eyes towards his figure so repeatedly, as to catch Miss
Tilney's notice. " My father," she whispered, " often
walks about the room in this way ; it is nothing unusual."

" So much the worse ! " thought Catherine ; such
ill-timed exercise was of a piece with the strange unsea-
sonableness of his morning walks, and boded nothing
good.

After an evening, the little variety and seeming length
of which made her peculiarly sensible of Henry's importance among them, she was heartily glad to be dismissed ;
though it was a look from the General not designed for
her observation which sent his daughter to the bell.
When the butler would have lit his master's candle,
however, he was forbidden. The latter was not going to
retire. " I have many pamphlets to finish," said he to
Catherine, " before I can close my eyes ; and perhaps
may be poring over the affairs of the nation for hours
after you are asleep. Can either of us be more meetly
employed ? *My* eyes will be blinding for the good of
others ; and *yours* preparing by rest for future mischief."

But neither the business alleged, nor the magnificent
compliment, could win Catherine from thinking, that
some very different object must occasion so serious
a delay of proper repose. To be kept up for hours, after
the family were in bed, by stupid pamphlets, was not
very likely. There must be some deeper cause : something was to be done which could be done only while the
household slept ; and the probability that Mrs. Tilney
yet

yet lived, shut up for causes unknown, and receiving from
the pitiless hands of her husband a nightly supply of
coarse food, was the conclusion which necessarily followed.
Shocking as was the idea, it was at least better than
a death unfairly hastened, as, in the natural course of
things, she must ere long be released. The suddenness of
her reputed illness ; the absence of her daughter, and
probably of her other children, at the time—all favoured
the supposition of her imprisonment.—Its origin—
jealousy perhaps, or wanton cruelty—was yet to be
unravelled.

In revolving these matters, while she undressed, it
suddenly struck her as not unlikely, that she might that
morning have passed near the very spot of this unfortunate woman's confinement—might have been within
a few paces of the cell in which she languished out her
days ; for what part of the Abbey could be more fitted
for the purpose than that which yet bore the traces of
monastic division ? In the high-arched passage, paved
with stone, which already she had trodden with peculiar
awe, she well remembered the doors of which the General
had given no account. To what might not those doors
lead ? In support of the plausibility of this conjecture,
it further occurred to her, that the forbidden gallery, in
which lay the apartments of the unfortunate Mrs. Tilney,
must be, as certainly as her memory could guide her,
exactly over this suspected range of cells, and the stair-case
by the side of those apartments of which she had caught
a transient glimpse, communicating by some secret means
with those cells, might well have favoured the barbarous
proceedings of her husband. Down that stair-case she
had perhaps been conveyed in a state of well-prepared
insensibility !

Catherine sometimes started at the boldness of her own
surmises, and sometimes hoped or feared that she had
gone too far ; but they were supported by such appearances as made their dismissal impossible.

The side of the quadrangle, in which she supposed the
                                                         guilty

guilty scene to be acting, being, according to her belief, just opposite her own, it struck her that, if judiciously watched, some rays of light from the General's lamp might glimmer through the lower windows, as he passed to the prison of his wife ; and, twice before she stepped into bed, she stole gently from her room to the corresponding window in the gallery, to see if it appeared ; but all abroad was dark, and it must yet be too early. The various ascending noises convinced her that the servants must still be up. Till midnight, she supposed it would be in vain to watch ; but then, when the clock had struck twelve, and all was quiet, she would, if not quite appalled by darkness, steal out and look once more. The clock struck twelve—and Catherine had been half an hour asleep.

CHAP-

CHAPTER IX.

THE next day afforded no opportunity for 'the proposed
examination of the mysterious apartments. It was
Sunday, and the whole time between morning and afternoon service was required by the General in exercise
abroad or eating cold meat at home ; and great as was
Catherine's curiosity, her courage was not equal to a wish
of exploring them after dinner, either by the fading light
of the sky between six and seven o'clock, or by the yet
more partial though stronger illumination of a treacherous
lamp. The day was unmarked therefore by any thing
to interest her imagination beyond the sight of a very
elegant monument to the memory of Mrs. Tilney, which
immediately fronted the family pew. By that her eye
was instantly caught and long retained ; and the perusal
of the highly-strained epitaph, in which every virtue
was ascribed to her by the inconsolable husband, who
must have been in some way or other her destroyer,
affected her even to tears.

That the General, having erected such a monument,
should be able to face it, was not perhaps very strange,
and yet that he could sit so boldly collected within its
view, maintain so elevated an air, look so fearlessly
around, nay, that he should even enter the church,
seemed wonderful to Catherine. Not however that many
instances of beings equally hardened in guilt might not be
produced. She could remember dozens who had per-
severed in every possible vice, going on from crime to
crime, murdering whomsoever they chose, without any
feeling of humanity or remorse ; till a violent death or
a religious retirement closed their black career. The
erection of the monument itself could not in the smallest
degree affect her doubts of Mrs. Tilney's actual decease.
Were she even to descend into the family vault where
her

her ashes were supposed to slumber, were she to behold
the coffin in which they were said to be enclosed—what
could it avail in such a case ? Catherine had read too
much not to be perfectly aware of the ease with which
a waxen figure might be introduced, and a supposititious
funeral carried on.

The succeeding morning promised something better.
The General's early walk, ill-timed as it was in every
other view, was favourable here ; and when she knew
him to be out of the house, she directly proposed to Miss
Tilney the accomplishment of her promise. Eleanor was
ready to oblige her ; and Catherine reminding her as they
went of another promise, their first visit in consequence
was to the portrait in her bed-chamber. It represented
a very lovely woman, with a mild and pensive countenance, justifying, so far, the expectations of its new
observer ; but they were not in every respect answered,
for Catherine had depended upon meeting with features,
air, complexion that should be the very counterpart, the
very image, if not of Henry's, of Eleanor's ;—the only
portraits of which she had been in the habit of thinking,
bearing always an equal resemblance of mother and child.
A face once taken was taken for generations. But here
she was obliged to look and consider and study for
a likeness. She contemplated it, however, in spite of this
drawback, with much emotion ; and, but for a yet
stronger interest, would have left it unwillingly.

Her agitation as they entered the great gallery was too
much for any endeavour at discourse ; she could only
look at her companion. Eleanor's countenance was
dejected, yet sedate ; and its composure spoke her
enured to all the gloomy objects to which they were
advancing. Again she passed through the folding-doors,
again her hand was upon the important lock, and Catherine,
hardly able to breathe, was turning to close the former
with fearful caution, when the figure, the dreaded figure
of the General himself at the further end of the gallery,
stood before her ! The name of " Eleanor " at the same
moment,

moment, in his loudest tone, resounded through the
building, giving to his daughter the first intimation of his
presence, and to Catherine terror upon terror. An
attempt at concealment had been her first instinctive
movement on perceiving him, yet she could scarcely hope
to have escaped his eye; and when her friend, who with
an apologizing look darted hastily by her, had joined and
disappeared with him, she ran for safety to her own room,
and, locking herself in, believed that she should never
have courage to go down again. She remained there at
least an hour, in the greatest agitation, deeply commiser-
ating the state of her poor friend, and expecting a summons herself from the angry General to attend him in his
own apartment. No summons however arrived; and at
last, on seeing a carriage drive up to the Abbey, she was
emboldened to descend and meet him under the protection of visitors. The breakfast-room was gay with
company; and she was named to them by the General,
as the friend of his daughter, in a complimentary style,
which so well concealed his resentful ire, as to make her
feel secure at least of life for the present. And Eleanor,
with a command of countenance which did honour to her
concern for his character, taking an early occasion of
saying to her, " My father only wanted me to answer
a note," she began to hope that she had either been
unseen by the General, or that from some consideration
of policy she should be allowed to suppose herself so.
Upon this trust she dared still to remain in his presence,
after the company left them, and nothing occurred to
disturb it.

In the course of this morning's reflections, she came to
a resolution of making her next attempt on the forbidden
door alone. It would be much better in every respect that
Eleanor should know nothing of the matter. To involve
her in the danger of a second detection, to court her into
an apartment which must wring her heart, could not be
the office of a friend. The General's utmost anger could
not be to herself what it might be to a daughter; and,
besides,

besides, she thought the examination itself would be more satisfactory if made without any companion. It would be impossible to explain to Eleanor the suspicions, from which the other had, in all likelihood, been hitherto happily exempt ; nor could she therefore, in *her* presence, search for those proofs of the General's cruelty, which however they might yet have escaped discovery, she felt confident of somewhere drawing forth, in the shape of some fragmented journal, continued to the last gasp. Of the way to the apartment she was now perfectly mistress ; and as she wished to get it over before Henry's return, who was expected on the morrow, there was no time to be lost. The day was bright, her courage high ; at four o'clock, the sun was now two hours above the horizon, and it would be only her retiring to dress half an hour earlier than usual.

It was done ; and Catherine found herself alone in the gallery before the clocks had ceased to strike. It was no time for thought ; she hurried on, slipped with the least possible noise through the folding doors, and without stopping to look or breathe, rushed forward to the one in question. The lock yielded to her hand, and, luckily, with no sullen sound that could alarm a human being. On tip-toe she entered ; the room was before her ; but it was some minutes before she could advance another step. She beheld what fixed her to the spot and agitated every feature.—She saw a large, well-proportioned apartment, an handsome dimity bed, arranged as unoccupied with an housemaid's care, a bright Bath stove, mahogany wardrobes and neatly-painted chairs, on which the warm beams of a western sun gaily poured through two sash windows ! Catherine had expected to have her feelings worked, and worked they were. Astonishment and doubt first seized them ; and a shortly succeeding ray of common sense added some bitter emotions of shame. She could not be mistaken as to the room ; but how grossly mistaken in every thing else !—in Miss Tilney's meaning, in her own calculation ! This apartment, to which she had

O

given

given a date so ancient, a position so awful, proved to be
one end of what the General's father had built. There
were two other doors in the chamber, leading probably
into dressing-closets ; but she had no inclination to open
either. Would the veil in which Mrs. Tilney had last
walked, or the volume in which she had last read, remain
to tell what nothing else was allowed to whisper ? No :
whatever might have been the General's crimes, he had
certainly too much wit to let them sue for detection.
She was sick of exploring, and desired but to be safe in
her own room, with her own heart only privy to its folly ;
and she was on the point of retreating as softly as she had
entered, when the sound of footsteps, she could hardly
tell where, made her pause and tremble. To be found
there, even by a servant, would be unpleasant ; but by
the General, (and he seemed always at hand when least
wanted,) much worse !—She listened—the sound had
ceased ; and resolving not to lose a moment, she passed
through and closed the door. At that instant a door
underneath was hastily opened ; some one seemed with
swift steps to ascend the stairs, by the head of which she
had yet to pass before she could gain the gallery. She
had no power to move. With a feeling of terror not very
definable, she fixed her eyes on the staircase, and in a few
moments it gave Henry to her view. " Mr. Tilney ! " she
exclaimed in a voice of more than common astonishment.
He looked astonished too. " Good God ! " she continued, not attending to his address, " how came you
here ?—how came you up that staircase ? "

" How came I up that staircase ! " he replied, greatly
surprized. " Because it is my nearest way from the
stable-yard to my own chamber ; and why should I not
come up it ? "

Catherine recollected herself, blushed deeply, and could
say no more. He seemed to be looking in her countenance for that explanation which her lips did not
afford. She moved on towards the gallery. " And may
I not, in my turn," said he, as he pushed back the folding
doors,

doors, " ask how *you* came here ?—This passage is at
least as extraordinary a road from the breakfast-parlour
to your apartment, as that staircase can be from the
stables to mine."

" I have been," said Catherine, looking down, " to see
your mother's room."

" My mother's room !—Is there any thing extraordinary
to be seen there ? "

" No, nothing at all.—I thought you did not mean to
come back till to-morrow."

" I did not expect to be able to return sooner, when
I went away ; but three hours ago I had the pleasure of
finding nothing to detain me.—You look pale.—I am
afraid I alarmed you by running so fast up those stairs.
Perhaps you did not know—you were not aware of their
leading from the offices in common use ? "

" No, I was not.—You have had a very fine day for
your ride."

" Very ;—and does Eleanor leave you to find your way
into all the rooms in the house by yourself ? "

" Oh ! no ; she shewed me over the greatest part on
Saturday—and we were coming here to these rooms—
but only—(dropping her voice)—your father was with us."

" And that prevented you ; " said Henry, earnestly
regarding her.—" Have you looked into all the rooms in
that passage ? "

" No, I only wanted to see——Is not it very late ?
I must go and dress."

" It is only a quarter past four, (shewing his watch) and
you are not now in Bath. No theatre, no rooms to
prepare for. Half an hour at Northanger must be enough."

She could not contradict it, and therefore suffered herself to be detained, though her dread of further questions
made her, for the first time in their acquaintance, wish to
leave him. They walked slowly up the gallery. " Have
you had any letter from Bath since I saw you ? "

" No, and I am very much surprized. Isabella promised so faithfully to write directly."

" Promised

" Promised so faithfully !—A faithful promise !—That puzzles me.—I have heard of a faithful performance. But a faithful promise—the fidelity of promising ! It is a power little worth knowing however, since it can deceive and pain you. My mother's room is very commodious, is it not ? Large and cheerful-looking, and the dressing closets so well disposed ! It always strikes me as the most comfortable apartment in the house, and I rather wonder that Eleanor should not take it for her own. She sent you to look at it, I suppose ? "

" No."

" It has been your own doing entirely ? "—Catherine said nothing—After a short silence, during which he had closely observed her, he added, " As there is nothing in the room in itself to raise curiosity, this must have proceeded from a sentiment of respect for my mother's character, as described by Eleanor, which does honour to her memory. The world, I believe, never saw a better woman. But it is not often that virtue can boast an interest such as this. The domestic, unpretending merits of a person never known, do not often create that kind of fervent, venerating tenderness which would prompt a visit like yours. Eleanor, I suppose, has talked of her a great deal ? "

" Yes, a great deal. That is—no, not much, but what she did say, was very interesting. Her dying so suddenly," (slowly, and with hesitation it was spoken,) " and you— none of you being at home—and your father, I thought— perhaps had not been very fond of her."

" And from these circumstances," he replied, (his quick eye fixed on her's,) " you infer perhaps the probability of some negligence—some—(involuntarily she shook her head)—or it may be—of something still less pardonable." She raised her eyes towards him more fully than she had ever done before. " My mother's illness," he continued, " the seizure which ended in her death *was* sudden. The malady itself, one from which she had often suffered, a bilious fever—its cause therefore constitutional. On the
third

third day, in short as soon as she could be prevailed on,
a physician attended her, a very respectable man, and one
in whom she had always placed great confidence. Upon
his opinion of her danger, two others were called in the
next day, and remained in almost constant attendance
for four-and-twenty hours. On the fifth day she died.
During the progress of her disorder, Frederick and I (*we*
were both at home) saw her repeatedly ; and from our
own observation can bear witness to her having received
every possible attention which could spring from the
affection of those about her, or which her situation in
life could command. Poor Eleanor *was* absent, and at
such a distance as to return only to see her mother in her
coffin."

"But your father," said Catherine, "was *he* afflicted ? "

"For a time, greatly so. You have erred in supposing
him not attached to her. He loved her, I am persuaded,
as well as it was possible for him to—We have not all,
you know, the same tenderness of disposition—and I will
not pretend to say that while she lived, she might not
often have had much to bear, but though his temper
injured her, his judgment never did. His value of her
was sincere ; and, if not permanently, he was truly
afflicted by her death."

"I am very glad of it," said Catherine, "it would have
been very shocking ! "——

"If I understand you rightly, you had formed a surmise
of such horror as I have hardly words to——Dear Miss
Morland, consider the dreadful nature of the suspicions
you have entertained. What have you been judging
from ? Remember the country and the age in which we
live. Remember that we are English, that we are
Christians. Consult your own understanding, your own
sense of the probable, your own observation of what is
passing around you—Does our education prepare us for
such atrocities ? Do our laws connive at them ? Could
they be perpetrated without being known, in a country
like this, where social and literary intercourse is on such
a footing ;

a footing ; where every man is surrounded by a neighbourhood of voluntary spies, and where roads and newspapers lay every thing open ? Dearest Miss Morland, what ideas have you been admitting ? "

They had reached the end of the gallery; and with tears of shame she ran off to her own room.

CHAP-

CHAPTER X.

THE visions of romance were over. Catherine was completely awakened. Henry's address, short as it had been, had more thoroughly opened her eyes to the extra-vagance of her late fancies than all their several disap-pointments had done. Most grievously was she humbled. Most bitterly did she cry. It was not only with herself that she was sunk—but with Henry. Her folly, which now seemed even criminal, was all exposed to him, and he must despise her for ever. The liberty which her imagina-tion had dared to take with the character of his father, could he ever forgive it ? The absurdity of her curiosity and her fears, could they ever be forgotten ? She hated herself more than she could express. He had—she thought he had, once or twice before this fatal morning, shewn something like affection for her.—But now—in short, she made herself as miserable as possible for about half an hour, went down when the clock struck five, with a broken heart, and could scarcely give an intelligible answer to Eleanor's inquiry, if she was well. The formid-able Henry soon followed her into the room, and the only difference in his behaviour to her, was that he paid her rather more attention than usual. Catherine had never wanted comfort more, and he looked as if he was aware of it.

The evening wore away with no abatement of this soothing politeness ; and her spirits were gradually raised to a modest tranquillity. She did not learn either to forget or defend the past ; but she learned to hope that it would never transpire farther, and that it might not cost her Henry's entire regard. Her thoughts being still chiefly fixed on what she had with such causeless terror felt and done, nothing could shortly be clearer, than that it had been all a voluntary, self-created delusion, each trifling circumstance receiving importance from an
imagination

imagination resolved on alarm, and every thing forced to
bend to one purpose by a mind which, before she entered
the Abbey, had been craving to be frightened. She
remembered with what feelings she had prepared for a
knowledge of Northanger. She saw that the infatuation
had been created, the mischief settled long before her
quitting Bath, and it seemed as if the whole might be
traced to the influence of that sort of reading which she
had there indulged.

Charming as were all Mrs. Radcliffe's works, and
charming even as were the works of all her imitators, it
was not in them perhaps that human nature, at least in
the midland counties of England, was to be looked for.
Of the Alps and Pyrenees, with their pine forests and
their vices, they might give a faithful delineation ; and
Italy, Switzerland, and the South of France, might be as
fruitful in horrors as they were there represented. Catherine dared not doubt beyond her own country, and even
of that, if hard pressed, would have yielded the northern
and western extremities. But in the central part of
England there was surely some security for the existence
even of a wife not beloved, in the laws of the land, and the
manners of the age. Murder was not tolerated, servants
were not slaves, and neither poison nor sleeping potions
to be procured, like rhubarb, from every druggist. Among
the Alps and Pyrenees, perhaps, there were no mixed
characters. There, such as were not as spotless as an
angel, might have the dispositions of a fiend. But in
England it was not so ; among the English, she believed,
in their hearts and habits, there was a general though
unequal mixture of good and bad. Upon this conviction,
she would not be surprized if even in Henry and Eleanor
Tilney, some slight imperfection might hereafter appear ;
and upon this conviction she need not fear to acknowledge
some actual specks in the character of their father, who,
though cleared from the grossly injurious suspicions which
she must ever blush to have entertained, she did believe,
upon serious consideration, to be not perfectly amiable.

Her

Her mind made up on these several points, and her resolution formed, of always judging and acting in future with the greatest good sense, she had nothing to do but to forgive herself and be happier than ever ; and the lenient hand of time did much for her by insensible gradations in the course of another day. Henry's astonishing generosity and nobleness of conduct, in never alluding in the slightest way to what had passed, was of the greatest assistance to her ; and sooner than she could have supposed it possible in the beginning of her distress, her spirits became absolutely comfortable, and capable, as heretofore, of continual improvement by any thing he said. There were still some subjects indeed, under which she believed they must always tremble ;—the mention of a chest or a cabinet, for instance—and she did not love the sight of japan in any shape : but even *she* could allow, that an occasional memento of past folly, however painful, might not be without use.

The anxieties of common life began soon to succeed to the alarms of romance. Her desire of hearing from Isabella grew every day greater. She was quite impatient to know how the Bath world went on, and how the Rooms were attended ; and especially was she anxious to be assured of Isabella's having matched some fine netting-cotton, on which she had left her intent ; and of her continuing on the best terms with James. Her only dependence for information of any kind was on Isabella. James had protested against writing to her till his return to Oxford ; and Mrs. Allen had given her no hopes of a letter till she had got back to Fullerton.—But Isabella had promised and promised again ; and when she promised a thing, she was so scrupulous in performing it ! this made it so particularly strange !

For nine successive mornings, Catherine wondered over the repetition of a disappointment, which each morning became more severe : but, on the tenth, when she entered the breakfast-room, her first object was a letter, held out by Henry's willing hand. She thanked him as heartily
as

as if he had written it himself. " 'Tis only from James,
however," as she looked at the direction. She opened
it ; it was from Oxford ; and to this purpose :—

" Dear Catherine,
        " Though, God knows, with little inclination for
writing, I think it my duty to tell you, that every thing
is at an end between Miss Thorpe and me.—I left her and
Bath yesterday, never to see either again. I shall not
enter into particulars, they would only pain you more.
You will soon hear enough from another quarter to know
where lies the blame ; and I hope will acquit your brother
of every thing but the folly of too easily thinking his
affection returned. Thank God ! I am undeceived in
time ! But it is a heavy blow !—After my father's consent had been so kindly given—but no more of this. She
has made me miserable for ever ! Let me soon hear from
you, dear Catherine ; you are my only friend ; *your* love
I do build upon. I wish your visit at Northanger may
be over before Captain Tilney makes his engagement
known, or you will be uncomfortably circumstanced.—
Poor Thorpe is in town : I dread the sight of him ; his
honest heart would feel so much. I have written to him
and my father. Her duplicity hurts me more than all ;
till the very last, if I reasoned with her, she declared
herself as much attached to me as ever, and laughed at
my fears. I am ashamed to think how long I bore with
it ; but if ever man had reason to believe himself loved,
I was that man. I cannot understand even now what
she would be at, for there could be no need of my being
played off to make her secure of Tilney. We parted at
last by mutual consent—happy for me had we never
met ! I can never expect to know such another woman !
Dearest Catherine, beware how you give your heart.
                                " Believe me," &c.

Catherine had not read three lines before her sudden
change of countenance, and short exclamations of sorrow-
ing wonder, declared her to be receiving unpleasant news ;
                                                    and

and Henry, earnestly watching her through the whole
letter, saw plainly that it ended no better than it began.
He was prevented, however, from even looking his
surprize by his father's entrance. They went to breakfast
directly ; but Catherine could hardly eat any thing.
Tears filled her eyes, and even ran down her cheeks as she
sat. The letter was one moment in her hand, then in her
lap, and then in her pocket ; and she looked as if she
knew not what she did. The General, between his cocoa
and his newspaper, had luckily no leisure for noticing her ;
but to the other two her distress was equally visible.
As soon as she dared leave the table she hurried away
to her own room ; but the house-maids were busy in it,
and she was obliged to come down again. She turned
into the drawing-room for privacy, but Henry and
Eleanor had likewise retreated thither, and were at that
moment deep in consultation about her. She drew back,
trying to beg their pardon, but was, with gentle violence,
forced to return ; and the others withdrew, after Eleanor
had affectionately expressed a wish of being of use or
comfort to her.

After half an hour's free indulgence of grief and reflection, Catherine felt equal to encountering her friends ;
but whether she should make her distress known to them
was another consideration. Perhaps, if particularly
questioned, she might just give an idea—just distantly
hint at it—but not more. To expose a friend, such
a friend as Isabella had been to her—and then their own
brother so closely concerned in it !—She believed she
must wave the subject altogether. Henry and Eleanor
were by themselves in the breakfast-room ; and each,
as she entered it, looked at her anxiously. Catherine
took her place at the table, and, after a short silence,
Eleanor said, " No bad news from Fullerton, I hope ?
Mr. and Mrs. Morland—your brothers and sisters—I hope
they are none of them ill ? "

" No, I thank you," (sighing as she spoke,) " they are
all very well. My letter was from my brother at Oxford."

Nothing

Nothing further was said for a few minutes ; and then speaking through her tears, she added, " I do not think I shall ever wish for a letter again ! "

" I am sorry," said Henry, closing the book he had just opened ; " if I had suspected the letter of containing any thing unwelcome, I should have given it with very different feelings."

" It contained something worse than any body could suppose !—Poor James is so unhappy !—You will soon know why."

" To have so kind-hearted, so affectionate a sister," replied Henry, warmly, " must be a comfort to him under any distress."

" I have one favour to beg," said Catherine, shortly afterwards, in an agitated manner, " that, if your brother should be coming here, you will give me notice of it, that I may go away."

" Our brother !—Frederick ! "

" Yes ; I am sure I should be very sorry to leave you so soon, but something has happened that would make it very dreadful for me to be in the same house with Captain Tilney."

Eleanor's work was suspended while she gazed with increasing astonishment ; but Henry began to suspect the truth, and something, in which Miss Thorpe's name was included, passed his lips.

" How quick you are ! " cried Catherine : " you have guessed it, I declare !—And yet, when we talked about it in Bath, you little thought of its ending so.   Isabella— no wonder *now* I have not heard from her—Isabella has deserted my brother, and is to marry your's !   Could you have believed there had been such inconstancy and fickleness, and every thing that is bad in the world ? "

" I hope, so far as concerns my brother, you are mis- informed.   I hope he has not had any material share in bringing on Mr. Morland's disappointment.   His marrying Miss Thorpe is not probable.   I think you must be deceived so far.   I am very sorry for Mr. Morland— sorry

sorry that any one you love should be unhappy ; but my
surprize would be greater at Frederick's marrying her,
than at any other part of the story."

" It is very true, however ; you shall read James's
letter yourself.—Stay——there is one part—— " recollecting with a blush the last line.

" Will you take the trouble of reading to us the passages
which concern my brother ? "

" No, read it yourself," cried Catherine, whose second
thoughts were clearer. " I do not know what I was
thinking of," (blushing again that she had blushed
before,)—" James only means to give me good advice."

He gladly received the letter ; and, having read it
through, with close attention, returned it saying, " Well,
if it is to be so, I can only say that I am sorry for it.
Frederick will not be the first man who has chosen a wife
with less sense than his family expected. I do not envy
his situation, either as a lover or a son."

Miss Tilney, at Catherine's invitation, now read the
letter likewise ; and, having expressed also her concern
and surprize, began to inquire into Miss Thorpe's connexions and fortune.

" Her mother is a very good sort of woman," was
Catherine's answer.

" What was her father ? "

" A lawyer, I believe.—They live at Putney."

" Are they a wealthy family ? "

" No, not very. I do not believe Isabella has any
fortune at all : but that will not signify in your family.—
Your father is so very liberal ! He told me the other
day, that he only valued money as it allowed him to
promote the happiness of his children." The brother
and sister looked at each other. " But," said Eleanor,
after a short pause, " would it be to promote his happiness,
to enable him to marry such a girl ?—She must be an
unprincipled one, or she could not have used your brother
so.—And how strange an infatuation on Frederick's
side ! A girl who, before his eyes, is violating an engage-
                                                    ment

ment voluntarily entered into with another man! Is
not it inconceivable, Henry? Frederick too, who always
wore his heart so proudly! who found no woman good
enough to be loved!"

"That is the most unpromising circumstance, the
strongest presumption against him. When I think of his
past declarations, I give him up.—Moreover, I have too
good an opinion of Miss Thorpe's prudence, to suppose
that she would part with one gentleman before the other
was secured. It is all over with Frederick indeed! He
is a deceased man—defunct in understanding. Prepare
for your sister-in-law, Eleanor, and such a sister-in-law
as you must delight in!—Open, candid, artless, guileless,
with affections strong but simple, forming no pretensions,
and knowing no disguise."

"Such a sister-in-law, Henry, I should delight in," said
Eleanor, with a smile.

"But perhaps," observed Catherine, "though she has
behaved so ill by our family, she may behave better by
your's. Now she has really got the man she likes, she
may be constant."

"Indeed I am afraid she will," replied Henry; "I am
afraid she will be very constant, unless a baronet should
come in her way; that is Frederick's only chance.—I will
get the Bath paper, and look over the arrivals."

"You think it is all for ambition then?—And, upon
my word, there are some things that seem very like it.
I cannot forget, that, when she first knew what my
father would do for them, she seemed quite disappointed
that it was not more. I never was so deceived in any
one's character in my life before."

"Among all the great variety that you have known
and studied."

"My own disappointment and loss in her is very great;
but, as for poor James, I suppose he will hardly ever
recover it."

"Your brother is certainly very much to be pitied at
present; but we must not, in our concern for his sufferings,

ings, undervalue your's. You feel, I suppose, that, in losing Isabella, you lose half yourself : you feel a void in your heart which nothing else can occupy. Society is becoming irksome ; and as for the amusements in which you were wont to share at Bath, the very idea of them without her is abhorrent. You would not, for instance, now go to a ball for the world. You feel that you have no longer any friend to whom you can speak with unreserve ; on whose regard you can place dependence ; or whose counsel, in any difficulty, you could rely on. You feel all this ? "

" No," said Catherine, after a few moments' reflection, " I do not—ought I ? To say the truth, though I am hurt and grieved, that I cannot still love her, that I am never to hear from her, perhaps never to see her again, I do not feel so very, very much afflicted as one would have thought."

" You feel, as you always do, what is most to the credit of human nature.—Such feelings ought to be investigated, that they may know themselves."

Catherine, by some chance or other, found her spirits so very much relieved by this conversation, that she could not regret her being led on, though so unaccountably, to mention the circumstance which had produced it.

CHAP-

CHAPTER XI.

FROM this time, the subject was frequently canvassed by the three young people ; and Catherine found, with some surprize, that her two young friends were perfectly agreed in considering Isabella's want of consequence and fortune as likely to throw great difficulties in the way of her marrying their brother. Their persuasion that the General would, upon this ground alone, independent of the objection that might be raised against her character, oppose the connexion, turned her feelings moreover with some alarm towards herself. She was as insignificant, and perhaps as portionless as Isabella ; and if the heir of the Tilney property had not grandeur and wealth enough in himself, at what point of interest were the demands of his younger brother to rest ? The very painful reflections to which this thought led, could only be dispersed by a dependence on the effect of that particular partiality, which, as she was given to understand by his words as well as his actions, she had from the first been so fortunate as to excite in the General ; and by a recollection of some most generous and disinterested sentiments on the subject of money, which she had more than once heard him utter, and which tempted her to think his disposition in such matters misunderstood by his children.

They were so fully convinced, however, that their brother would not have the courage to apply in person for his father's consent, and so repeatedly assured her that he had never in his life been less likely to come to Northanger than at the present time, that she suffered her mind to be at ease as to the necessity of any sudden removal of her own. But as it was not to be supposed that Captain Tilney, whenever he made his application, would give his father any just idea of Isabella's conduct, it occurred to her as highly expedient that Henry should

lay

lay the whole business before him as it really was, enabling
the General by that means to form a cool and impartial
opinion, and prepare his objections on a fairer ground
than inequality of situations. She proposed it to him
accordingly ; but he did not catch at the measure so
eagerly as she had expected. "No," said he, "my
father's hands need not be strengthened, and Frederick's
confession of folly need not be forestalled. He must tell
his own story."

"But he will tell only half of it."

"A quarter would be enough."

A day or two passed away and brought no tidings of
Captain Tilney. His brother and sister knew not what
to think. Sometimes it appeared to them as if his silence
would be the natural result of the suspected engagement,
and at others that it was wholly incompatible with it.
The General, meanwhile, though offended every morning
by Frederick's remissness in writing, was free from any
real anxiety about him ; and had no more pressing
solicitude than that of making Miss Morland's time at
Northanger pass pleasantly. He often expressed his
uneasiness on this head, feared the sameness of every
day's society and employments would disgust her with
the place, wished the Lady Frasers had been in the
country, talked every now and then of having a large
party to dinner, and once or twice began even to calculate
the number of young dancing people in the neighbourhood. But then it was such a dead time of year, no
wild-fowl, no game, and the Lady Frasers were not in the
country. And it all ended, at last, in his telling Henry
one morning, that when he next went to Woodston, they
would take him by surprize there some day or other, and
eat their mutton with him. Henry was greatly honoured
and very happy, and Catherine was quite delighted with
the scheme. "And when do you think, sir, I may look
forward to this pleasure ?—I must be at Woodston on
Monday to attend the parish meeting, and shall probably
be obliged to stay two or three days."

"Well,

" Well, well, we will take our chance some one of those
days. There is no need to fix. You are not to put
yourself at all out of your way. Whatever you may
happen to have in the house will be enough. I think
I can answer for the young ladies making allowance for
a bachelor's table. Let me see ; Monday will be a busy
day with you, we will not come on Monday ; and Tuesday
will be a busy one with me. I expect my surveyor from
Brockham with his report in the morning ; and afterwards I cannot in decency fail attending the club. I really
could not face my acquaintance if I staid away now ;
for, as I am known to be in the country, it would be taken
exceedingly amiss ; and it is a rule with me, Miss Morland,
never to give offence to any of my neighbours, if a small
sacrifice of time and attention can prevent it. They are
a set of very worthy men. They have half a buck from
Northanger twice a year ; and I dine with them whenever
I can. Tuesday, therefore, we may say is out of the
question. But on Wednesday, I think, Henry, you may
expect us ; and we shall be with you early, that we may
have time to look about us. Two hours and three
quarters will carry us to Woodston, I suppose ; we shall
be in the carriage by ten ; so, about a quarter before one
on Wednesday, you may look for us."

A ball itself could not have been more welcome to
Catherine than this little excursion, so strong was her
desire to be acquainted with Woodston ; and her heart
was still bounding with joy, when Henry, about an hour
afterwards, came booted and great coated into the room
where she and Eleanor were sitting, and said, " I am
come, young ladies, in a very moralizing strain, to observe
that our pleasures in this world are always to be paid for,
and that we often purchase them at a great disadvantage,
giving ready-monied actual happiness for a draft on the
future, that may not be honoured. Witness myself,
at this present hour. Because I am to hope for
the satisfaction of seeing you at Woodston on Wednesday, which bad weather, or twenty other causes may
prevent,

prevent, I must go away directly, two days before
I intended it."

"Go away!" said Catherine, with a very long face;
"and why?"

"Why!—How can you ask the question?—Because
no time is to be lost in frightening my old housekeeper
out of her wits,—because I must go and prepare a dinner
for you to be sure."

"Oh! not seriously!"

"Aye, and sadly too—for I had much rather stay."

"But how can you think of such a thing, after what
the General said? when he so particularly desired you not
to give yourself any trouble, because *any thing* would do."

Henry only smiled. "I am sure it is quite unnecessary
upon your sister's account and mine. You must know
it to be so; and the General made such a point of your
providing nothing extraordinary :—besides, if he had not
said half so much as he did, he has always such an excellent
dinner at home, that sitting down to a middling one for
one day could not signify."

"I wish I could reason like you, for his sake and my
own. Good bye. As to-morrow is Sunday, Eleanor,
I shall not return."

He went; and, it being at any time a much simpler
operation to Catherine to doubt her own judgment than
Henry's, she was very soon obliged to give him credit
for being right, however disagreeable to her his going.
But the inexplicability of the General's conduct dwelt
much on her thoughts. That he was very particular in
his eating, she had, by her own unassisted observation,
already discovered; but why he should say one thing so
positively, and mean another all the while, was most
unaccountable! How were people, at that rate, to be
understood? Who but Henry could have been aware of
what his father was at?

From Saturday to Wednesday, however, they were now
to be without Henry. This was the sad finale of every
reflection :—and Captain Tilney's letter would certainly

come

come in his absence ; and Wednesday she was very sure
would be wet. The past, present, and future, were all
equally in gloom. Her brother so unhappy, and her loss
in Isabella so great ; and Eleanor's spirits always affected
by Henry's absence ! What was there to interest or
amuse her ? She was tired of the woods and the shrubberies—always so smooth and so dry ; and the Abbey in
itself was no more to her now than any other house.
The painful remembrance of the folly it had helped to
nourish and perfect, was the only emotion which could
spring from a consideration of the building. What a
revolution in her ideas ! she, who had so longed to be
in an abbey ! Now, there was nothing so charming to her
imagination as the unpretending comfort of a well-
connected Parsonage, something like Fullerton, but better :
Fullerton had its faults, but Woodston probably had
none.—If Wednesday should ever come !

It did come, and exactly when it might be reasonably
looked for. It came—it was fine—and Catherine trod
on air. By ten o'clock, the chaise-and-four conveyed
the trio from the Abbey ; and, after an agreeable drive
of almost twenty miles, they entered Woodston, a large
and populous village, in a situation not unpleasant.
Catherine was ashamed to say how pretty she thought it,
as the General seemed to think an apology necessary for
the flatness of the country, and the size of the village ;
but in her heart she preferred it to any place she had
ever been at, and looked with great admiration at
every neat house above the rank of a cottage, and at
all the little chandler's shops which they passed. At the
further end of the village, and tolerably disengaged from
the rest of it, stood the Parsonage, a new-built substantial
stone house, with its semi-circular sweep and green gates ;
and, as they drove up to the door, Henry, with the friends
of his solitude, a large Newfoundland puppy and two or
three terriers, was ready to receive and make much of
them.

Catherine's mind was too full, as she entered the house,
for

for her either to observe or to say a great deal ; and, till
called on by the General for her opinion of it, she had
very little idea of the room in which she was sitting.
Upon looking round it then, she perceived in a moment
that it was the most comfortable room in the world ; but
she was too guarded to say so, and the coldness of her
praise disappointed him.

" We are not calling it a good house," said he.—" We
are not comparing it with Fullerton and Northanger—
We are considering it as a mere Parsonage, small and
confined, we allow, but decent perhaps, and habitable ;
and altogether not inferior to the generality ;—or, in
other words, I believe there are few country parsonages
in England half so good. It may admit of improvement,
however. Far be it from me to say otherwise ; and any
thing in reason—a bow thrown out, perhaps—though,
between ourselves, if there is one thing more than another
my aversion, it is a patched-on bow."

Catherine did not hear enough of this speech to understand or be pained by it ; and other subjects being
studiously brought forward and supported by Henry,
at the same time that a tray full of refreshments was
introduced by his servant, the General was shortly
restored to his complacency, and Catherine to all her
usual ease of spirits.

The room in question was of a commodious, well-
proportioned size, and handsomely fitted up as a dining
parlour ; and on their quitting it to walk round the
grounds, she was shewn, first into a smaller apartment,
belonging peculiarly to the master of the house, and made
unusually tidy on the occasion ; and afterwards into
what was to be the drawing-room, with the appearance of
which, though unfurnished, Catherine was delighted
enough even to satisfy the General. It was a prettily-
shaped room, the windows reaching to the ground, and
the view from them pleasant, though only over green
meadows ; and she expressed her admiration at the
moment with all the honest simplicity with which she
felt

felt it. "Oh! why do not you fit up this room, Mr.
Tilney? What a pity not to have it fitted up! It is
the prettiest room I ever saw;—it is the prettiest room
in the world!"

"I trust," said the General, with a most satisfied smile,
"that it will very speedily be furnished: it waits only
for a lady's taste!"

"Well, if it was my house, I should never sit any where
else. Oh! what a sweet little cottage there is among the
trees—apple trees too! It is the prettiest cottage!"—

"You like it—you approve it as an object;—it is
enough. Henry, remember that Robinson is spoken to
about it. The cottage remains."

Such a compliment recalled all Catherine's consciousness, and silenced her directly; and, though pointedly
applied to by the General for her choice of the prevailing
colour of the paper and hangings, nothing like an opinion
on the subject could be drawn from her. The influence
of fresh objects and fresh air, however, was of great use
in dissipating these embarrassing associations; and,
having reached the ornamental part of the premises,
consisting of a walk round two sides of a meadow, on which
Henry's genius had begun to act about half a year ago,
she was sufficiently recovered to think it prettier than
any pleasure-ground she had ever been in before, though
there was not a shrub in it higher than the green bench
in the corner.

A saunter into other meadows, and through part of the
village, with a visit to the stables to examine some
improvements, and a charming game of play with a litter
of puppies just able to roll about, brought them to four
o'clock, when Catherine scarcely thought it could be
three. At four they were to dine, and at six to set off on
their return. Never had any day passed so quickly!

She could not but observe that the abundance of the
dinner did not seem to create the smallest astonishment
in the General; nay, that he was even looking at the
side-table for cold meat which was not there. His son
and

and daughter's observations were of a different kind.
They had seldom seen him eat so heartily at any table
but his own; and never before known him so little dis-
concerted by the melted butter's being oiled.

At six o'clock, the General having taken his coffee,
the carriage again received them; and so gratifying had
been the tenor of his conduct throughout the whole visit,
so well assured was her mind on the subject of his expectations, that, could she have felt equally confident of the
wishes of his son, Catherine would have quitted Woodston
with little anxiety as to the How or the When she might
return to it.

CHAP.

CHAPTER XII.

THE next morning brought the following very unexpected letter from Isabella :—

Bath, April ——

My dearest Catherine,

I received your two kind letters with the greatest delight, and have a thousand apologies to make for not answering them sooner. I really am quite ashamed of my idleness ; but in this horrid place one can find time for nothing. I have had my pen in my hand to begin a letter to you almost every day since you left Bath, but have always been prevented by some silly trifler or other. Pray write to me soon, and direct to my own home. Thank God ! we leave this vile place to-morrow. Since you went away, I have had no pleasure in it—the dust is beyond any thing ; and every body one cares for is gone. I believe if I could see you I should not mind the rest, for you are dearer to me than any body can conceive. I am quite uneasy about your dear brother, not having heard from him since he went to Oxford ; and am fearful of some misunderstanding. Your kind offices will set all right :—he is the only man I ever did or could love, and I trust you will convince him of it. The spring fashions are partly down ; and the hats the most frightful you can imagine. I hope you spend your time pleasantly, but am afraid you never think of me. I will not say all that I could of the family you are with, because I would not be ungenerous, or set you against those you esteem ; but it is very difficult to know whom to trust, and young men never know their minds two days together. I rejoice to say, that the young man whom, of all others, I particularly abhor, has left Bath. You will know, from this description, I must mean Captain Tilney, who, as you

may

may remember, was amazingly disposed to follow and
tease me, before you went away. Afterwards he got
worse, and became quite my shadow. Many girls might
have been taken in, for never were such attentions ; but
I knew the fickle sex too well. He went away to his
regiment two days ago, and I trust I shall never be
plagued with him again. He is the greatest coxcomb I
ever saw, and amazingly disagreeable. The last two
days he was always by the side of Charlotte Davis :
I pitied his taste, but took no notice of him. The last
time we met was in Bath-street, and I turned directly
into a shop that he might not speak to me ;—I would
not even look at him. He went into the Pump-room
afterwards ; but I would not have followed him for all
the world. Such a contrast between him and your
brother !—pray send me some news of the latter—I am
quite unhappy about him, he seemed so uncomfortable
when he went away, with a cold, or something that
affected his spirits. I would write to him myself, but
have mislaid his direction ; and, as I hinted above, am
afraid he took something in my conduct amiss. Pray
explain every thing to his satisfaction ; or, if he still
harbours any doubt, a line from himself to me, or a call
at Putney when next in town, might set all to rights.
I have not been to the Rooms this age, nor to the Play,
except going in last night with the Hodges's, for a frolic,
at half-price : they teased me into it ; and I was determined they should not say I shut myself up because
Tilney was gone. We happened to sit by the Mitchells,
and they pretended to be quite surprized to see me out.
I knew their spite :—at one time they could not be civil
to me, but now they are all friendship ; but I am not
such a fool as to be taken in by them. You know I have
a pretty good spirit of my own. Anne Mitchell had tried
to put on a turban like mine, as I wore it the week before
at the Concert, but made wretched work of it—it happened
to become my odd face I believe, at least Tilney told me
so at the time, and said every eye was upon me ; but he
is the

is the last man whose word I would take. I wear nothing
but purple now : I know I look hideous in it, but no
matter—it is your dear brother's favourite colour. Lose
no time, my dearest, sweetest Catherine, in writing to
him and to me,

Who ever am, &c.

Such a strain of shallow artifice could not impose even
upon Catherine. Its inconsistencies, contradictions, and
falsehood, struck her from the very first. She was
ashamed of Isabella, and ashamed of having ever loved
her. Her professions of attachment were now as dis-
gusting as her excuses were empty, and her demands
impudent. " Write to James on her behalf !—No,
James should never hear Isabella's name mentioned by
her again."

On Henry's arrival from Woodston, she made known
to him and Eleanor their brother's safety, congratulating
them with sincerity on it, and reading aloud the most
material passages of her letter with strong indignation.
When she had finished it,—" So much for Isabella," she
cried, " and for all our intimacy ! She must think me
an idiot, or she could not have written so ; but perhaps
this has served to make her character better known to
me than mine is to her. I see what she has been about.
She is a vain coquette, and her tricks have not answered.
I do not believe she had ever any regard either for James
or for me, and I wish I had never known her."

" It will soon be as if you never had," said Henry.

" There is but one thing that I cannot understand.
I see that she has had designs on Captain Tilney, which
have not succeeded ; but I do not understand what
Captain Tilney has been about all this time. Why should
he pay her such attentions as to make her quarrel with
my brother, and then fly off himself ? "

" I have very little to say for Frederick's motives, such
as I believe them to have been. He has his vanities as
well as Miss Thorpe, and the chief difference is, that,
having

having a stronger head, they have not yet injured himself.
If the *effect* of his behaviour does not justify him with you,
we had better not seek after the cause."

" Then you do not suppose he ever really cared about
her ? "

" I am persuaded that he never did."

" And only made believe to do so for mischief's sake ? "
Henry bowed his assent.

" Well, then, I must say that I do not like him at all.
Though it has turned out so well for us, I do not like him
at all. As it happens, there is no great harm done,
because I do not think Isabella has any heart to lose.
But, suppose he had made her very much in love with
him ? "

" But we must first suppose Isabella to have had
a heart to lose,—consequently to have been a very
different creature ; and, in that case, she would have
met with very different treatment."

" It is very right that you should stand by your
brother."

" And if you would stand by *your's*, you would not be
much distressed by the disappointment of Miss Thorpe.
But your mind is warped by an innate principle of general
integrity, and therefore not accessible to the cool reason-
ings of family partiality, or a desire of revenge."

Catherine was complimented out of further bitterness.
Frederick could not be unpardonably guilty, while Henry
made himself so agreeable. She resolved on not answering
Isabella's letter ; and tried to think no more of it.

CHAP-

CHAPTER XIII.

Soon after this, the General found himself obliged to go to London for a week ; and he left Northanger earnestly regretting that any necessity should rob him even for an hour of Miss Morland's company, and anxiously recommending the study of her comfort and amusement to his children as their chief object in his absence. His departure gave Catherine the first experimental conviction that a loss may be sometimes a gain. The happiness with which their time now passed, every employment voluntary, every laugh indulged, every meal a scene of ease and good-humour, walking where they liked and when they liked, their hours, pleasures and fatigues at their own command, made her thoroughly sensible of the restraint which the General's presence had imposed, and most thankfully feel their present release from it. Such ease and such delights made her love the place and the people more and more every day ; and had it not been for a dread of its soon becoming expedient to leave the one, and an apprehension of not being equally beloved by the other, she would at each moment of each day have been perfectly happy ; but she was now in the fourth week of her visit ; before the General came home, the fourth week would be turned, and perhaps it might seem an intrusion if she staid much longer. This was a painful consideration whenever it occurred ; and eager to get rid of such a weight on her mind, she very soon resolved to speak to Eleanor about it at once, propose going away, and be guided in her conduct by the manner in which her proposal might be taken.

Aware that if she gave herself much time, she might feel it difficult to bring forward so unpleasant a subject, she took the first opportunity of being suddenly alone with Eleanor, and of Eleanor's being in the middle of
a speech

a speech about something very different, to start forth
her obligation of going away very soon. Eleanor looked
and declared herself much concerned. She had " hoped
for the pleasure of her company for a much longer time—
had been misled (perhaps by her wishes) to suppose that
a much longer visit had been promised—and could not
but think that if Mr. and Mrs. Morland were aware of the
pleasure it was to her to have her there, they would be
too generous to hasten her return."—Catherine explained.
—" Oh ! as to *that*, papa and mamma were in no hurry
at all. As long as she was happy, they would always be
satisfied."

" Then why, might she ask, in such a hurry herself to
leave them ? "

" Oh ! because she had been there so long."

" Nay, if you can use such a word, I can urge you no
farther. If you think it long—"

" Oh ! no, I do not indeed. For my own pleasure,
I could stay with you as long again."—And it was directly
settled that, till she had, her leaving them was not even
to be thought of. In having this cause of uneasiness so
pleasantly removed, the force of the other was likewise
weakened. The kindness, the earnestness of Eleanor's
manner in pressing her to stay, and Henry's gratified
look on being told that her stay was determined, were
such sweet proofs of her importance with them, as left
her only just so much solicitude as the human mind can
never do comfortably without. She did—almost always
—believe that Henry loved her, and quite always that
his father and sister loved and even wished her to belong
to them ; and believing so far, her doubts and anxieties
were merely sportive irritations.

Henry was not able to obey his father's injunction of
remaining wholly at Northanger in attendance on the
ladies, during his absence in London ; the engagements
of his curate at Woodston obliging him to leave them on
Saturday for a couple of nights. His loss was not now
what it had been while the General was at home ; it
lessened

lessened their gaiety, but did not ruin their comfort;
and the two girls agreeing in occupation, and improving
in intimacy, found themselves so well-sufficient for the
time to themselves, that it was eleven o'clock, rather
a late hour at the Abbey, before they quitted the supper-
room on the day of Henry's departure. They had just
reached the head of the stairs, when it seemed, as far as
the thickness of the walls would allow them to judge,
that a carriage was driving up to the door, and the next
moment confirmed the idea by the loud noise of the
house-bell. After the first perturbation of surprize had
passed away, in a " Good Heaven! what can be the
matter ? " it was quickly decided by Eleanor to be
her eldest brother, whose arrival was often as sudden,
if not quite so unseasonable, and accordingly she hurried
down to welcome him.

Catherine walked on to her chamber, making up her
mind as well as she could, to a further acquaintance with
Captain Tilney, and comforting herself under the unpleasant impression his conduct had given her, and the
persuasion of his being by far too fine a gentleman to
approve of her, that at least they should not meet under
such circumstances as would make their meeting mate-
rially painful. She trusted he would never speak of Miss
Thorpe ; and indeed, as he must by this time be ashamed
of the part he had acted, there could be no danger of it ;
and as long as all mention of Bath scenes were avoided,
she thought she could behave to him very civilly. In
such considerations time passed away, and it was certainly in his favour that Eleanor should be so glad to
see him, and have so much to say, for half an hour was
almost gone since his arrival, and Eleanor did not come up.

At that moment Catherine thought she heard her step
. in the gallery, and listened for its continuance ; but all
was silent. Scarcely, however, had she convicted her
fancy of error, when the noise of something moving close
to her door made her start ; it seemed as if some one was
touching the very doorway—and in another moment
a slight

a slight motion of the lock proved that some hand must be on it. She trembled a little at the idea of any one's approaching so cautiously; but resolving not to be again overcome by trivial appearances of alarm, or misled by a raised imagination, she stepped quietly forward, and opened the door. Eleanor, and only Eleanor, stood there. Catherine's spirits however were tranquillized but for an instant, for Eleanor's cheeks were pale, and her manner greatly agitated. Though evidently intending to come in, it seemed an effort to enter the room, and a still greater to speak when there. Catherine, supposing some uneasiness on Captain Tilney's account, could only express her concern by silent attention; obliged her to be seated, rubbed her temples with lavender-water, and hung over her with affectionate solicitude. "My dear Catherine, you must not—you must not indeed—" were Eleanor's first connected words. "I am quite well. This kindness distracts me—I cannot bear it—I come to you on such an errand!"

"Errand!—to me!"

"How shall I tell you!—Oh! how shall I tell you!"

A new idea now darted into Catherine's mind, and turning as pale as her friend, she exclaimed, "'Tis a messenger from Woodston!"

"You are mistaken, indeed," returned Eleanor, looking at her most compassionately—"it is no one from Woodston. It is my father himself." Her voice faltered, and her eyes were turned to the ground as she mentioned his name. His unlooked-for return was enough in itself to make Catherine's heart sink, and for a few moments she hardly supposed there were any thing worse to be told. She said nothing; and Eleanor endeavouring to collect herself and speak with firmness, but with eyes still cast down, soon went on. "You are too good, I am sure, to think the worse of me for the part I am obliged to perform. I am indeed a most unwilling messenger. After what has so lately passed, so lately been settled between us—how joyfully, how thankfully on my side!—

as

as to your continuing here as I hoped for many, many
weeks longer, how can I tell you that your kindness is not
to be accepted—and that the happiness your company
has hitherto given us is to be repaid by——but I must
not trust myself with words. My dear Catherine, we are
to part. My father has recollected an engagement that
takes our whole family away on Monday. We are going
to Lord Longtown's, near Hereford, for a fortnight.
Explanation and apology are equally impossible. I cannot attempt either."

"My dear Eleanor," cried Catherine, suppressing her
feelings as well as she could, "do not be so distressed.
A second engagement must give way to a first. I am
very, very sorry we are to part—so soon, and so suddenly
too ; but I am not offended, indeed I am not. I can
finish my visit here you know at any time ; or I hope you
will come to me. Can you, when you return from this
lord's, come to Fullerton ? "

"It will not be in my power, Catherine."

"Come when you can, then."—

Eleanor made no answer ; and Catherine's thoughts
recurring to something more directly interesting, she
added, thinking aloud, "Monday—so soon as Monday ;—
and you *all* go. Well, I am certain of——I shall be able
to take leave however. I need not go till just before you
do, you know. Do not be distressed, Eleanor, I can go
on Monday very well. My father and mother's having
no notice of it is of very little consequence. The General
will send a servant with me, I dare say, half the way—
and then I shall soon be at Salisbury, and then I am only
nine miles from home."

"Ah, Catherine ! were it settled so, it would be somewhat less intolerable, though in such common attentions
you would have received but half what you ought.
But—how can I tell you ?—To-morrow morning is fixed
for your leaving us, and not even the hour is left to your
choice ; the very carriage is ordered, and will be here at
seven o'clock, and no servant will be offered you."

Catherine

Catherine sat down, breathless and speechless. " I
could hardly believe my senses, when I heard it ;—and
no displeasure, no resentment that you can feel at this
moment, however justly great, can be more than I myself——but I must not talk of what I felt. Oh ! that
I could suggest any thing in extenuation ! Good God !
what will your father and mother say ! After courting
you from the protection of real friends to this—almost
double distance from your home, to have you driven out
of the house, without the considerations even of decent
civility ! Dear, dear Catherine, in being the bearer of
such a message, I seem guilty myself of all its insult ;
yet, I trust you will acquit me, for you must have been
long enough in this house to see that I am but a nominal
mistress of it, that my real power is nothing."

" Have I offended the General ? " said Catherine in
a faltering voice.

" Alas ! for my feelings as a daughter, all that I know,
all that I answer for is, that you can have given him no
just cause of offence. He certainly is greatly, very
greatly discomposed ; I have seldom seen him more so.
His temper is not happy, and something has now occurred
to ruffle it in an uncommon degree ; some disappointment,
some vexation, which just at this moment seems important ; but which I can hardly suppose you to have any
concern in, for how is it possible ? "

It was with pain that Catherine could speak at all ;
and it was only for Eleanor's sake that she attempted it.
" I am sure," said she, " I am very sorry if I have offended
him. It was the last thing I would willingly have done.
But do not be unhappy, Eleanor. An engagement you
know must be kept. I am only sorry it was not recollected
sooner, that I might have written home. But it is of very
little consequence."

" I hope, I earnestly hope that to your real safety it
will be of none ; but to every thing else it is of the greatest
consequence ; to comfort, appearance, propriety, to your
family, to the world. Were your friends, the Allens, still

in Bath, you might go to them with comparative ease;
a few hours would take you there; but a journey of
seventy miles, to be taken post by you, at your age,
alone, unattended ! "

" Oh, the journey is nothing. Do not think about that.
And if we are to part, a few hours sooner or later, you
know, makes no difference. I can be ready by seven.
Let me be called in time." Eleanor saw that she wished
to be alone; and believing it better for each that they
should avoid any further conversation, now left her with
" I shall see you in the morning."

Catherine's swelling heart needed relief. In Eleanor's
presence friendship and pride had equally restrained
her tears, but no sooner was she gone than they burst
forth in torrents. Turned from the house, and in such
a way !—Without any reason that could justify, any
apology that could atone for the abruptness, the rudeness,
nay, the insolence of it. Henry at a distance—not able
even to bid him farewell. Every hope, every expectation
from him suspended, at least, and who could say how
long ?—Who could say when they might meet again ?—
And all this by such a man as General Tilney, so polite,
so well-bred, and heretofore so particularly fond of her !
It was as incomprehensible as it was mortifying and
grievous. From what it could arise, and where it would
end, were considerations of equal perplexity and alarm.
The manner in which it was done so grossly uncivil ;
hurrying her away without any reference to her own
convenience, or allowing her even the appearance of
choice as to the time or mode of her travelling ; of two
days, the earliest fixed on, and of that almost the earliest
hour, as if resolved to have her gone before he was stirring
in the morning, that he might not be obliged even to see
her. What could all this mean but an intentional
affront ? By some means or other she must have had
the misfortune to offend him. Eleanor had wished to
spare her from so painful a notion, but Catherine could
not believe it possible that any injury or any misfortune
could

could provoke such ill-will against a person not connected, or, at least, not supposed to be connected with it.

Heavily past the night. Sleep, or repose that deserved the name of sleep, was out of the question. That room, in which her disturbed imagination had tormented her on her first arrival, was again the scene of agitated spirits and unquiet slumbers. Yet how different now the source of her inquietude from what it had been then—how mournfully superior in reality and substance! Her anxiety had foundation in fact, her fears in probability; and with a mind so occupied in the contemplation of actual and natural evil, the solitude of her situation, the darkness of her chamber, the antiquity of the building were felt and considered without the smallest emotion; and though the wind was high, and often produced strange and sudden noises throughout the house, she heard it all as she lay awake, hour after hour, without curiosity or terror.

Soon after six Eleanor entered her room, eager to show attention or give assistance where it was possible; but very little remained to be done. Catherine had not loitered; she was almost dressed, and her packing almost finished. The possibility of some conciliatory message from the General occurred to her as his daughter appeared. What so natural, as that anger should pass away and repentance succeed it? and she only wanted to know how far, after what had passed, an apology might properly be received by her. But the knowledge would have been useless here, it was not called for; neither clemency nor dignity was put to the trial—Eleanor brought no message. Very little passed between them on meeting; each found her greatest safety in silence, and few and trivial were the sentences exchanged while they remained up stairs, Catherine in busy agitation completing her dress, and Eleanor with more good-will than experience intent upon filling the trunk. When every thing was done they left the room, Catherine lingering only half a minute behind her friend to throw a parting glance on every well-known

cherished

cherished object, and went down to the breakfast-parlour,
where breakfast was prepared. She tried to eat, as well
to save herself from the pain of being urged, as to make
her friend comfortable ; but she had no appetite, and
could not swallow many mouthfuls. The contrast between
this and her last breakfast in that room, gave her fresh
misery, and strengthened her distaste for every thing
before her. It was not four-and-twenty hours ago since
they had met there to the same repast, but in circumstances how different ! With what cheerful ease, what
happy, though false security, had she then looked around
her, enjoying every thing present, and fearing little in
future, beyond Henry's going to Woodston for a day !
Happy, happy breakfast ! for Henry had been there,
Henry had sat by her and helped her. These reflections
were long indulged undisturbed by any address from her
companion, who sat as deep in thought as herself ; and
the appearance of the carriage was the first thing to
startle and recall them to the present moment. Catherine's
colour rose at the sight of it ; and the indignity with
which she was treated striking at that instant on her
mind with peculiar force, made her for a short time
sensible only of resentment. Eleanor seemed now
impelled into resolution and speech.

"You *must* write to me, Catherine," she cried, " you
must let me hear from you as soon as possible. Till
I know you to be safe at home, I shall not have an hour's
comfort. For *one* letter, at all risks, all hazards, I must
entreat. Let me have the satisfaction of knowing that
you are safe at Fullerton, and have found your family
well, and then, till I can ask for your correspondence as
I ought to do, I will not expect more. Direct to me at
Lord Longtown's, and, I must ask it, under cover to
Alice."

"No, Eleanor, if you are not allowed to receive a letter
from me, I am sure I had better not write. There can be
no doubt of my getting home safe."

Eleanor only replied, " I cannot wonder at your
feelings.

feelings. I will not importune you. I will trust to your own kindness of heart when I am at a distance from you." But this, with the look of sorrow accompanying it, was enough to melt Catherine's pride in a moment, and she instantly said, "Oh, Eleanor, I *will* write to you indeed."

There was yet another point which Miss Tilney was anxious to settle, though somewhat embarrassed in speaking of. It had occurred to her, that after so long an absence from home, Catherine might not be provided with money enough for the expenses of her journey, and, upon suggesting it to her with most affectionate offers of accommodation, it proved to be exactly the case. Catherine had never thought on the subject till that moment ; but, upon examining her purse, was convinced that but for this kindness of her friend, she might have been turned from the house without even the means of getting home ; and the distress in which she must have been thereby involved filling the minds of both, scarcely another word was said by either during the time of their remaining together. Short, however, was that time. The carriage was soon announced to be ready ; and Catherine, instantly rising, a long and affectionate embrace supplied the place of language in bidding each other adieu ; and, as they entered the hall, unable to leave the house without some mention of one whose name had not yet been spoken by either, she paused a moment, and with quivering lips just made it intelligible that she left " her kind remembrance for her absent friend." But with this approach to his name ended all possibility of restraining her feelings ; and, hiding her face as well as she could with her handkerchief, she darted across the hall, jumped into the chaise, and in a moment was driven from the door.

CHAP-

CHAPTER XIV.

CATHERINE was too wretched to be fearful. The journey in itself had no terrors for her ; and she began it without either dreading its length, or feeling its solitariness. Leaning back in one corner of the carriage, in a violent burst of tears, she was conveyed some miles beyond the walls of the Abbey before she raised her head ; and the highest point of ground within the park was almost closed from her view before she was capable of turning her eyes towards it. Unfortunately, the road she now travelled was the same which only ten days ago she had so happily passed along in going to and from Woodston ; and, for fourteen miles, every bitter feeling was rendered more severe by the review of objects on which she had first looked under impressions so different. Every mile, as it brought her nearer Woodston, added to her sufferings, and when within the distance of five, she passed the turning which led to it, and thought of Henry, so near, yet so unconscious, her grief and agitation were excessive.

The day which she had spent at that place had been one of the happiest of her life. It was there, it was on that day that the General had made use of such expressions with regard to Henry and herself, had so spoken and so looked as to give her the most positive conviction of his actually wishing their marriage. Yes, only ten days ago had he elated her by his pointed regard—had he even confused her by his too significant reference ! And now—what had she done, or what had she omitted to do, to merit such a change ?

The only offence against him of which she could accuse herself, had been such as was scarcely possible to reach his knowledge. Henry and her own heart only were privy to the shocking suspicions which she had so idly entertained ; and equally safe did she believe her secret with

with each. Designedly, at least, Henry could not have betrayed her. If, indeed, by any strange mischance his father should have gained intelligence of what she had dared to think and look for, of her causeless fancies and injurious examinations, she could not wonder at any degree of his indignation. If aware of her having viewed him as a murderer, she could not wonder at his even turning her from his house. But a justification so full of torture to herself, she trusted would not be in his power.

Anxious as were all her conjectures on this point, it was not, however, the one on which she dwelt most. There was a thought yet nearer, a more prevailing, more impetuous concern. How Henry would think, and feel, and look, when he returned on the morrow to Northanger and heard of her being gone, was a question of force and interest to rise over every other, to be never ceasing, alternately irritating and soothing; it sometimes suggested the dread of his calm acquiescence, and at others was answered by the sweetest confidence in his regret and resentment. To the General, of course, he would not dare to speak ; but to Eleanor—what might he not say to Eleanor about her ?

In this unceasing recurrence of doubts and inquiries, on any one article of which her mind was incapable of more than momentary repose, the hours passed away, and her journey advanced much faster than she looked for. The pressing anxieties of thought, which prevented her from noticing any thing before her, when once beyond the neighbourhood of Woodston, saved her at the same time from watching her progress ; and though no object on the road could engage a moment's attention, she found no stage of it tedious. From this, she was preserved too by another cause, by feeling no eagerness for her journey's conclusion ; for to return in such a manner to Fullerton was almost to destroy the pleasure of a meeting with those she loved best, even after an absence such as her's— an eleven weeks absence. What had she to say that would not humble herself and pain her family ; that
would

would not increase her own grief by the confession of it,
extend an useless resentment, and perhaps involve the
innocent with the guilty in undistinguishing ill-will ?
She could never do justice to Henry and Eleanor's merit ;
she felt it too strongly for expression ; and should a dislike
be taken against them, should they be thought of un-
favourably, on their father's account, it would cut her
to the heart.

With these feelings, she rather dreaded than sought for
the first view of that well-known spire which would
announce her within twenty miles of home. Salisbury
she had known to be her point on leaving Northanger ;
but after the first stage she had been indebted to the
post-masters for the names of the places which were then
to conduct her to it ; so great had been her ignorance of
her route. She met with nothing, however, to distress or
frighten her. Her youth, civil manners and liberal pay,
procured her all the attention that a traveller like herself
could require ; and stopping only to change horses, she
travelled on for about eleven hours without accident
or alarm, and between six and seven o'clock in the evening
found herself entering Fullerton.

A heroine returning, at the close of her career, to her
native village, in all the triumph of recovered reputation,
and all the dignity of a countess, with a long train of
noble relations in their several phaetons, and three
waiting-maids in a travelling chaise-and-four, behind her,
is an event on which the pen of the contriver may well
delight to dwell ; it gives credit to every conclusion, and
the author must share in the glory she so liberally bestows.
—But my affair is widely different ; I bring back my
heroine to her home in solitude and disgrace ; and no
sweet elation of spirits can lead me into minuteness.
A heroine in a hack post-chaise, is such a blow upon
sentiment, as no attempt at grandeur or pathos can
withstand. Swiftly therefore shall her post-boy drive
through the village, amid the gaze of Sunday groups, and
speedy shall be her descent from it.

But,

But, whatever might be the distress of Catherine's mind, as she thus advanced towards the Parsonage, and whatever the humiliation of her biographer in relating it, she was preparing enjoyment of no every-day nature for those to whom she went ; first, in the appearance of her carriage—and secondly, in herself. The chaise of a traveller being a rare sight in Fullerton, the whole family were immediately at the window ; and to have it stop at the sweep-gate was a pleasure to brighten every eye and occupy every fancy—a pleasure quite unlooked for by all but the two youngest children, a boy and girl of six and four years old, who expected a brother or sister in every carriage. Happy the glance that first distinguished Catherine !—Happy the voice that proclaimed the discovery !—But whether such happiness were the lawful property of George or Harriet could never be exactly understood.

Her father, mother, Sarah, George, and Harriet, all assembled at the door, to welcome her with affectionate eagerness, was a sight to awaken the best feelings of Catherine's heart ; and in the embrace of each, as she stepped from the carriage, she found herself soothed beyond any thing that she had believed possible. So surrounded, so caressed, she was even happy ! In the joyfulness of family love every thing for a short time was subdued, and the pleasure of seeing her, leaving them at first little leisure for calm curiosity, they were all seated round the tea-table, which Mrs. Morland had hurried for the comfort of the poor traveller, whose pale and jaded looks soon caught her notice, before any inquiry so direct as to demand a positive answer was addressed to her.

Reluctantly, and with much hesitation, did she then begin what might perhaps, at the end of half an hour, be termed by the courtesy of her hearers, an explanation; but scarcely, within that time, could they at all discover the cause, or collect the particulars of her sudden return. They were far from being an irritable race ; far from any quickness in catching, or bitterness in resenting affronts :—

but

but here, when the whole was unfolded, was an insult not to be overlooked, nor, for the first half hour, to be easily pardoned. Without suffering any romantic alarm, in the consideration of their daughter's long and lonely journey, Mr. and Mrs. Morland could not but feel that it might have been productive of much unpleasantness to her ; that it was what they could never have voluntarily suffered ; and that, in forcing her on such a measure, General Tilney had acted neither honourably nor feelingly—neither as a gentleman nor as a parent. Why he had done it, what could have provoked him to such a breach of hospitality, and so suddenly turned all his partial regard for their daughter into actual ill-will, was a matter which they were at least as far from divining as Catherine herself ; but it did not oppress them by any means so long ; and, after a due course of useless conjecture, that, " it was a strange business, and that he must be a very strange man," grew enough for all their indignation and wonder ; though Sarah indeed still indulged in the sweets of incomprehensibility, exclaiming and conjecturing with youthful ardour.—" My dear, you give yourself a great deal of needless trouble," said her mother at last ; " depend upon it, it is something not at all worth understanding."

" I can allow for his wishing Catherine away, when he recollected this engagement," said Sarah, " but why not do it civilly ? "

" I am sorry for the young people," returned Mrs. Morland ; " they must have a sad time of it ; but as for any thing else, it is no matter now ; Catherine is safe at home, and our comfort does not depend upon General Tilney." Catherine sighed. " Well," continued her philosophic mother, " I am glad I did not know of your journey at the time ; but now it is all over perhaps there is no great harm done. It is always good for young people to be put upon exerting themselves ; and you know, my dear Catherine, you always were a sad little shatter-brained creature ; but now you must have been
forced

forced to have your wits about you, with so much changing
of chaises and so forth ; and I hope it will appear that
you have not left any thing behind you in any of the
pockets."

Catherine hoped so too, and tried to feel an interest in
her own amendment, but her spirits were quite worn
down ; and, to be silent and alone becoming soon her only
wish, she readily agreed to her mother's next counsel of
going early to bed. Her parents seeing nothing in her
ill-looks and agitation but the natural consequence of
mortified feelings, and of the unusual exertion and
fatigue of such a journey, parted from her without any
doubt of their being soon slept away ; and though, when
they all met the next morning, her recovery was not
equal to their hopes, they were still perfectly unsuspicious
of there being any deeper evil. They never once thought
of her heart, which, for the parents of a young lady of
seventeen, just returned from her first excursion from
home, was odd enough !

As soon as breakfast was over, she sat down to fulfil
her promise to Miss Tilney, whose trust in the effect of
time and distance on her friend's disposition was already
justified, for already did Catherine reproach herself with
having parted from Eleanor coldly ; with having never
enough valued her merits or kindness ; and never enough
commiserated her for what she had been yesterday left to
endure. The strength of these feelings, however, was far
from assisting her pen ; and never had it been harder
for her to write than in addressing Eleanor Tilney. To
compose a letter which might at once do justice to her
sentiments and her situation, convey gratitude without
servile regret, be guarded without coldness, and honest
without resentment—a letter which Eleanor might not be
pained by the perusal of—and, above all, which she might
not blush herself, if Henry should chance to see, was an
undertaking to frighten away all her powers of performance ; and, after long thought and much perplexity, to
be very brief was all that she could determine on with
any

any confidence of safety. The money therefore which Eleanor had advanced was inclosed with little more than grateful thanks, and the thousand good wishes of a most affectionate heart.

"This has been a strange acquaintance," observed Mrs. Morland, as the letter was finished ; " soon made and soon ended.—I am sorry it happens so, for Mrs. Allen thought them very pretty kind of young people ; and you were sadly out of luck too in your Isabella. Ah ! poor James ! Well, we must live and learn ; and the next new friends you make I hope will be better worth keeping."

Catherine coloured as she warmly answered, " No friend can be better worth keeping than Eleanor."

" If so, my dear, I dare say you will meet again some time or other ; do not be uneasy. It is ten to one but you are thrown together again in the course of a few years ; and then what a pleasure it will be ! ''

Mrs. Morland was not happy in her attempt at consolation. The hope of meeting again in the course of a few years could only put into Catherine's head what might happen within that time to make a meeting dreadful to her. She could never forget Henry Tilney, or think of him with less tenderness than she did at that moment ; but he might forget her ; and in that case to meet !—— Her eyes filled with tears as she pictured her acquaintance so renewed ; and her mother, perceiving her comfortable suggestions to have had no good effect, proposed, as another expedient for restoring her spirits, that they should call on Mrs. Allen.

The two houses were only a quarter of a mile apart ; and, as they walked, Mrs. Morland quickly dispatched all that she felt on the score of James's disappointment. " We are sorry for him," said she ; " but otherwise there is no harm done in the match going off ; for it could not be a desirable thing to have him engaged to a girl whom we had not the smallest acquaintance with, and who was so entirely without fortune ; and now, after such behaviour,

viour, we cannot think at all well of her. Just at present it comes hard to poor James ; but that will not last for ever ; and I dare say he will be a discreeter man all his life, for the foolishness of his first choice."

This was just such a summary view of the affair as Catherine could listen to ; another sentence might have endangered her complaisance, and made her reply less rational ; for soon were all her thinking powers swallowed up in the reflection of her own change of feelings and spirits since last she had trodden that well-known road. It was not three months ago since, wild with joyful expectation, she had there run backwards and forwards some ten times a-day, with an heart light, gay, and independent ; looking forward to pleasures untasted and unalloyed, and free from the apprehension of evil as from the knowledge of it. Three months ago had seen her all this ; and now, how altered a being did she return !

She was received by the Allens with all the kindness which her unlooked-for appearance, acting on a steady affection, would naturally call forth ; and great was their surprize, and warm their displeasure, on hearing how she had been treated,—though Mrs. Morland's account of it was no inflated representation, no studied appeal to their passions. " Catherine took us quite by surprize yesterday evening," said she. "She travelled all the way post by herself, and knew nothing of coming till Saturday night ; for General Tilney, from some odd fancy or other, all of a sudden grew tired of having her there, and almost turned her out of the house. Very unfriendly, certainly ; and he must be a very odd man ;—but we are so glad to have her amongst us again ! And it is a great comfort to find that she is not a poor helpless creature, but can shift very well for herself."

Mr. Allen expressed himself on the occasion with the reasonable resentment of a sensible friend ; and Mrs. Allen thought his expressions quite good enough to be immediately made use of again by herself. His wonder, his conjectures, and his explanations, became in succession
her's,

her's, with the addition of this single remark—" I really
have not patience with the General "—to fill up every
accidental pause. And, " I really have not patience with
the General," was uttered twice after Mr. Allen left the
room, without any relaxation of anger, or any material
digression of thought. A more considerable degree of
wandering attended the third repetition ; and, after completing the fourth, she immediately added, " Only think,
my dear, of my having got that frightful great rent in my
best Mechlin so charmingly mended, before I left Bath,
that one can hardly see where it was. I must shew it you
some day or other. Bath is a nice place, Catherine, after
all. I assure you I did not above half like coming away.
Mrs. Thorpe's being there was such a comfort to us, was
not it ? You know you and I were quite forlorn at first."

" Yes, but *that* did not last long," said Catherine, her
eyes brightening at the recollection of what had first
given spirit to her existence there.

" Very true : we soon met with Mrs. Thorpe, and then
we wanted for nothing. My dear, do not you think
these silk gloves wear very well ? I put them on new
the first time of our going to the Lower Rooms, you know,
and I have worn them a great deal since. Do you
remember that evening ? "

" Do I ! Oh ! perfectly."

" It was very agreeable, was not it ? Mr. Tilney drank
tea with us, and I always thought him a great addition,
he is so very agreeable. I have a notion you danced
with him, but am not quite sure. I remember I had my
favourite gown on."

Catherine could not answer ; and, after a short trial
of other subjects, Mrs. Allen again returned to—" I really
have not patience with the General ! Such an agreeable,
worthy man as he seemed to be ! I do not suppose,
Mrs. Morland, you ever saw a better-bred man in your
life. His lodgings were taken the very day after he left
them, Catherine. But no wonder ; Milsom-street you
know."—

As

As they walked home again, Mrs. Morland endeavoured to impress on her daughter's mind the happiness of having such steady well-wishers as Mr. and Mrs. Allen, and the very little consideration which the neglect or unkindness of slight acquaintance like the Tilneys ought to have with her, while she could preserve the good opinion and affection of her earliest friends. There was a great deal of good sense in all this; but there are some situations of the human mind in which good sense has very little power; and Catherine's feelings contradicted almost every position her mother advanced. It was upon the behaviour of these very slight acquaintance that all her present happiness depended; and while Mrs. Morland was successfully confirming her own opinions by the justness of her own representations, Catherine was silently reflecting that *now* Henry must have arrived at Northanger; *now* he must have heard of her departure; and *now*, perhaps, they were all setting off for Hereford.

CHAP-

CHAPTER XV.

CATHERINE's disposition was not naturally sedentary, nor had her habits been ever very industrious ; but whatever might hitherto have been her defects of that sort, her mother could not but perceive them now to be greatly increased. She could neither sit still, nor employ herself for ten minutes together, walking round the garden and orchard again and again, as if nothing but motion was voluntary ; and it seemed as if she could even walk about the house rather than remain fixed for any time in the parlour. Her loss of spirits was a yet greater alteration. In her rambling and her idleness she might only be a caricature of herself ; but in her silence and sadness she was the very reverse of all that she had been before.

For two days Mrs. Morland allowed it to pass even without a hint ; but when a third night's rest had neither restored her cheerfulness, improved her in useful activity, nor given her a greater inclination for needle-work, she could no longer refrain from the gentle reproof of, " My dear Catherine, I am afraid you are growing quite a fine lady. I do not know when poor Richard's cravats would be done, if he had no friend but you. Your head runs too much upon Bath ; but there is a time for every thing—a time for balls and plays, and a time for work. You have had a long run of amusement, and now you must try to be useful."

Catherine took up her work directly, saying, in a dejected voice, that " her head did not run upon Bath——much."

" Then you are fretting about General Tilney, and that is very simple of you ; for ten to one whether you ever see him again. You should never fret about trifles." After a short silence—" I hope, my Catherine, you are not getting out of humour with home because it is not so grand

grand as Northanger. That would be turning your visit
into an evil indeed. Wherever you are you should
always be contented, but especially at home, because
there you must spend the most of your time. I did not
quite like, at breakfast, to hear you talk so much about
the French-bread at Northanger."

" I am sure I do not care about the bread. It is all the
same to me what I eat."

" There is a very clever Essay in one of the books up
stairs upon much such a subject, about young girls that
have been spoilt for home by great acquaintance—' The
Mirror,' I think. I will look it out for you some day or
other, because I am sure it will do you good."

Catherine said no more, and, with an endeavour to do
right, applied to her work ; but, after a few minutes,
sunk again, without knowing it herself, into languor and
listlessness, moving herself in her chair, from the irritation
of weariness, much oftener than she moved her needle.—
Mrs. Morland watched the progress of this relapse ; and
seeing, in her daughter's absent and dissatisfied look, the
full proof of that repining spirit to which she had now
begun to attribute her want of cheerfulness, hastily left
the room to fetch the book in question, anxious to lose
no time in attacking so dreadful a malady. It was some
time before she could find what she looked for ; and
other family matters occurring to detain her, a quarter
of an hour had elapsed ere she returned down stairs with
the volume from which so much was hoped. Her avoca-
tions above having shut out all noise but what she created
herself, she knew not that a visitor had arrived within
the last few minutes, till, on entering the room, the first
object she beheld was a young man whom she had never
seen before. With a look of much respect, he immediately rose, and being introduced to her by her conscious
daughter as " Mr. Henry Tilney," with the embarrassment of real sensibility began to apologise for his appearance there, acknowledging that after what had passed
he had little right to expect a welcome at Fullerton, and

stating his impatience to be assured of Miss Morland's
having reached her home in safety, as the cause of his
intrusion. He did not address himself to an uncandid
judge or a resentful heart. Far from comprehending him
or his sister in their father's misconduct, Mrs. Morland
had been always kindly disposed towards each, and
instantly, pleased by his appearance, received him with
the simple professions of unaffected benevolence; thank-
ing him for such an attention to her daughter, assuring
him that the friends of her children were always welcome
there, and intreating him to say not another word of
the past.

He was not ill inclined to obey this request, for, though
his heart was greatly relieved by such unlooked-for
mildness, it was not just at that moment in his power
to say any thing to the purpose. Returning in silence to
his seat, therefore, he remained for some minutes most
civilly answering all Mrs. Morland's common remarks
about the weather and roads. Catherine meanwhile,—
the anxious, agitated, happy, feverish Catherine,—said
not a word; but her glowing cheek and brightened eye
made her mother trust that this good-natured visit would
at least set her heart at ease for a time, and gladly therefore did she lay aside the first volume of the Mirror for
a future hour.

Desirous of Mr. Morland's assistance, as well in giving
encouragement, as in finding conversation for her guest,
whose embarrassment on his father's account she earnestly
pitied, Mrs. Morland had very early dispatched one of
the children to summon him; but Mr. Morland was from
home—and being thus without any support, at the end
of a quarter of an hour she had nothing to say. After
a couple of minutes unbroken silence, Henry, turning to
Catherine for the first time since her mother's entrance,
asked her, with sudden alacrity, if Mr. and Mrs. Allen
were now at Fullerton? and on developing, from amidst
all her perplexity of words in reply, the meaning, which
one short syllable would have given, immediately expressed

pressed his intention of paying his respects to them, and,
with a rising colour, asked her if she would have the
goodness to shew him the way. " You may see the house
from this window, sir," was information on Sarah's side,
which produced only a bow of acknowledgment from the
gentleman, and a silencing nod from her mother ; for
Mrs. Morland, thinking it probable, as a secondary consideration in his wish of waiting on their worthy neighbours, that he might have some explanation to give of
his father's behaviour, which it must be more pleasant
for him to communicate only to Catherine, would not on
any account prevent her accompanying him. They
began their walk, and Mrs. Morland was not entirely
mistaken in his object in wishing it. Some explanation
on his father's account he had to give ; but his first
purpose was to explain himself, and before they reached
Mr. Allen's grounds he had done it so well, that Catherine
did not think it could ever be repeated too often. She
was assured of his affection ; and that heart in return
was solicited, which, perhaps, they pretty equally knew
was already entirely his own ; for, though Henry was
now sincerely attached to her, though he felt and delighted
in all the excellencies of her character and truly loved
her society, I must confess that his affection originated
in nothing better than gratitude, or, in other words, that
a persuasion of her partiality for him had been the only
cause of giving her a serious thought. It is a new circumstance in romance, I acknowledge, and dreadfully
derogatory of an heroine's dignity ; but if it be as new
in common life, the credit of a wild imagination will at
least be all my own.

A very short visit to Mrs. Allen, in which Henry talked
at random, without sense or connection, and Catherine,
wrapt in the contemplation of her own unutterable
happiness, scarcely opened her lips, dismissed them to the
extasies of another tête-à-tête ; and before it was suffered
to close, she was enabled to judge how far he was sanc-
tioned by parental authority in his present application.

On

On his return from Woodston, two days before, he had been met near the Abbey by his impatient father, hastily informed in angry terms of Miss Morland's departure, and ordered to think of her no more.

Such was the permission upon which he had now offered her his hand. The affrighted Catherine, amidst all the terrors of expectation, as she listened to this account, could not but rejoice in the kind caution with which Henry had saved her from the necessity of a conscientious rejection, by engaging her faith before he mentioned the subject; and as he proceeded to give the particulars, and explain the motives of his father's conduct, her feelings soon hardened into even a triumphant delight. The General had had nothing to accuse her of, nothing to lay to her charge, but her being the involuntary, unconscious object of a deception which his pride could not pardon, and which a better pride would have been ashamed to own. She was guilty only of being less rich than he had supposed her to be. Under a mistaken persuasion of her possessions and claims, he had courted her acquaintance in Bath, solicited her company at Northanger, and designed her for his daughter in law. On discovering his error, to turn her from the house seemed the best, though to his feelings an inadequate proof of his resentment towards herself, and his contempt of her family.

John Thorpe had first misled him. The General, perceiving his son one night at the theatre to be paying considerable attention to Miss Morland, had accidentally inquired of Thorpe, if he knew more of her than her name. Thorpe, most happy to be on speaking terms with a man of General Tilney's importance, had been joyfully and proudly communicative;—and being at that time not only in daily expectation of Morland's engaging Isabella, but likewise pretty well resolved upon marrying Catherine himself, his vanity induced him to represent the family as yet more wealthy than his vanity and avarice had made him believe them. With whomsoever he was, or

was

was likely to be connected, his own consequence always
required that theirs should be great, and as his intimacy
with any acquaintance grew, so regularly grew their
fortune. The expectations of his friend Morland, therefore, from the first over-rated, had ever since his introduction to Isabella, been gradually increasing ; and by
merely adding twice as much for the grandeur of the
moment, by doubling what he chose to think the amount
of Mr. Morland's preferment, trebling his private fortune,
bestowing a rich aunt, and sinking half the children,
he was able to represent the whole family to the General
in a most respectable light. For Catherine, however, the
peculiar object of the General's curiosity, and his own
speculations, he had yet something more in reserve, and
the ten or fifteen thousand pounds which her father could
give her, would be a pretty addition to Mr. Allen's estate.
Her intimacy there had made him seriously determine on
her being handsomely legacied hereafter ; and to speak
of her therefore as the almost acknowledged future
heiress of Fullerton naturally followed. Upon such
intelligence the General had proceeded ; for never had it
occurred to him to doubt its authority. Thorpe's interest
in the family, by his sister's approaching connection with
one of its members, and his own views on another, (circumstances of which he boasted with almost equal open-
ness,) seemed sufficient vouchers for his truth ; and to
these were added the absolute facts of the Allens being
wealthy and childless, of Miss Morland's being under
their care, and—as soon as his acquaintance allowed him
to judge—of their treating her with parental kindness.
His resolution was soon formed. Already had he discerned a liking towards Miss Morland in the countenance
of his son ; and thankful for Mr. Thorpe's communication,
he almost instantly determined to spare no pains in
weakening his boasted interest and ruining his dearest
hopes. Catherine herself could not be more ignorant at
the time of all this, than his own children. Henry and
Eleanor, perceiving nothing in her situation likely to
engage

engage their father's particular respect, had seen with
astonishment the suddenness, continuance and extent
of his attention ; and though latterly, from some hints
which had accompanied an almost positive command to
his son of doing every thing in his power to attach her,
Henry was convinced of his father's believing it to be an
advantageous connection, it was not till the late explanation at Northanger that they had the smallest idea of the
false calculations which had hurried him on. That they
were false, the General had learnt from the very person
who had suggested them, from Thorpe himself, whom he
had chanced to meet again in town, and who, under the
influence of exactly opposite feelings, irritated by
Catherine's refusal, and yet more by the failure of a very
recent endeavour to accomplish a reconciliation between
Morland and Isabella, convinced that they were separated
for ever, and spurning a friendship which could be no
longer serviceable, hastened to contradict all that he had
said before to the advantage of the Morlands ;—confessed
himself to have been totally mistaken in his opinion of
their circumstances and character, misled by the rhodo-
montade of his friend to believe his father a man of
substance and credit, whereas the transactions of the two
or three last weeks proved him to be neither ; for after
coming eagerly forward on the first overture of a marriage
between the families, with the most liberal proposals, he
had, on being brought to the point by the shrewdness of
the relator, been constrained to acknowledge himself
incapable of giving the young people even a decent
support. They were, in fact, a necessitous family ;
numerous too almost beyond example ; by no means
respected in their own neighbourhood, as he had lately
had particular opportunities of discovering ; aiming at
a style of life which their fortune could not warrant ;
seeking to better themselves by wealthy connexions ;
a forward, bragging, scheming race.

The terrified General pronounced the name of Allen
with an inquiring look ; and here too Thorpe had learnt
his

his error. The Allens, he believed, had lived near them too long, and he knew the young man on whom the Fullerton estate must devolve. The General needed no more. Enraged with almost every body in the world but himself, he set out the next day for the Abbey, where his performances have been seen.

I leave it to my reader's sagacity to determine how much of all this it was possible for Henry to communicate at this time to Catherine, how much of it he could have learnt from his father, in what points his own conjectures might assist him, and what portion must yet remain to be told in a letter from James. I have united for their ease what they must divide for mine. Catherine, at any rate, heard enough to feel, that in suspecting General Tilney of either murdering or shutting up his wife, she had scarcely sinned against his character, or magnified his cruelty.

Henry, in having such things to relate of his father, was almost as pitiable as in their first avowal to himself. He blushed for the narrow-minded counsel which he was obliged to expose. The conversation between them at Northanger had been of the most unfriendly kind. Henry's indignation on hearing how Catherine had been treated, on comprehending his father's views, and being ordered to acquiesce in them, had been open and bold. The General, accustomed on every ordinary occasion to give the law in his family, prepared for no reluctance but of feeling, no opposing desire that should dare to clothe itself in words, could ill brook the opposition of his son, steady as the sanction of reason and the dictate of conscience could make it. But, in such a cause, his anger, though it must shock, could not intimidate Henry, who was sustained in his purpose by a conviction of its justice. He felt himself bound as much in honour as in affection to Miss Morland, and believing that heart to be his own which he had been directed to gain, no unworthy retraction of a tacit consent, no reversing decree of unjustifiable anger, could shake his fidelity, or influence the resolutions it prompted.

He

He steadily refused to accompany his father into Herefordshire, an engagement formed almost at the moment, to promote the dismissal of Catherine, and as steadily declared his intention of offering her his hand. The General was furious in his anger, and they parted in dreadful disagreement. Henry, in an agitation of mind which many solitary hours were required to compose, had returned almost instantly to Woodston ; and, on the afternoon of the following day, had begun his journey to Fullerton.

CHAP-

CHAPTER XVI.

MR. and Mrs. Morland's surprize on being applied to
by Mr. Tilney, for their consent to his marrying their
daughter, was, for a few minutes, considerable ; it having
never entered their heads to suspect an attachment on
either side ; but as nothing, after all, could be more
natural than Catherine's being beloved, they soon learnt
to consider it with only the happy agitation of gratified
pride, and, as far as they alone were concerned, had not
a single objection to start. His pleasing manners and
good sense were self-evident recommendations ; and
having never heard evil of him, it was not their way to
suppose any evil could be told. Good-will supplying the
place of experience, his character needed no attestation.
" Catherine would make a sad heedless young housekeeper to be sure," was her mother's foreboding remark ;
but quick was the consolation of there being nothing like
practice.

There was but one obstacle, in short, to be mentioned ;
but till that one was removed, it must be impossible for
them to sanction the engagement. Their tempers were
mild, but their principles were steady, and while his
parent so expressly forbad the connexion, they could not
allow themselves to encourage it. That the General
should come forward to solicit the alliance, or that he
should even very heartily approve it, they were not
refined enough to make any parading stipulation ; but
the decent appearance of consent must be yielded, and
that once obtained—and their own hearts made them
trust that it could not be very long denied—their willing
approbation was instantly to follow. His *consent* was all
that they wished for. They were no more inclined than
entitled to demand his *money*. Of a very considerable
fortune, his son was, by marriage settlements, eventually
secure ;

secure ; his present income was an income of independence
and comfort, and under every pecuniary view, it was
a match beyond the claims of their daughter.

The young people could not be surprized at a decision
like this. They felt and they deplored—but they could
not resent it ; and they parted, endeavouring to hope
that such a change in the General, as each believed
almost impossible, might speedily take place, to unite
them again in the fullness of privileged affection. Henry
returned to what was now his only home, to watch over
his young plantations, and extend his improvements for
her sake, to whose share in them he looked anxiously
forward ; and Catherine remained at Fullerton to cry.
Whether the torments of absence were softened by
a clandestine correspondence, let us not inquire. Mr. and
Mrs. Morland never did—they had been too kind to
exact any promise ; and whenever Catherine received
a letter, as, at that time, happened pretty often, they
always looked another way.

The anxiety, which in this state of their attachment
must be the portion of Henry and Catherine, and of all
who loved either, as to its final event, can hardly extend,
I fear, to the bosom of my readers, who will see in the
tell-tale compression of the pages before them, that we
are all hastening together to perfect felicity. The means
by which their early marriage was effected can be the
only doubt ; what probable circumstance could work
upon a temper like the General's ? The circumstance
which chiefly availed, was the marriage of his daughter
with a man of fortune and consequence, which took place
in the course of the summer—an accession of dignity that
threw him into a fit of good-humour, from which he did
not recover till after Eleanor had obtained his forgiveness
of Henry, and his permission for him " to be a fool if he
liked it ! "

The marriage of Eleanor Tilney, her removal from all
the evils of such a home as Northanger had been made
by Henry's banishment, to the home of her choice and
the

the man of her choice, is an event which I expect to give
general satisfaction among all her acquaintance. My
own joy on the occasion is very sincere. I know no one
more entitled, by unpretending merit, or better prepared
by habitual suffering, to receive and enjoy felicity. Her
partiality for this gentleman was not of recent origin ;
and he had been long withheld only by inferiority of
situation from addressing her. His unexpected accession
to title and fortune had removed all his difficulties ;
and never had the General loved his daughter so well in
all her hours of companionship, utility, and patient
endurance, as when he first hailed her, " Your Ladyship ! "
Her husband was really deserving of her ; independent
of his peerage, his wealth, and his attachment, being to
a precision the most charming young man in the world.
Any further definition of his merits must be unnecessary ;
the most charming young man in the world is instantly
before the imagination of us all. Concerning the one in
question therefore I have only to add—(aware that the
rules of composition forbid the introduction of a character
not connected with my fable)—that this was the very
gentleman whose negligent servant left behind him that
collection of washing-bills, resulting from a long visit at
Northanger, by which my heroine was involved in one
of her most alarming adventures.

The influence of the Viscount and Viscountess in their
brother's behalf was assisted by that right understanding
of Mr. Morland's circumstances which, as soon as the
General would allow himself to be informed, they were
qualified to give. It taught him that he had been scarcely
more misled by Thorpe's first boast of the family wealth,
than by his subsequent malicious overthrow of it ; that
in no sense of the word were they necessitous or poor,
and that Catherine would have three thousand pounds.
This was so material an amendment of his late expectations, that it greatly contributed to smooth the descent
of his pride ; and by no means without its effect was the
private intelligence, which he was at some pains to
                                                procure,

procure, that the Fullerton estate, being entirely at the disposal of its present proprietor, was consequently open to every greedy speculation.

On the strength of this, the General, soon after Eleanor's marriage, permitted his son to return to Northanger, and thence made him the bearer of his consent, very courteously worded in a page full of empty professions to Mr. Morland. The event which it authorized soon followed : Henry and Catherine were married, the bells rang and every body smiled ; and, as this took place within a twelve-month from the first day of their meeting, it will not appear, after all the dreadful delays occasioned by the General's cruelty, that they were essentially hurt by it. To begin perfect happiness at the respective ages of twenty-six and eighteen, is to do pretty well ; and pro-fessing myself moreover convinced, that the General's unjust interference, so far from being really injurious to their felicity, was perhaps rather conducive to it, by improving their knowledge of each other, and adding strength to their attachment, I leave it to be settled by whomsoever it may concern, whether the tendency of this work be altogether to recommend parental tyranny, or reward filial disobedience.

FINIS.

CHINUA ACHEBE
Things Fall Apart

THE ARABIAN NIGHTS
(tr. Husain Haddawy)

MARCUS AURELIUS
Meditations

JANE AUSTEN
Emma
Mansfield Park
Northanger Abbey
Persuasion
Pride and Prejudice
Sense and Sensibility

HONORÉ DE BALZAC
Cousin Bette
Eugénie Grandet
Old Goriot

WILLIAM BLAKE
Poems and Prophecies

JAMES BOSWELL
The Life of Samuel Johnson

CHARLOTTE BRONTË
Jane Eyre
Villette

EMILY BRONTË
Wuthering Heights

MIKHAIL BULGAKOV
The Master and Margarita

SAMUEL BUTLER
The Way of all Flesh

WILLA CATHER
Death Comes for the Archbishop

MIGUEL DE CERVANTES
Don Quixote

GEOFFREY CHAUCER
Canterbury Tales

ANTON CHEKHOV
The Steppe and Other Stories
My Life and Other Stories

KATE CHOPIN
The Awakening

SAMUEL TAYLOR COLERIDGE
Poems

WILLIAM WILKIE COLLINS
The Moonstone
The Woman in White

JOSEPH CONRAD
Lord Jim
Nostromo
Typhoon and Other Stories
Under Western Eyes
The Secret Agent

DANIEL DEFOE
Moll Flanders
Robinson Crusoe

CHARLES DICKENS
Bleak House
David Copperfield
Great Expectations
Hard Times
Little Dorrit
Oliver Twist

DENIS DIDEROT
Memoirs of a Nun

JOHN DONNE
The Complete English Poems

FYODOR DOSTOEVSKY
The Brothers Karamazov

GEORGE ELIOT
Adam Bede
Middlemarch
The Mill on the Floss

HENRY FIELDING
Joseph Andrews
Tom Jones

FORD MADOX FORD
The Good Soldier
Parade's End

E. M. FORSTER
Howards End
A Passage to India

IVAN GONCHAROV
Oblomov

GRAHAM GREENE
The Human Factor

THOMAS HARDY
Far From The Madding Crowd
Jude the Obscure
The Return of the Native
Tess of the d'Urbervilles

NATHANIEL HAWTHORNE
The Scarlet Letter

HINDU SCRIPTURES
(tr. R. C. Zaehner)

JAMES HOGG
Confessions of a Justified Sinner

HOMER
The Iliad
The Odyssey

HENRY JAMES
The Bostonians
The Golden Bowl
The Portrait of a Lady
The Princess Casamassima

JAMES JOYCE
Dubliners
A Portrait of the Artist as a Young
Man

FRANZ KAKFA
The Castle
The Trial

JOHN·KEATS
The Poems

THE KORAN
(tr. Marmaduke Pickthall)

CHODERLOS DE LACLOS
Les Liaisons dangereuses

GIUSEPPE TOMASI DI
LAMPEDUSA
The Leopard

D. H. LAWRENCE
Sons and Lovers
Women in Love

MIKHAIL LERMONTOV
A Hero of Our Time

NICCOLÒ MACHIAVELLI
The Prince

THOMAS MANN
Death in Venice and Other Stories
Doctor Faustus

KATHERINE MANSFIELD
The Garden Party and Other
Stories

HERMAN MELVILLE
Moby-Dick

JOHN STUART MILL
On Liberty and Utilitarianism

JOHN MILTON
The Complete English Poems

MARY WORTLEY MONTAGU
Letters

THOMAS MORE
Utopia

MURASAKI SHIKIBU
The Tale of Genji

VLADIMIR NABOKOV
Lolita
Pale Fire

GEORGE ORWELL
Nineteen Eighty-Four

BORIS PASTERNAK
Doctor Zhivago

PLATO
The Republic

Everyman's Library, founded in 1906 and relaunched in 1991, aims to offer the most complete library in the English language of the world's classics. Each volume is printed in a classic typeface on acid-free, cream-wove paper with a sewn full cloth binding.